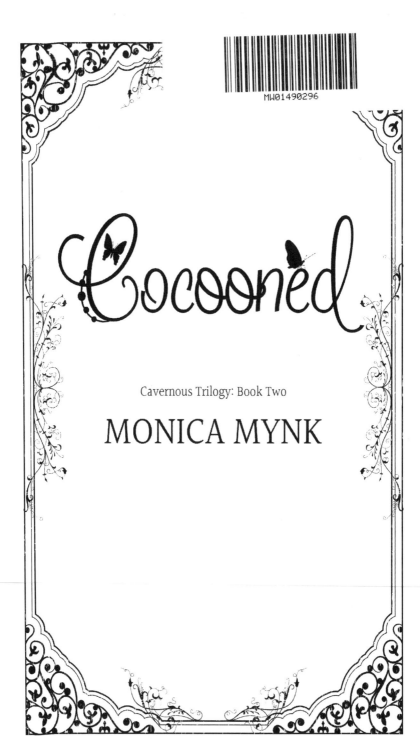

# Cocooned

Cavernous Trilogy: Book Two

## MONICA MYNK

Cover and interior images by Christa Holland of
Paper and Sage Design (http://paperandsage.com).

Published in the United States of America by
Prodigal Daughter Publishing
416 Wellington Way
Winchester, KY 40391

# Dedication

To my husband and my beautiful children
And to God, whose promises are new every morning

*The humble shall see this and be glad;*
*And you who seek God, your hearts shall live.*
*For the Lord hears the poor,*
*And does not despise His prisoners.*
*Psalm 69:32-33*

**OTHER BOOKS BY MONICA MYNK**

*The Cavernous Trilogy*
*Cavernous*
*Cocooned*
*Conceded (November 2017)*

*The Goddess to Daughter Series*
*Pandora's Deed*
*Medusa's Hands*
*Athena's Baby (2018)*

*The Billboard Bride (June 2017)*

# Chapter One

## ETHAN

**A BRIGHT FLASH**. A huge boom. Screams. Then, darkness spreads over me like a blanket covering the clear, blue sky.

Another scream, in my ear. "Ethan!"

To my right, Amber lunges forward, toppling to the pavement. As I face the arena, my heart thumps outside my chest like a trapped rocket is bursting from within it.

Callie's in there. I have to go back for her.

Martin's eyes widen to epic proportions as a pyroclastic cloud bumbles toward us with a deafening roar, its debris-filled tentacles clawing in every direction. The smell of dirt and sulfur sting my nostrils. Moments ago, we had a plan. Get to the train. Ride to the helipad and head back to America. Wait for James Caudill, the thirtysomething rebel who promised to help us escape, to meet us there with Callie. But now? Run. And hope that James gets her out of the building, let alone the country.

Maybe we can get to the other side…

With a death grip on Amber's stark white hand, Martin jerks her to her feet. She lifts her gaze to her father as his eyes dart between her and the arena, more childlike than I've ever seen her. This sure wasn't how we'd pictured life after high school.

I know what he's thinking. Which daughter should he save? Strong, brave Callie, who's in the hands of his maniac twin brother Adrian, or helpless drug addict college-failure Amber, who's defied him so many times?

"Move!" With my hefty shove, he falls into fretful steps with the fleeing crowd. The monstrous dust cloud towers over us as though it's alive, sending a sprinkle of sharp debris raining around us.

Another abysmal scream escapes Amber's throat. Martin tugs her down the long alley that runs between the arena and the huge concrete parking structure beside it.

Who is responsible for this? Surely not the flippant Adrian Lamb. He'd probably be too busy being a dictator and figuring out how to further divide the nation. I mean, wasn't this his grandiose meeting? Why bomb his own party?

Has the American government decided to put an end to the Alliance and its garish rule? It doesn't seem likely they'd bomb a place with a bunch of American citizens, even though several have denounced their citizenship. And not when so many are trapped in the Alliance beyond their own will.

We lead the pack, though not from Amber's contribution. As the bodies press against us, some of them pass him, and she gets entangled in a sea of arms.

In the movies, it's always so easy to predict the guy or girl who will die in this situation, and it's always the Amber-type character. The dregs of society. The ones who rebelliously live beyond anyone's law. But no way will Martin let that happen. He's too good for her.

*Greater love has no one than this, than one to lay down his life for his friends.* The verse smacks me in the face like the tiny sharp sticks and rocks surrounding me. Martin is a Christian. Period. He'll save Amber, no matter how rotten she is.

A tall, muscular guy in a leather jacket scoops her up and slings her over his shoulder, freeing Martin to run on his own.

"Thanks!" His shout fades against the rumbles behind us.

That should have been me. Why couldn't I soften my heart and help her? We've both been through so much together since I moved to Union City back in high school. Prom, graduation, our first year of college, all those crazy parties when I had to keep her from drowning in her own puke. And both of us hurting Callie. Guess I've been a rotten person, too.

Though I know it's a terrible mistake, my gaze is drawn back to the arena. Like Lot's wife and the pillar of salt, I can't let go. Not of

Callie. Not when I just found her again.

Those words, cast over the mountains of Virginia, fill my heart. How freeing it felt to confess my love for her at the time. Ironic it was the very thing that entrapped us.

I have to find a way back into that building. I have to save her.

My knees buckle as someone bumps into my left side, and I topple to the ground.

Martin lurches, landing on the steps of a nearby building. He extends his hand toward me.

Dodging feet, I crawl to him. Another man trips over me as Martin pulls me to him, sending several others cascading like dominoes. They scramble up and race onward.

"You okay?"

A sea of faces blur as they pass me, and the words fade into the abyss. No idea who asked the question. I can only nod as the smoke inches closer. A small break forms in the crowd, and Martin and I fall back into the line of frantic runners.

My lungs constrict. Keeping my jaws clamped tight, I turn with the runners to a wide space in front of the arena that opens to a city park. Ahead of me, droves of people climb over its fences. Others line up along the porch of the arena, shielding their faces and crawling under benches and trash bins. To the right of the arena, more blasts sound and another cloud inches toward us. No chance of getting to Callie that way.

So, which way should we go?

The good Samaritan who carried Amber rushes past, and Martin grabs at him, catching her sleeve and pulling her close. He motions the man on and drags Amber toward the fences, but I hesitate. The door of a white van parked on the street beside me slides open. A hand reaches out and swings at my arm. Captor or savior, I don't know, but he clamps onto me with a vice grip, drags me in, and fights off others who try to climb in after me.

Amber stops in her tracks. "Ethan! Wait for us!" She drags Martin back toward the van.

"We can't take any more!" A deep male voice booms beside me. Escaping his grasp is futile. "Go on. I'll find you!"

Grim-faced, Martin and Amber race back toward the fences.

The van door closes. I turn to the guy who brought me in as the engine roars to life. Even crouching, he stands a foot taller than me. Denim jacket. Thick, bushy eyebrows and dark, shifty eyes. Enough stubble to prove that he could grow a manly beard if he wanted. Dark hair tousled in rebellious curls. Not my kind of guy.

He offers a smooth hand for a shake. "Davey Brinkle."

"Ethan Thomas." I stifle my wince as he squeezes the life from my fingers. "Thanks for saving me."

"Ethan Thomas." He clamps his hand over his mouth to block his snickers. "As in, 'I love you, Callie' Ethan Thomas? I mean, I recognize you from the Twitter pic, now that you mention it. Man, it's my lucky day. Pleasure to meet you."

This guy's out of his mind. "I can't imagine why you'd find that funny. Or lucky."

"Not funny. Ironic. Have a seat. Buckle up, because we're moving fast." He braces himself against the side of the van and grips a handle on the seat. "Ethan Thomas."

Weirdo. "Where are we going? Can you drive behind the arena? Callie's still in there."

Out the back window of the van, the giant smoke cloud marches closer. Davey nods to the driver. "She's not still in there. We have teams working to get everyone to safety. We'll help you get reconnected with your girlfriend soon."

Three other guys, probably about twenty-one like me, occupy seats encircling the van walls rather than sitting in rows. The space smells like sweat and fear, but what choice do I have? As the van jolts into motion, I land on leather and secure myself in.

"Robbie." The guy next to me points to his scrawny chest.

"I'm Al," says a redhead across from us, "and my brother Chris."

Davey falls into the seat beside Chris and pulls a cell phone from his pocket. He taps the screen and brings it to his ear.

Al frowns. "How are you making a call? I thought there wasn't any cell service in the Alliance."

With a crisp laugh, Davey shakes his head. "Only to the little people. We'll issue you phones soon if you earn your keep. Got to get you to the facility first."

Facility? I open my mouth to ask then clamp it shut. Who is this guy? He obviously isn't inclined to follow any of the Alliance rules.

"We're on the way," he speaks into the phone. "I have four. And you're not going to believe this one. Remember that Thomas kid? Randomly stumbled by. Talk about your good fortune. Peace out, bro."

"What do you mean?" I wrap my arms over my chest as he ends the call. "What facility? Why do you care about me?"

"Let me give you boys a more formal introduction." He tucks the phone back into his pocket and sits straighter. "I represent an organization called ASP. That stands for the Allied Security Patriots." His shoulders shake as he snickers again. What an annoying habit. "Well, I might as well be honest. I'm eighth in command, but I run the whole operation these days. All the big guys are too old to do anything but foot the bill."

Inertia drives my elbow into Robbie's arm. "Sorry, man." I lean forward and grip the bottom of the seat. "What does ASP do? Are you Alliance loyalists?"

"Not even close." Davey flicks his chin up and grins. "A certain subculture has always existed in America. The elitist, if you will. They have secret societies and highfalutin parties. You know, Skull and Bones, the Knights Templar, the Freemasons…" He gives an exaggerated wink. "ASP."

"A secret society? In 2020?" Chris squints through thick-lens glasses. "Are those things even real? I didn't think they existed anymore."

Davey cups his hands around his mouth sucks in a deep breath. "They do." His loud whisper carries the vibration as the van jostles from a huge bump.

"Okay, so ASP is a secret society." Should I believe this guy? And if he is part of some secret society, why come to the arena and snatch up guys like me? Are we kidnapped? Was he responsible for the bombs? "Do you guys have meetings in the woods and jump off of buildings holding umbrellas?"

"No." Davey brushes invisible dust from his shoulder. "You know how these things work. The people with the money have the power to do whatever they want. How do you think the Alliance was formed in the first place? ASP was part of that movement in the beginning. Millions of dollars sent under the table to make it happen, and certain perks were given in return." He points to his pocket. "Like cell phones, for example. And gasoline. Ever notice how most of the Alliance struggles to get gasoline, but there are always cars on the road? All of our wealthy parents bribe people and use their influence. Deals are made and cell service is extended to places where it shouldn't exist. It's not like the technology went away."

"I've seen a lot of private planes in Monongahela." Chris leans closer to the window.

My ears prick. Monongahela? The West Virginia forest where Adrian first held Callie?

"My parents' property backed up to a private airstrip. Since Dad volunteered to be an Alliance officer, we were allowed to stay." Condensation from Chris's breath collects on the glass, and he wipes it with his elbow. "No one used it until Adrian Lamb became our so-called Lord and Master."

Al winces. "You need to stop saying stuff like that, Chris. You're going to end up stuffed in a barrel."

Davey snorts. "I'm the last person you'd have to worry about in that regard. And yes, Ethan, you're right. We used to be one of those frivolous party-boy societies. Had big shindigs with ridiculous rules and pulled off stunts that could have landed us all in jail. But now, we have a single agenda. Destroy the Alliance to reunite America."

"Well, I can get behind that." Al scratches his stubbly red chin. "What will we be? Like rebel soldiers or something?"

"Not exactly." Davey points to a row of weapons lining the back of the van. "We specialize in distractions and extractions. Those bombings were distractions so we could free entrapped Alliance citizens."

My blood boils. "People could have died as they fled the scene. Trampled or anything."

"True. But our agents always comb the scenes. They haven't found anyone dead yet." Davey's halo practically glitters. I'd love to knock that smirk off his face.

"You still haven't explained why you consider me such good fortune." I dig my fingernails into my palms.

"We've been looking for you, Ethan Thomas. We'd love your

12

help to pull off the ultimate extraction. Everyone knows that you're in love with Callie Lamb—"

"Noland." My jaw tightens.

"Callie Noland, rather. And everyone knows that she's Adrian's dearest pet. Losing her would devastate him."

"I'd love to help you extract Callie, but I don't see how that stops the Alliance. Adrian isn't the only person running the country."

Davey scoffs. "Adrian isn't running the country. Are you out of your mind? He's a figurehead. A charismatic puppet who keeps the people confused and entertained with his smooth speeches and flashy smiles. He's no more in charge of the Alliance than the White House receptionist is in charge of American policy."

"Does ASP have a plan to get her to America safely?"

"Of course." Davey fiddles with the hem of his jacket. "We come and go as we please as long as the money trickles into the Alliance pockets. They don't realize, of course, that we're siphoning it back off from the bottom of their cookie jar."

I raise my palm then let it fall to my lap. "Well, we had a plan. We'd let Adrian introduce Callie as his First Daughter, and one of the rebels was going to help her escape. After we left the arena we were headed to the train station and meeting Callie at the helipad. Me, her dad, her sister… And we were all supposed to be in America within the next couple of hours. You've kept that from happening. Callie didn't make it out of the building, and Martin and Amber are lost in the fleeing crowd. Who knows where they are now." My skin itches, like tiny bugs crawl on the inside of my hands. Bet my blood pressure's up to its max. Deep breaths. In and out. "So did you have a team that went into the arena to get her?"

A smirk slides up the right side of Davey's cheek like he's the Grinch at Christmastime. "Guess you didn't know Callie planned to publicly defy Adrian."

"What?" I slap my palm over my mouth.

"She did, as well as told everyone in attendance that 'Lord Adrian' and his so-called Bible was a farce. And they shot her. Straight in the chest."

My breath fails me. Callie, shot? "Is she..."

"Dead?" A bubble of laughter burst from his twisted lips.

"Hardly. And truly it helps our cause. One of ASP's waiting ambulances was right outside the door, posing as an Alliance one. I'm sure she's in our custody. We have sixteen operatives onsite posing as emergency personnel on Adrian's special team."

Operatives. This guy is playing CIA, and he's messing with my girlfriend's life. Words could never express how much I'd like to punch him. Still, what's happened has happened. I have to get to her now.

"Will she be where you take us?"

"Should be." Davey pulls up a map on his phone and waves it in front of me. "It's a big mansion with an underground training compound and a ton of security. Even though it's not in true America, it's as American as any soil you'll rest your feet on. You can count on that. And you'll both be safe there." He taps the screen and it goes dark. "And who were the others running with you?"

Like he doesn't know. "Martin and Amber Noland. Callie's dad and sister."

He swipes his phone screen and types. Within seconds, Amber's mug shot pops up. He laughs. "This beauty? She looks like a meth head."

"She's got issues."

He presses the buttons to capture the image then pulls up one of Martin from the University. "Your girlfriend's dad?"

"That's him." Why does he toy with me? He knows who we are. I bet he already had the pictures queued up to show me. He knew exactly where I was before the bombing and waited for me to run past the van.

His fingers tap his phone screen, and I drum my fingers against my pants leg. What choice do I have but to trust and go along with him right now? I have no money, no ID, and no hope. My backpack sits in the helicopter James arranged for us, and I'll never see it again.

I flick my gaze to the ceiling of the van and close my eyes. *God, I know you're in charge of all this, but I'm terrified. Please, watch over Callie and keep her safe. Help Martin and Amber find their way to America and to avoid being trampled in that crowd. Keep them from Adrian's claws, and lead us to a place where we can serve and praise you without fear of persecution. And please, if trusting this guy is the wrong move, show me. In Jesus' name, amen.*

When I open my eyes, Davey glares in my direction, his lips twisted like he's trying to bite the inside of his cheek.

"Lost you for a sec, there. So, what do you say? Are you interested in helping us save your girlfriend, Ethan Thomas? Will you become part of ASP and join our extraction team?"

The other guys all lean forward like they're hanging on my answer. I take a slow, deep breath and hold it a few seconds before releasing it with a whoosh. At the least, I need to stay on his good side. Forcing my fist to relax, I rest my hands on my thighs. "If you can get me to Callie, I will."

# Chapter Two

## CALLIE

**MY SPEECH**. The arena. Gunshots, and the look on Adrian's face as the bullets hit me. Pure hatred.

Oh, how I betrayed him. To say that his rewritten Bible was a farce. To call his loyal followers to remember the true God and to decry the Alliance. To pledge allegiance to America. How dare I? But then again, how dare I not?

The cold stage floor presses against my cheek. I must have regained consciousness seconds after blacking out. Either that, or time froze.

The crowd sings on, heedless of the rows of officers in their crisp red uniforms or the bullets spraying among them. "He has loosed the fateful lightning of his terrible swift sword…"

Fearless in the face of terror. Maybe this is a shift in the tide.

Feet shuffle, forming a line between me and the hands and arms scrambling at the side of the stage. One by one, they fall away, and their singing morphs into screams.

An agonizing burn pulses my side and jolts through my knee as warm blood pools around my fingers. This wasn't how I'd imagined death.

"Our God is marching on…"

Right. He marches on, using my death to forward His will. Have I been good enough? Faithful enough? I've tried, but now…

An old sermon comes back to me, one Dad preached years ago when he filled in for our full-time minister. He talked about the continual cleansing of sin for those who walk in the light, as Jesus walks in the light. How for the Christian, we can have reassurance of our home in heaven. I have walked in the light. But still... I don't feel ready to die. Not at the hand of Adrian's goons.

When the bullets first struck, they winded me, but now I draw labored breaths. For about thirty seconds, I struggle to find my voice. "Lord, please spare my life."

Like my whisper, the voices weaken. The screams intensify. My heart feels... tired.

But my mind—alive, for the first time since Ethan kissed me. And if I do manage to survive, I want to understand everything going on around me. I dig my nails into my palms.

Adrian darts about the stage, jumping around like a startled black poodle. "Get her under the blanket, you morons. And get my wretched wife out of here. Fix her. But make her feel every ounce of the pain." He ducks behind the curtain and his pill bottle rattles.

Between an officer's legs, Mom reaches for me. Blood stains her collar and mats the hair at the base of her neck, seeping along the zipper of her dress.

Though she's a mess and can barely stand, they cuff her, beat her, and drag her out of my line of sight, leaving behind a sea of faces frozen in fear. Her gaze holds mine until the last second.

Her love, strength, and fear pass through me as though I'm part of her. Adrian infested her like a parasite and destroyed her from within, but she saved a little room for me. He can take everything else, but not that.

A piercing blast shakes the stage, and the faces blur into a frenzy of rushing arms and legs. Dust and concrete rain down on me, and I close my eyes, shutting out the sandy grit. Wails from the audience drown Adrian's perpetual muttering.

After a second blast, and then a third, Adrian kneels and lifts my arm. "I want them alive. Both of them alive. Get them out of here."

Bullets whiz by us, one striking him in the chest and bouncing off his protective gear. As he tumbles to the floor, he lunges for the nearest officer. "What are you imbeciles doing? We're taking fire. Did you not hear me? Get us out of here."

I crane my neck toward him, wincing at the influx of fresh pain.

He dives behind the podium while several officers step in front of him and spray more bullets over the crowd. Tears spring and my chest tightens as James joins the line. Whose side is he on, anyway? After all, this bulletproof vest was supposed to spare me. And then I get hit in my exposed side? It's as if someone knew. Can I trust anyone?

"The cameras!" He waves to the videographer. "Get her on film and get her out of here! Hurry before they blow the whole place!"

A bearded officer rushes to me, his face hardening. "Stupid girl. Close your eyes. Do you have a death wish?"

His hiss gives me chills, which sets off new spasms of pain. As I obey, he rolls my chin back toward the chaos. "Your First Daughter! Rest her soul."

"No!" The muffled sounds of flight cease, and tearful cries from the crowd prick my heart. Hope I pricked theirs, and at least got them thinking about God again.

I cough, and blood trickles down my chin. *Lord, if it's Your will for me to die, I pray that You've accepted my repentance and found me a faithful servant. Please, watch out for Ethan and Amber, and be with Mom and Dad...*

The screams resume, then another blasts sends tiny shards into my ankles. *And please, Lord... all these people. I pray they heard my words, how Adrian's bible is false—hat they'll stand up to Adrian and they'll seek You and Your truth.*

Fabric lands on my cheek, stiff like new linen. It settles on my arms, hip, and then my legs. I open my eyes as the officer's knee plunks beside me.

He touches my forehead like the supervisors did to Ben, a student who died at my first academy. "Did anyone get the shots?"

"Done. Medic! Hurry!" The shout comes from my right. "And close that curtain."

Waves of misery wash over me as hands grope me everywhere. Something rough brushes my upper right thigh, then a tight squeeze. I scream, but don't have the air to sustain it.

"Tourniquet complete. Toss me the syringe."

My head presses into the rough stage boards, grinding back and forth as an unusual sensation sends my nerves into a spiral.

"Sponges in, dressing."

Another tight squeeze, and they shove my knee to the side. Someone rips open the satin covering my Kevlar vest.

"Superficial. Bullet bounced off and skirted her chest. Caught in the lace. Let's move."

The bearded officer scoops me into his arms and slings me over his left shoulder, covering his uniform in my blood. He carries me down the steps through the back hall out a side door. Propping it with his hip, he shifts my weight to his right. As my head strikes his clavicle, my world fades once more.

I wake to bright lights and electric volts of agony, strapped to a gurney in a small, boxy room and covered in wires and tubes. Some sort of makeshift ambulance rather than a normal one. Would Adrian sink so low?

"She's with us. Eyes open. Good girl." A blue-eyed woman in a shower cap leans over me, shining a flashlight in my eyes, loose tendrils of her tawny hair framing her catlike face.

My sister? Amber? No, it can't be.

"Callie, blink twice if you can hear me."

Moaning, I stretch my shoulders and regret it. Raging fire soars through my veins. After two small blinks, I try to swallow, gagging on the plastic tube hanging from my mouth.

She adjusts the tube. "You're lucky, Callie. Adrian made us stock this new stuff, these spongy things. We stopped your bleeding before we even got you out of the building."

"Ah... gwa..." Amber? Ethan? My chest heaves. Where are we? Three little words, and I can't even start to say them. But I need to be grateful. Wincing, I close my eyes. *Lord, thank you for that breath. And all the others.*

The room shakes, and the woman grabs my arm. "That must have been a tough one. I'd give you something for the pain if I could."

If she could? A numbing rage surges through my veins. Did Adrian forbid her? Surely he's got enough pain pills to spare a couple for his own daughter. Stupid dopehead. Well... maybe she has to keep me conscious or something. Or they thought since Amber was a pillhead... Amber... Ethan.

19

I push myself up, catching on the polyester restraints.

"No need to get all anxious. We're still in transit, that's all. When we get to the hospital, I'm sure they'll have something for you." The woman runs her finger across my neck. "Such a beautiful tattoo. Did you know that's a noble leafwing? One of the prettiest, in my opinion. I've read that it can span up to three inches."

She grins, her freckles stretching around dimpled cheeks. "They're a little more brown than red, I think, but I doubt that would have suited Adrian."

Cool metal brushes my skin, and she lifts my head. "Found this necklace in your shoe. Figured you might want to wear it. Grandma's, right?"

My dark hair spills over the edge of the stretcher pad, and she twists it into a loose braid. "I'm Court, by the way. Adrian told me to take good care of you." She leans closer and brushes her lips against my ear. "He must love you very much."

I gasp and gurgle, my saliva catching at the base of my throat. "Why?" The word bursts forth from my very soul.

Court pats my right hand, flexing the needle and sending spasms over my whole body. "Even with your betrayal, he's gone to great lengths to protect you. The Alliance thinks you're dead. Now, no one will try to harm you for your foolishness."

Half expecting her eyes to fill with mystic spirals, I jerk away, my wrists rubbing against the restraints. Would anyone besides Adrian want to harm me? Would she?

Her laugh fills the ambulance, and she writes something on a clipboard. "Don't worry. I'm paid well to follow his orders."

That face. So much like Amber's. For a moment, I'm thrown back in time to a special vacation we took when I was little. Amber and I sat on a big, mossy rock while Dad read to us from Alice in Wonderland. She wore the same expression as this girl.

More than once, Adrian's world has felt like a trip down the rabbit hole. The characters all seem to have their own twisted agenda. Maybe we were right in thinking the Alliance citizens weren't buying into his crazy rules, but how many of them are being opportunistic? After all, if Adrian's empire topples, who will rise to build it again? All it would take is one good rally to make them believe things could be better.

The ambulance jostles as we drive over what must be the biggest pothole in history. New pain shoots through my angle. Right. The shrapnel. The explosions. Who planned them? And why?

As if reading my mind, Court holds up her fist, then extends her fingers and makes a blasting noise. "Aww. You know, I don't see any reason why I don't go ahead and tell you." She leans to my ear again. "I don't work for Adrian."

It takes all my strength to hold my face muscles stoic. Should I rejoice or quiver?

Snorting, she grips the edge of my stretcher. "My organization is the antidote to the Alliance." Her nostrils flare, and she frees the tape from my cheek then removes the plastic tube from my mouth. "Here. This isn't any fun if you can't talk back to me. It's not like that tube did anything anyway."

My eyes widen before I can stop them. Aren't they treating me for the gunshot wounds? I'm bandaged, yes, but... A quick tug of my wrists reminds me of the polyester straps holding me firm to the table. I clamp my mouth closed. No way am I talking to this lunatic.

"Anyhoo..." Court sounds like Adrian. She chirps on about how she helped stage my kidnapping while I focus on the ceiling trim. "...so this guy, Davey Brinkle dreamed the whole thing up. He plans an exchange, of course, but to send you back, Adrian's going to have to do some serious negotiation."

It's odd. She's so familiar with Adrian, even so far as to call him by first name when most of the Alliance citizens call him Lord. Her profile matches his. The nose, and that chin. Her lips, pouty like Amber's, and tawny hair, stringy like mine. "You're my sister?"

My voice comes out raspy. She startles, but straightens. "Something like that. Although he never treated me like a princess."

I lift my head. "Don't... under... stand."

As I drop back to the pillow, she snorts. "You wouldn't. Let's say Daddy Dearest better get ready to pay up if he wants to see his precious again."

The ambulance screeches to a halt, and Court rushes toward the driver.

"Are you out of your mind?" Her screech even sounds like Amber's.

"We're surrounded, Court. What do you want me to do?" The driver shuts off the ignition, and they both charge toward me as sunlight floods the cabin.

Shouts ring out from what must be a herd of people. I lay still as possible while Court and the driver move toward the door, twist the handle, raise their hands, and kick it open.

"We surrender!" Court's snarky voice, no longer steady, fades into the crisp, cool air.

"Of course you surrender." Adrian's snicker matches hers. "I should lock you up with your mother, you insolent witch." He laughs. "But you know what's more fun? Why don't you go ahead and run off? Be free. Come on. Walk away. But never stop wondering when I'll be back for you."

"Moron." She clears her throat. "Davey will have you killed by then."

"I'll have you know, they intercepted your buddy Davey a few miles from the freeway an hour before the program. His entire plan..." Adrian cackled. "Up in smoke. Train station and everything."

My heart plummets. *Lord, please... tell me Dad, Amber, and Ethan never made that train.*

Metal clangs, then footsteps, and seconds later, Adrian stands beside me. "Well, if it isn't the little traitor. Aren't you lucky to have survived, to spend the rest of your life in an Alliance prison, knowing Martin and your boyfriend never made it past the edge of town?"

He huffs, throws his head back, and pivots. I glare over the bridge of my nose at his retreating figure and grip the sheet between the stretcher and me. Officers flood the cabin, and the ambulance starts up again.

Uttering silent prayer after silent prayer, I squeeze my eyes closed and hold the sheet tighter as needles and equipment prod me. Someone reinserts the plastic tube in my mouth, and my gag reflex chokes me. The machine breathes for me again and my head grows fuzzy. *Protect them. Help me be strong. Watch over Mom, and... Lord, I don't understand why You've permitted Adrian such power.*

*Please, if it's Your will, let his terrorized citizens free themselves from his grasp. I pray they seek You instead.*

Sharpness surges through my knee, and I writhe against the restraints as a cool, metallic pain deepens to my bone. My distorted scream weakens. How much longer will I have to endure this excruciation?

My brain fogs, and I open my eyes to blurry swirls of grays and reds.

"How are her vitals?" A man coughs twice.

"Good. She's not in immediate danger." Another man answers him.

Danger of dying? Or of something worse? I strain to lift my heavy eyelids.

"Steady." A woman releases what must be ten full lungs of air.

She taps something on the metal table that swings over the stretcher... Or... maybe it's not a table. Maybe I'm not on a stretcher.

With a quick move, she punctures my arm with a monstrous needle. Its contents blaze a path into my veins, sending an eerie calm over me. As my toes and fingers turn to jelly, I blink one last time before the stupor sets in.

# Chapter Three

## ETHAN

**THE VAN VEERS RIGHT**, and inertia sends us all bumping into the next guy's shoulders. I stifle my own yawn as Al's mouth stretches wide enough to see into his bulging stomach.

He scratches his curly red head, leans forward, and faces Davey. "Not to be a complainer, but are we there yet?"

"About ten more minutes." Davey glances at his cell screen as the van slows to a stop. The driver leans out the window and presses buttons on a silvery panel embedded into a brick post. He cups his hands over his mouth. "Fahrenheit 451."

"Ray Bradbury," comes the answer from a feeble man's voice.

Out the windshield, the gate in front of us swings apart, providing the way to a long blacktopped road that leads to a monster house at the top of a grassy hill. I'm talking at least four floors, three or four entrances, and more windows than anyone could ever count. At least Davey had told the truth about that.

The driver approaches the house, and we all fidget.

Davey's cell blares. He rolls his eyes, swipes the screen, and taps the speaker icon.

"Brinkle?" A deep male voice carries urgency. "The daughter is alive. We did snag her according to plan, but Lamb intercepted Court. Think he knew we were coming?"

Davey's face has blanched to near transparent. "Is she okay? Court, I mean. Is she okay?"

"He let her go." Dead silence filled the man's pause. "Took the Noland girl and let Court go. She's on her way to the safe house."

"Thank goodness." Davey's chest deflates.

I clutch my pecs, the thumps of my heart resonating into my fingertips. "Adrian caught Callie? We have to save her."

Davey holds up a finger.

"Lamb's goons stabilized the Noland girl on the stage," says the man on the phone. "Our operatives rolled her right into our ambulance without a hitch, but they were caught after about four miles. The man coughs, deep and low. "Gotta go. Smoke's getting thick here. I'll keep in touch."

I arch my back, leaning out past Chris and Al, who have unbuckled and scooted to the edge of their seats. "Who is Court?"

"A family friend of Ms. Noland's." Davey's jaw flinches.

This Court girl must mean a lot to him. Maybe a girlfriend? Why is he hiding it from me?

"Thought you knew about her." He gestures to the other guys, including the driver. "All of you, out."

As they scramble out of the van, I unbuckle and move to the seat opposite his. "I don't know anything about anyone named Court."

"She's… well, I'll tell you that later. Here's what you need to know." He stretches his legs out in front of him and crosses them at the ankles. "My organization has ruthless means at times, sure, but we have a worthy goal. Destroy the Alliance and extract trapped citizens so they can get back to America."

"So you kidnapped my girlfriend to destroy the Alliance?" And me? Did he kidnap me? Is that what this is? Or, am I free to walk away?

He folds his hands in his lap and twists his college ring. "My family has indispensable income. We have power. And, we have resources to get her out of the country within a few hours. We thought we could kill two birds with one stone, so to speak. Use her to destroy Adrian, and save her in the process."

I flick a piece of lint from the seat to the van floor. "How noble of you. How'd you get into this business, anyway?"

He tosses his hair out of his eyes. "I was quarterback for the University of Charleston. Bode my time for three seasons to start for them, then lost it all when the university went belly-up after the Alliance formed. I could have transferred to any US college, but that was my team. This place was my home. I wanted it back."

"So you became a rogue criminal?" I cannot hide my sneer. His lips twitch. "Something like that. More like the Alliance's version of Robin Hood. Steal from the crazies and give to the poor, downtrodden citizens."

"Are you sure? Because I thought your organization bombed innocent people, wreaked havoc…" My fingernails dig into my flesh.

"Only when we have to." Davey reaches into his jacket pocket and hands me a cell phone. "Yours if you want it."

"Why?" I flip the device over in my hands. It's an old-school model, but fully charged with five bars. Even Internet access. Wonder if it's traceable.

He shrugs. "I thought you'd want one. The Alliance is a farce. America still maneuvers this place wherever they want. And most Americans prefer cell phone service. The Alliance only exists because no one in Washington wants to bomb a whole bunch of innocent victims. We take it upon ourselves to seek out the true enemy and do the job for them."

"No, thanks. I never much liked to have a cell, anyway." Besides, who would I call? I hand him back the phone. "You bombed officers, then? Did you know that a good third of the officers in Adrian's inner circle are Christian rebels and not true Alliance supporters? You could have bombed me."

This time, Davey's laugh comes from deep in his chest. "Christian rebels. Now there's an oxymoron for you." His nose crumples as a snarl snags his upper lip. "Those self-righteous so-called Christian people are the reason we're in this mess in the first place."

"I don't think you know what a true Christian is. Have you ever even read the Bible?"

"Cover to cover." Davey sneers. "Spent every single Saturday, Sunday, and weekday in the front row pew of the Evangelical Repentant Baptismal Tabernacle of the First Church of the… Well, whatever it was called. I don't even know. I think we were Baptist. But we went every day until the day I turned sixteen. Decided Hell couldn't be any worse than the torture of that awful place. Thank goodness my father finally talked some sense into Mom, and we all quit going."

"So, what do you know about Jesus?"

"He overturned the table on the moneychangers. Dude had a temper."

I blink. "I wish you wouldn't do that."

"Do what?"

"Disrespect my Lord by calling him dude. Did you know about the pain and suffering Jesus tolerated so sinners like me and you could have hope of eternal salvation?"

"Church babble. So, you admit you're a sinner, then?"

Man, do I wish Callie could be here. We'd tag team this guy and have his head spinning within minutes. He wouldn't dare insult the Bible again after that. "I am a sinner. The Bible says 'all have sinned and fallen short of the glory of God,' but assures us that Christ's blood offers continual cleansing of our sins. Thank goodness."

"If you're a sinner, then how are you saved?" He leans his head against the van and closes his eyes. "With a magic wand?"

"Look. I can see you're ready for a spiritual flame war, but I have no intention of arguing. If you want to listen, I'm happy to talk Christ crucified. If you insist on insults and disrespect, drop it. Davey, do you know Jesus?"

He scuffs his shoe across the carpet, loosening packed mud. "I know enough to know all you crazies speak His name every time you get online and start homosexual bashing and stuff. I took a girl's virginity against her will back in eighth grade, but I can become a Christian, and it's like it never happened. Erased. Poor girl can't undo the years of therapy and trauma, but I can be clean."

What do I even say to that? I'm going to have to put some thought into it before I talk to him about this again.

I jump to the grass and stand aside as he follows, then we start toward the mansion where Chris, Al, and Robbie wait. "If I'm going to be a part of this um… organization, am I captive or free to go whenever? How did you know where to find us, and what do you expect us to do if you capture… rescue Callie?"

With a shrug, he throws up his hands. "Leave now if you want. But this could be your golden ticket, you know. The founders of ASP are aging, and they've turned things over to the younger guys. We were on Adrian Lamb's side in the beginning, and he used us to secure the borders when the Alliance became a nation. We parted ways when his goons started rough-handing and blackmailing anyone in opposition." He lifts his face to the sky, like he's reading it to find what to tell me. "I'm sure you saw the news. They assassinated the President and Vice President. And you know, Mr. Noland's wife was part of ASP, even back as far as college. She handled some of their social media accounts. I followed her on Twitter long before the Alliance was conceived. Elizabeth Lamb."

"That explains a lot."

Amber's lip twitches come to mind, the ones ending in her inevitable pouts. How many times did she complain about her mom being on the Internet all the time? And the embarrassment of her Facebook and Twitter posts?

"Anyway, when we realized Lamb planned to steer the new nation in a direction they didn't want us to go, some of our members turned on him. There was a thwarted assassination plot, and our members divided. Those loyal to the Alliance left to become officers. Though we had some members who infiltrated the officer ranks as spies. Here, you hungry?" Davey snags a protein bar from his backpack and breaks it into two pieces. "It was so easy. Takes no effort to get disgruntled people to throw each other under the bus."

"So ASP was responsible for the bombings across the Eastern US when the Alliance first formed?" I bite into the grainy protein bar and chew. Bitterness mixes with my saliva, and I choke it down. One of these days I'm going to eat steak again.

"They were." Davey practically swallows his half of the bar whole. "I wasn't part of it then, of course. But now, I'm integral. And if you stick with me, I can help destroy Adrian Lamb."

"What happened in that arena today?"

"We planted small pipe bombs high enough that no one would be injured from the direct explosion. Sure, there's bound to be someone struck by shrapnel, but our goal has never been to kill. We wanted to create a distraction big enough that our waiting team could extract your girlfriend. Of course, we couldn't predict that she'd get herself shot. And, we detonated explosives in nearby abandoned buildings for visual effect."

"You knew the route we'd be leaving, and that we were headed for the train." My teeth grind together, and I force even breaths. "If not for you, we'd already be out of the country."

Davey grabs a second bar, rips it open with his teeth, and takes a huge bite. He chews for a few seconds and then gulps it down, his Adam's apple bobbing like it's detached from his neck. "That train station is no more. Blown to smithereens, and all the people waiting to board were gunned down. The sharpshooters were all Alliance officers. You would have never made that train."

The warmth drains from my face. Is he telling the truth?

He lets the wrapper drift to the ground. "Regardless, are you with me? I mean, really with me? I can help you find Callie. All I need is your cooperation in helping to draw out Adrian Lamb so we can make him publicly pay for his crimes against humanity."

Do I dance with the devil or face his wrath? With gritted teeth, I take several deep breaths. "Fine. Tell me what you want me to do."

# Chapter Four

## CALLIE

**A WOODSY SMELL** replaces the strong antiseptic that tingles my nose. I turn to the right as a large, masculine hand clamps over my mouth. Where am I?

My pulse hits Mach III and my eyes pop wide open to a dim hospital room. To my right, a monitor flashes an erratic stream of waves. My heart will break the sound barrier and give me away. So much for fearless.

The hand moves away as tears sting my eyes. I rub them with the heel of my palm, dragging along the IV taped to my wrist.

Someone pokes my door open and flicks on the light. Before I can adjust, they flip the switch off and leave the room. Whoever's in here with me must have ducked behind the chair.

Seconds tick by on the analog clock, the sound intensifying the tension in the room. I fumble with my feet, trying to scoot higher against my pillow. Futile.

The person clears his throat.

My dry skin burns as I try to roll across the stiff cotton sheet and crane my neck to see who he is. Pointless. Didn't even manage to turn an inch. Am I paralyzed?

James Caudill stands to my right, against a backdrop of plastic tubes and old-school equipment. "Callie. You're awake."

"Yeah." The word sticks in my voice box, coming out as a whistling rasp.

"Don't try to talk." He looks bulky in his faded brown T-shirt and jogging pants, a far cry from his red officer attire. A jagged scar stretches down his cheek, and resignation oozes from his hollow eyes.

"They're releasing you soon." His whisper bears no evidence of urgency. "Maybe tomorrow."

I furrow my brow. "I just got here. I was shot." My voice emerges like I've had laryngitis for days. With my unrestrained left arm, I make a labored attempt to feel under the sheets for the bandages covering my torso. It's as if my muscles have forgotten how to move.

When my fingers brush a thick, bumpy scar on my abdomen, a gasp comes out louder than I intend. No dressing. No bleeding. Not even a hint of a scab.

"You're doing great, Callie." James uncovers my right knee and helps me bend it so I can see another scar. A healed wound. How is that possible?

"How long have I been here?"

"Months."

"Months? Are you serious?" With his help, I strain to reach the purple streak, tracing my fingers across my kneecap. "So are you not an officer now?"

He shrugs. "When I feel like it. I seldom do guard duty anymore, just inspections. It's easier for the rebels when I don't show up, and no one bothers to check. Sometimes I go on prison runs with Adrian to watch him torment people and document it. The Alliance is dying. It's a matter of time before the US sweeps in and takes over."

He rolls back my electronic monitor, which looks like something from a cheesy eighties movie. This must have been a nice hospital once, and now it's a relic. And I'm a relic, I guess. What would Ethan think if he could see me now? My heart rate quickens, and warmth floods my cheeks. Dizzy, I dissolve into the pillow. "Why not take over before?"

"You know how it goes. Big debate in Washington over what they're supposed to do. Can't come in bombing because there are tons of innocent people holed up in caves and such. Adrian's foot soldiers are armed lunatics, many of them former military, so they have extensive training, and the US has had trouble at the borders because they won't listen to reason. The new president has had to resort to old-school tactics, sort of squeezing the Alliance in from the sides. His name's Cooper, by the way. President Cooper."

I raise my head about an inch, holding it a couple seconds before dropping back to the bed. "Have I been in a coma? Did I almost die?"

"Your injuries were serious, but Adrian's doctors stabilized you right away. Shrapnel more than the gunshot wounds, from bombs that exploded over the stage. They've had you drugged on and off for months. I've visited so many times, hoping you'd be awake, and trying to make sure they didn't overdo it with the sedatives. Thankfully, they used a new one that doesn't have so many long-term effects. But I've been so afraid for you..." He straightens my leg and covers it back up with the sheet. "Today, for whatever reason, they didn't give you any. Plans are to move you to an Alliance prison. We wanted to break you out, but he's got too much security. Best I can do right now is warn you and let you know we're still trying."

We're still trying? Who's still trying? Does he mean Dad and Ethan? Maybe some of the other officers?

His sharp nose twitches, and he tightens his jaw. "We've been trying for a long time."

Pressing my shoulders into the pillow, I try to lift my head again. Five full seconds this time. Every swallow feels like a slice with a knife. "I saw you... in the ambulance."

James quirks his brow. "What ambulance? I never saw you in an ambulance. Adrian's medics took you off in a helicopter. I have visited you several times in the hospital, though. I've tried to make sure you're getting good care."

"Don't remember a helicopter. Just the street. When they arrested that girl." I lick my chapped lips, and try to gather up enough saliva to ease my aching throat. Mistake. "What was her name? She looked like Amber. Court. That was it."

Shaking his head, James moves to the window. "I don't know anyone named Court. Maybe you were hallucinating from the drugs they gave you."

"She felt... real. She touched me." I try again to sit up, and he rushes over, lifting me higher and propping pillows. After a couple minutes, I wince and swallow again. "Dad? And Ethan? Were they able to get to the train? And Amber?"

He kneels beside the bed and takes my hand. "The train never left the station. There was an explosion. We don't know for sure if Martin and Ethan escaped, but their remains weren't found at the station, and they weren't on the security feed. Amber, either."

"Mom?"

"Well, they shot her from several angles. Hit her spine in two places, which paralyzed her, but I'm not sure how permanent. She's in a facility, like you, but alive. Very critical for a while, and a slow recovery. Doubtful she'll ever walk again."

Not sure how I feel about that. On the one hand, Mom deserves it for all her betrayal. On the other… that look in her eyes before they dragged her away. My arm hairs prickle. "You had a plan." Bracing myself for a blast of pain, I stretch my toes. The dull resistance of unused muscles remains. "What happened?"

"I'm not sure." James stands. "The arena scene was like a war between three groups of people. We learned at the last minute of a second group of rebels. Adrian's loyalists tried to restrain them with guns. They set off a series of pipe bombs at the edge of the crowd. We think they planned to kidnap you. But…"

Glaring over the bridge of my nose, I twitch my lips. He told us we'd be safe. Can I trust him? I'm sure I was in an ambulance. I talked to that girl. Didn't I? And she told me they planned to kidnap me.

Wait. Grandma's necklace.

I scratch at my collarbone with my chin. It's there. Maybe I did hallucinate, but someone put that necklace on me. Some other girl who looked like Amber… what would be the odds?

There must be some sensible explanation for all this.

"I have to go." James brushes wispy strands of hair away from my forehead. "Know we haven't forgotten you, and we're still trying to work out an extraction."

He pulls back the long drape covering the window and peeks outside. A burst of sunlight floods my room, and a handful of clanks and bangs trickle through the crack under the door. The knob turns as James hides behind the curtain.

As the door widens, a dark, curly head pops in. My breath catches. Adrian. But it's not Adrian. Just a twinzie follower wearing a dark perm to show her loyalty. A woman somewhere in her forties, wearing faded blue scrubs and worn tennis shoes. A clipboard pokes out from under her arm, and she clutches a huge leather bag with white knuckles.

"Hi Callie. I'm Morgan. I'm your physical therapist." She sets the bag on the floor and extends her hand, her eyes narrowing as I struggle to lift mine. "Even out of consciousness, you've come a long way."

"Yeah." I've had physical therapy? Why bother, if I'm going to rot in an Alliance prison? Tears drip to my pillow.

"What I wouldn't give for an iPad. These archaic hospitals are driving me crazy." She pulls several plastic bands from her bag and drapes them over the back of a chair, while James slips behind her and ducks out of the room. Her face darkens. "Guess I won't have to worry about that much longer."

My shoulders slacken. What does she mean? Is she sick or dying? "Thanks for helping me."

"No problem. I'd like to do more." She rolls a small white towel into a cylinder. "If I see you again, it will be in the prison. I don't know how often that will be, so I've left instructions for this equipment to travel with you. I doubt they'll permit that for a prisoner, but we'll try."

I blink my itching eyes. "Thanks."

"I'm going to show you some different ways to hook the bands around door frames and such, and teach you all the exercises. Then, we'll explore ways you can use your own body for resistance."

Her point shatters my core. This will be like a long-term stint in the thinking room. Solitude. And I'll die there. Doubtful I'll ever see her or anyone again.

"Let's start small." She hands me a red plastic band. "I want you to hold this with your palms facing upward, and try to stretch it out a few inches, then let it relax inward again." Turning my hands, she places them in my lap and wraps my fingers around the band, moving my IV lines out of the way.

"Okay." Quivering, I struggle to grip the plastic and tug sideways. When it relaxes, I lower my clenched fists to the bed and fill my lungs before trying again. "It feels impossible."

"You'll get stronger." She prods my upper arm with her jagged fingernail. "Oops. Sorry. Didn't mean to scratch you. Take baby steps. We've been exercising your muscles while you slept, so maybe it will be faster than you think."

"I hope so."

"Okay, let's do some simple stretches. Can you raise your right hand above your head?"

It takes a couple of minutes, but I get it there then flop my arm on the pillow. "Why am I so weak?"

"Several reasons. Intravenous diet, no true exercise… You will gain strength. You have to believe and keep trying."

We work for a couple hours, making little progress and taking several breaks for water and rest. After a while, I swallow easier.

When my muscles start convulsing from repeated pathetic attempts at using them, she leans back against the windowsill and frowns. "Callie, you have a strong spirit. Keep at those isometric exercises. Stretch and flex every muscle every chance you get. Once you regain control…" She steps away from the window and swings her arm in a wide arc. "You can do some range of motion moves. Sit on a bed or chair and straighten your leg. Most important is to keep the blood flowing."

"Sounds good." Still scratchy, but at least my voice is stronger.

"If there are any objects in your room at all, you can use them as weights or resistance. Lift the corner of your bed or chair an inch or so. Push against the wall or floor." She casts me a rueful smile. "Wish I could give you printouts of the exercises, but we haven't had ink cartridges in months. But try to remember. If you keep at it, you can move to squats, lunges, and overhead presses. Maybe planks and stuff like that."

After showing me examples of several different types of complex exercises, she leaves me to my thoughts. I play her actions over and over again. Maybe someday, as long as I remember them.

Yawns overtake me. I rest against the headboard, letting Ethan's kisses fill my mind. Wonder where he is right now. Did he manage to cross the border to America? And if not, is he safe? Does he have enough food? With Dad, he's sure to at least have a chance at survival.

And Amber… Wonder if they picked up where they left off since I'm out of the picture. My lungs ache as I inhale deep and exhale long. Good thing my tears have all dried up, or I'd drown this place.

James's words come flooding back to me. The train. An explosion. Is Ethan even alive? I'll burn for him enough as it is. Maybe it's just as well that we didn't dive into a deep romance.

"Lunchtime." The voice screeches at my door, and seconds later a tiny, withered woman pops into view, carrying a cafeteria tray. She sets it on a bedside table and swings it in front of me. "How do you feel about taking in your first real food in months?"

I grimace. A few tiny carrots and potatoes swim in the beefy broth, which smells like mildewed shoes. Three small corn muffins sit beside it, a fatty butter-like substance filling the crack in their top. How do I feel? Grateful, I guess. Glad to be alive. But I'd much rather have a cheeseburger, thank you very much.

The woman plants a spoon next to the bowl and pops open a milk carton. Curdles have built around the mouth, and my stomach churns. Should I even be drinking milk right now?

"Do you want me to feed you, or would you like to try it yourself?"

I inch my unsteady hand to the tray, and she places her wrinkled one on top of mine. "Here. I'll help you today, and you can try next time."

Her face darkens. I know what she's thinking. There won't be a next time for her. "Okay."

"Let's start with a muffin." She spreads butter over the sandy-looking bread and breaks off a small piece. When she brings it to my lips, I let her place it in my mouth, and regret it. The gritty cornmeal, coarse against my aching throat, sticks in a lump at the back of my tongue. I sputter and gag.

"Drink?" She holds up a wrapped straw. "Think you can sip it or do you need this?"

"St—" I choke, but she must understand, and unwraps it. At least it would let me avoid the curds. Ugh.

When my lips close around it, I muster enough breath to suck a mouthful, and brace myself for the bitter taste. It's not spoiled, though, so I have a couple more drinks.

She smiles. "Good girl. You'll make it fine. Now, let's have some soup."

After about twenty spoonfuls of the bland broth and a few more battles with the thick, crumby bread, I lower my chin. "Thanks. Don't think I can eat any more."

With a wicked grin, she digs into her apron pocket then holds up a couple of Hershey's Kisses. "How about these? I smuggled them in for you. But you have to unwrap them and feed yourself."

Chocolate. The thought of sugar rushes through my veins like the Percocets I took when I had dental work. My mouth waters, and I can almost taste them through the foil. After about five minutes of laboring, the milky goodness melts on my tongue, and I close my eyes, letting the Kiss dissolve in a slow, deliberate stream down my throat.

"See? I told you. You're going to be fine." The woman laughs, then her face goes slack. "We're all pulling for you, Callie. Far as I can tell, ten of us know you're still alive, and we've been more or less imprisoned here while you've been under our care. Word of your supposed death has spread like wildfire, stifling the rebellion. But it's alive in many of our hearts."

"Aren't you afraid to talk about it?" The chocolate sticks to the roof of my mouth, and my words come out muddled.

She gives me a sip of milk. "Not anymore. I'm an old woman, at the end of my life anyway. They'll dispose of us all when you are moved to the prison to preserve the secret. Some, like Morgan, might be fortunate enough to go with you." Tucking a lock of my matted hair behind my ear, she cups my cheek. "I wanted to give you some hope. Never, ever give up."

# Chapter Five

## ETHAN

**TWO YEARS AGO**, I'd have never seen myself as a regular passenger in a helicopter. Five months ago, I stood in an arena planning to flee in one with Callie.

Now, Al, Chris, Robbie and I fly over the landscape every day for our various missions. In a way, it's exciting. Fulfilling. It's awesome to be actively helping Alliance prisoners escape back to America, and even better to be able to scope the sites for signs of Callie. But… there's a certain rebellious angle. Dangerous, defiant, and invincible. And I'm not entirely sure where ASP's true allegiance lies or even if Davey's really in charge.

Davey put Al, Chris, Robbie, and me on his personal team. After nearly five months into the missions, I feel like nothing more than a hamster in a cage, and definitely no closer to finding Callie—if she's even still alive.

Each mission is the same. Catch the Alliance guards not paying attention, create a disturbance, and use the Alliance-developed and so-called nonlethal incapacitating grenades to render everyone senseless while Davey's crew storms the prison and frees the captives. If he's telling the truth, he gets them to America, and everyone's happy-go-lucky.

This all blows my mind. It's like a large-scale game of Cowboys and Indians except there are real weapons, real casualties, and real prisoners to free. But today, it all melds into one surreal… disaster.

The dead man lies across the lawn twelve feet in front of me, his arm outstretched beyond his head as he lurched toward the bushes where we were hiding. Everyone has retreated except Chris and me, but we can't seem to get our feet to carry us to the helicopter.

"What are you doing?" Robbie, who I've come to call Davey Jr., snatches me by the collar and pivots me toward the chopper. He does the same to Chris, and we set off in a sprint. We duck the blades, find our seats, and rest our hands in our laps with white knuckles.

"What do you think happened?" Al is always the first to speak, though his voice quivers.

"Too much agent in the grenades?" Chris massages his temple. "Remember how we learned that in training? That a single dose is near-lethal by injection, so they dilute the agent in the grenades to a level that should only cause paralysis? Maybe they messed something up with the dilution."

When we land, a small group of suited men approaches our crew. We've met them before. The board. A handful of former Wall Street gurus and Washington lobbyists. Self-proclaimed militia men and borderline terrorists. Robbie lunges past us as Al, Chris, and I linger in the door. He lands in the grass, rolls for a second, then sits up.

"What's going on?" One of the suited men steps in front of the group, lifting his Teddy Roosevelt glasses. No doubt Davey's father, the one board member I haven't seen before. The white-haired man's jaw line matches his son's perfectly.

"Nothing, sir." Robbie stands, brushes off the grass, and extends his hand to Mr. Brinkle. "Returning from our mission. Decompressing, you know. Boys being boys."

"We brought you on to be men." Mr. Brinkle stiffens. "All of you need to come with us." He points to a bungalow standing to the right of the mansion where we all stay. They lead us up a set of brick stairs, past a concrete porch, and into a hardwood foyer where each older man prods one of us younger guys down a long hallway into separate rooms.

I follow a bulky man whose tufts of bright red hair poke about like a crown on his shiny bald head.

"Sit," he says, pointing to a brown leather chair backing up to a dark-stained walnut desk.

"Yes, sir." I plant myself down as he walks around to the chair on the opposite side.

39

"Leonard Mueller." He extends his hand across a pile of neatly stacked manila folders. "I believe we've met before."

"We have." My fingers shrink under his tight grip. "Ethan Thomas."

"The Christian." Mr. Mueller smiles. "I'm a Christian, too, son, and in complete distress over this accident." His face sobers, and he folds his hands on the desk. "I know you must be terribly disturbed by what happened today. My own heart is broken. 'For all who take the sword will perish by the sword.' "

"I know the verse." My voice is flat and grim, like someone else is playing it back on low volume. "I've never seen men drop dead like that before." I force down a thick swallow. "Killing is wrong, Mr. Mueller. Even when it's one man and not mass casualties. How can you subscribe to these bombings and such, and call yourself a Christian? I don't mean to be disrespectful. I don't understand."

His face remains stoic. He picks up a crystal paperweight and turns it over in his hands. "War is never pleasant, Ethan, and that's essentially what we're in. A civil war. Sure, we aren't all trained military experts, and with the limited Alliance resources, our strategies are crude and rudimentary. Sometimes things backfire." Flaring his nostrils, he lets out a long, hard breath. "I do not subscribe to the bombings or the killings, but I do subscribe to freeing the oppressed citizens so they can have the right to worship God. Think about it, Ethan. Are you opposed to bombing Syrian warlords or ISIS operatives?"

Sort of makes sense, I guess. A lot of Christians support war. And I guess I do, too. But killing other American citizens, Alliance or not… it feels wrong. It is wrong. My shoulders heave. Maybe I don't know what I believe anymore. "Why did you separate us?"

"Nothing sinister." Mr. Mueller reaches behind him for a clipboard. "We need to get your statement about what happened. And if we separate you, we get the truth from everyone. You don't have time to cook up a story."

"Oh. That's easy." I try to brush the goose bumps from my arm as it all flashes back to the forefront of my mind. "We hid in the overgrown park surrounding the complex. The guards got bored and

Robbie approached with the dogs." My face involuntarily contorts. And the dogs mauled each other before the guards shot them.

"I see." Mr. Mueller makes a few notes.

"That's another part of our missions that I hate. Dogfighting is illegal in America. Barbarian and inhumane. I don't see how we can justify using them."

He shifts the clipboard to the right side of his desk. "Ethan, you're safe to say this in front of me, but you might consider being more cautious with your tongue. Several of our board members fully support young Mr. Brinkle's tactics."

Point taken.

"So, the dogs were released, and they fought?"

I nod. "Yes, and of course the guards all rushed over. We all put our gas masks on and launched the grenades like we've done every time before."

"And?"

"This time the cloud of gas swarmed the men. They grabbed their faces and screamed like normal, but…" I shudder. "You know, I watched this video on Sarin once. Well, or one of those other chemical warfare agents. It was like that. The men started twitching and writhing, and they all dropped. One almost got away, I think. He collapsed twelve feet in front of me. But it was too late."

"Why do you think they died?"

I scrape my teeth across my lower lip. "Maybe the grenades carried too strong a dose."

"But you don't think so. No?"

"I wonder if it was a different chemical entirely. Different side effects, you know. And were we in danger? I mean, I know we are expendable, but—"

He gives me a curt nod then puts his finger to his lips as a dark-haired mustached man walks by.

My gulp breaks the lingering silence between us.

"You can trust me, Ethan." He stands and closes the door. "I need you to tell me the truth about everything that happened."

Can I? "Mr. Mueller, I want no part of this. I want to find Callie Noland, rescue her, and get her home. Like I told you all at the beginning. I've told you all I know about the grenade. When we released it, the men fell across the field in haphazard angles. And they died within minutes. I felt blessed to be out of its path."

He makes a few notes on his clipboard. "Ethan, we're looking for Callie, as we promised. You'll be the first to know if we find her." Balancing his pen on a half-full coffee mug, he flicks his gaze toward the window behind him. "Sometimes we go along with things that are locally reprehensible because we know they are for the greater global good. Now, let's finish this interview and you promise to trust me for a few days. I'll see what I can do about finding you a different assignment."

"I'd appreciate that."

He asks a few more questions about the incident then stands. "Meditate and pray, Ethan."

"I pray every day, sir."

He leans closer. "Davey Brinkle is not in charge here, no matter what he'd like you to think."

"Thank you, sir."

We shake hands, and he escorts me to the hall where the other guys lean and pace. Mr. Brinkle approaches, and we all stand at attention.

"Take some leisure time, boys. We'll give you a three-day hiatus from missions." He nods to the black-haired, mustached man. "One of our members was a psychologist in his former life. If you need to talk to someone, you can use him. What happened today was a tragedy. A grave mistake, or a dastardly crime? Well, that remains to be seen, and we can assure you there will be an investigation. Regardless, operations at the lab are suspended for the moment, and we will find the cause."

Leisure time. For me, that translates into more time to pray for Callie. And, to think about the future.

All the way back to the barracks, I blink away the shrill screams and convulsing bodies that haunt me to my core. Once in my room, I dive under the covers and curl up on my cot. My last coherent thought—Callie's breathtaking smile as my head hits the pillow.

Sunrise comes, mealtime follows, and sunset falls. For three days, I eat, drink, and sleep the much-needed rest. A conviction grows, deep in my soul. I can't do this anymore. Someway, somehow, I have to move on from here. Hopefully, Mr. Mueller will come through for me.

On the fourth morning, Davey's face appears an inch from my nose.

"Rise and shine, buttercup."

Davey kicks the feet of my cot and I scoot back, bumping my head on the concrete wall behind me.

"I'm not going on any more missions."

He jerks to attention. "We feed you. We pay you and give you a place to live. You have no identification. What else would you do? Go back to the streets? This is important stuff we're handling. Rescuing, extracting... I thought that'd be right up your alley. Plus, we comb every single one of those prisons trying to find your girlfriend."

"I'm tired of your important stuff. It's essentially entrapment. And your search for Callie has been fruitless." I rake my hand through my too-long hair and drag my fingers across my prickly cheek. "You told me at the beginning I was free to go whenever. I don't want to do this anymore. I don't want to be a part of ASP."

His face contorts, and he draws his fist back like he might strike me as someone rounds the corner of my room.

"Good morning, Ethan. David." Mr. Mueller appears in jeans and a camo sweatshirt, his balding head covered in a cap.

David. It's hard to hide my snicker as Davey glowers. "Good morning, sir." I swing my legs over the side of the cot, stand, and meet Mr. Mueller's handshake and twinkling eyes. Is it too much to hope for good news?

"David, you may go to breakfast."

Davey huffs and shuffles out of the room, giving the door a good slam on the way.

"I couldn't tell you this the other day, not until the board met and approved for you to know. We've found Martin Noland and will release you to his custody. Together, you can both continue your search for Callie." Mr. Mueller hands me an envelope containing a stack of cash, my driver's license, and my passport. "Here is compensation for your service. I'm taking you to him today."

To Martin's custody? Does this guy not know I'm almost twenty-one? "The board is okay with this?"

Mr. Mueller nods. "To most of them, you're a liability. If word got out that you're one of us, the Alliance would come after us with a vengeance. At first, David felt confident we could use you for negotiations, but the board voted against it."

I shake my head. "He acts like he's all-powerful. Like he's in total control of everything."

"His father gives him too much control, that's for sure." Wrinkle lines tighten around Mr. Mueller's lips. "But no, the board is over everything, and they are not pleased with the way things have been handled recently. The older generation managed their business with class and dignity, even when more... delicate strategies were used. These young guys are heavy-fisted and hot-headed."

No kidding. I follow him out of the living quarters, down a long hall, and outside through the double doors of the mansion. He crosses the front lot to a Lexus and opens the passenger door for me. Inside, a backpack sits in the floorboard, and a wrapped homemade breakfast sandwich rests in the stiff leather seat.

"Go ahead and eat." He walks around the car and slides behind the wheel.

"I appreciate this. More than you could ever know." My hands grip the sandwich, which is still warm against my fingers. "Where are we going?"

"A community of squatters called Northwood." Mr. Mueller pulls out of the lot and speeds down the hill. "Once I release you, you'll be completely on your own and unprotected. You do have another alternative. I can secure your passage to America now, if you'd like."

"I'm not going to America without Callie." I bite into the sandwich and roll my tongue over the cheesy biscuit.

"Understood."

"What did you tell Davey?"

Mr. Mueller chuckles. "That you've been chosen for a special assignment."

We drive for almost an hour, and then he makes a sudden right turn. The car winds through a woodsy neighborhood, past a pay lake, and then even deeper into trees as he approaches a cluster of cabins. "I own this property. All these rentals are mine, and all the squatters who pass through here do so with my blessing." He points to the cabin on the very end. "And, I arranged for Martin to meet us here. You can stay for a couple days, but it will be important that he moves you on quickly. It wouldn't surprise me at all for David to track you here and retaliate. He was very upset by your departure. I had no choice but to tell his father where we were going."

"Okay."

When he pulls into the drive of the dark-stained cabin, a wisp of a man steps onto the porch. His face disappears behind his salt-and-pepper beard, which has grown down to his chest. Martin.

Amber staggers out behind him, her tawny hair twisted into ratty clumps. She grips her face with both hands. "Ethan! I can't believe you're here!"

The three of us fall into an embrace, me gripping so tight my fingers ache. A few moments of tears pass before we finally part, and Amber disappears inside the house.

"Thank you, Leonard." Martin reaches into his coat pocket and pulls out a small paper bag. "I whittled you a few more fishhooks."

Mr. Mueller holds up a beautifully crafted pine hook. "Amazing craftsmanship. One of these days when all this Alliance stuff settles, we'll try them out." He hands Martin an overstuffed envelope and heads back to his Lexus. "I'll be two houses down if you need anything," he calls back to us. "And I'm leaving tomorrow."

Martin and I embrace again before crossing the threshold into the house. I draw in a long, deep breath. "Any news on Callie?"

"No." His shoulders sag, and his voice cracks. "But we'll keep trying."

I clench my fists at my side. "We *will* find her. Whatever it takes."

# Chapter Six

## CALLIE

**INIQUITY.**

I scratch the letters into the oak table with a drywall nail. Words now cover half its surface, from the base of the wobbly legs to the peeling polyurethane top. I've been in my new prison a mere few weeks, but it's been long enough for Adrian's daily visits to grate my nerves.

Five months, most of them in an Alliance hospital, have passed since I betrayed him.

Though my physical wounds healed, my body aches from head to toe. Mostly my heart. The not knowing whether or not Dad and Ethan escaped with Amber…

My prison is nothing more than a basement in an old Monongahela School. A wooden frame with remnants of drywall covers moldy concrete walls. In the corner, dry-rotted panels separate a toilet and sink from the main room. It smells like old dirty socks down here, but Adrian doesn't seem to mind. His nostrils are burned out from snorting stuff anyway. And for whatever reason, he tolerates my etching.

I've considered ways to escape, but they're pointless. Guards and electric fences still surround the facility. From what I've gathered, Adrian's put so many people in jail they've started filling the churches and schools, which encourages me. The rebellion is alive.

I glance at a wad of paper on the floor by my feet. Adrian sits across the room on a worn leather couch, his legs crossed like a woman's. His heart throbs through his skin-tight shirt and his waxy curls bounce from the pulse on his temple.

Let him be mad. I'm not picking it up. It's another forgery, like the last supposed note he brought me.

"Aren't you even curious?" He smirks. "The boy is, after all, the love of your life."

"He's free." I carve a loop near the top corner of the left table leg. Adrian wants me to think he caught Ethan, but he refuses to look me in the eye. So I have faith.

"Free with your sister."

Pangs sear my chest. I etch them away. "Don't you have any original material for torture?" I lean closer to the table, scraping a small circle to dot the I. "This is growing tiresome. You talk about Amber and Ethan to get a rise from me; I don't care, which frustrates you. Your blood pressure soars, and you go home to pop pills. You have more important things to do than sit around this cell with me."

A centipede pokes its head out of a crack in the concrete wall. I shuffle over and catch it on my nail. Beside me, a huge spider hovers. I drop the centipede on its web. "Eat away, little buddy." And stay away from my cot. I turn to Adrian. "Are you hungry? I could catch you one, too."

Coughing, he raises his feet from the floor. Then he scratches his chin. Bet he's thinking about his next fix.

I return to the centipede's crevice, running my fingers along the surrounding wood beams that once held plastered walls. Tracing my etchings, I murmur, "I am convinced that neither death nor life, neither angels nor demons, neither the present nor the future, nor any powers, neither height nor depth, nor anything else in all creation, will be able to separate us from the love of God that is in Christ Jesus our Lord."

"You're wasting your time with those verses. We're going to burn this place in a few weeks anyway, after we move the prisoners into our new facility. Construction will be complete soon."

My pulse races. "Don't care." I return to the table and etch some more. "Shouldn't you go run your little country?"

"I have men who do that."

I shrug, though my hand shakes. "Yes, you've told me."

He stands then paces by the heavy steel door barring me from the world. "I visited your mother. She's healing from her last punishment. I think she lifted her arms over her head with no pain. And we've managed to secure her a wheelchair."

I have to force my lips to speak. "Good."

"She says hello. And that you should ask forgiveness for betraying me. Three little words, and I'll let you come back to the mansion."

"Not happening." I finish the last curve on the S and inspect my work, scratching deeper over the letters. Does he think I'd want to go back?

His face contorts. After a pause, he smiles. "How's your knee? You're not getting around so well today. Is your shoe on too tight?"

I stifle a grimace. My knee throbs. Speaking of shoes... His question makes me think of an old Bible joke Dad and I shared. "You ever hear of Bildad the Shuhite?"

Adrian tosses a glance at the ceiling. "The name doesn't ring a bell."

It wouldn't. "Shortest man in the Bible. You know, shoe-height?" I snort as Adrian scowls. "The book of Job. Bildad, who accused Job of wickedness the way you are accusing me. It's interesting, what he said, how dominion and fear belong to God."

Pressing his hands against his thighs, Adrian draws in the musty air. "I fail to understand how you could have lost everything and still choose to believe. It disgusts me."

"So kill me. Put me out of my misery." I rest my elbows on the table and fold my hands together. "Oh, that my words were written! Oh, that they were inscribed in a book! That they were engraved on a rock with an iron pen and lead forever! For I know that my redeemer lives, and that he shall stand last on the Earth. And after my skin is destroyed, this I know. That in my flesh I shall see God."

Adrian scoffs, his pacing growing more frenzied. "You're a lunatic."

Says the lunatic. I tap my knuckles against the table. "Xanax today? Need something for those nerves?"

He stops short, grinding his teeth. Beads of sweat sprinkle his forehead. "I hate you, Callie."

"I forgive you, Adrian." I cast him a cheeky smile. "I still don't understand why you keep me around. Ultimate betrayal and all. And if it's true, what you say… you know, how everyone thinks I'm dead. That's a lot of expense for a funeral for someone who you didn't manage to kill."

His breath quickens. He spins on his heels and grabs the doorknob. "Killing you would end your suffering. I'd rather it go on."

"As the Apostle Paul said, 'I've learned to be content in whatever state I am.' You're wasting your time."

Adrian harrumphs and storms through the door. When it slams, a piece of the wooden frame clatters to the concrete floor.

I crouch beside the table, wincing as pain shoots through my knee and up my thigh. Finding an empty spot on one of the legs, I dig the nail into the soft wood. The hair on my skin prickles as my eyes fill. Shallow breaths quell my trembling. I etch a line across the leg, separating the last verse from the new one.

Adrian's empty words still haunt me. The same message, day after day. The Alliance is strong as ever. America has had a financial breakdown, and nine other states are prepared to secede and form their own nation on the Pacific coast, splitting the US into thirds. Parents are sending their kids to the Alliance schools in droves, and the Alliance government has constructed more to accommodate the demand. Lies, but I have no way of knowing.

Every day he promises to set fire to this place and destroy it. Will he destroy me, too? Shivers race up my spine. I'm fine with dying, but I don't want to burn.

A roach skitters by, racing from the table to the wobbly bookshelf housing Adrian's trinkets. Months of gifts. A silver crown, studded with diamonds, rests in velvet on the top shelf, his reminder of what could have been. On the shelf below it, the Alliance Bible gathers dust, surrounded by little tchotchkes and figurines like the ones he'd given Mom.

Thoughts of Ethan encompass me. I taste the chocolate and peanuts from his last kiss and feel his smooth lips pressed against mine. Rubbing my arms, I squeeze, pretending he's holding me instead. Whether this is self-inflicted torture or guilty pleasure, I haven't decided, but it's become part of my routine. It keeps me sane, as does praying and reciting Scripture.

But today, I tremble.

*Be still, and know that I am God.*

I pull myself to a stand and hobble to my cot, tears trickling down my cheeks. Be still. I'm listening.

Curling in a ball, I slide under the thin sheet and wrap myself in my arms. Other than praying, being still is all I can do right now. That, and wait.

Someone knocks at the door, and I hold my breath. Hasn't Adrian bugged me enough today? As the lock clicks and the knob turns, I sit up straight, crossing my arms and lifting my chin. He'll not find me this way, broken and balled-up.

Instead, a middle-aged guard sweeps the door open enough to pass through, and cracks it behind him. His salt-and-pepper hair reminds me of Dad's. After depositing my poor excuse for food on the table, he squashes a roach and kicks it out of the way. "I hope you don't mind company. Name's Alex." He sits at the foot of my cot. "It's endless torture to sit in that dark hall with nothing but insects for hours, and I thought you might sing for me."

"Sing?" I gather my hair and twist it, letting it fall on my left shoulder.

"I love listening to your songs." The tips of his boots flex as he stretches his legs. "They give me hope."

Hope. He has been listening. "You know they're church songs, right? Adrian would have you shot."

Alex stares toward my etchings then crosses the room, tracing his fingers over the wooden beams. "Wow. You've done all this?"

"Have to do something to keep my mind occupied." I shrug. Should I trust this guy? He seems earnest. "So you aren't afraid of being exposed to my forbidden religion?"

He leans closer to the beam. "It looks more like poetry. I love this. 'For I know the thoughts that I think toward you, says the Lord, thoughts of peace and not of evil, to give you a future and a hope.' "

"One of my favorites." I give him a warm smile. "Try the verse about four down. Romans 12:12 'Rejoice in hope, be patient in tribulation, be constant in prayer.' "

"Well, you're keeping up your end of the bargain in being patient in tribulation." Alex picks up the Alliance Bible and carries it back to my cot. "I used to go to church years ago. Stopped going because I got tired of people judging me for every choice I made. And I never got anything out of the service."

"There's your problem. Worship is not for you. It's your personal offering of praise to God." I walk over to him and crouch beside one of the beams, a flicker of pain shooting through my knee. "Did it ever occur to you that maybe He never got anything out of your worship?" Where did I put that verse?

"Never thought about it like that. Guess God didn't like me sitting in the church all bitter every Sunday."

"Oh. Here it is. This is Romans 1:18-25. Adrian… um, I mean Lord Lamb—"

"You don't have to call that lunatic Lord on my account." Alex kneels beside me, tracing the letters.

I laugh. Maybe I can trust him. "Good to know. Anyway, Adrian has twisted this passage for the Alliance, but he didn't understand what it meant. Listen to this first part, verses 18 and 19. 'For the wrath of God is revealed from heaven against all ungodliness and unrighteousness of men, who suppress the truth in unrighteousness, because what may be known of God is manifest in them, for God has shown it to them.' "

"What does that mean? Manifest?" Alex sits cross-legged on the concrete floor, forgetting the open door. Isn't he worried I'll try to escape?

"Manifest is like clear, or obvious. It's saying that those men should have known better. God showed them what they could know about him, and they chose to suppress the truth." I sit next to him, extending my leg to ease my aching knee.

"So you mean they knew who God was and decided to ignore it."

"Right. So they could continue doing the wrong things they wanted instead of the righteous, godly things they should have been doing. Selfish ambition and stuff like that. You know, like Philippians 2 says. 'Do nothing out of selfish ambition or vain conceit.' "

Alex's eyes widen. He didn't know.

He shakes his head. "Everything Adrian does is for selfish ambition. His religion is based on it. Do what's best for yourself. Deny everything so you can have a good life."

"Well, now, the Bible does teach to deny self. But it also says to take up your cross and follow Jesus."

A centipede skitters beside him, and I chuckle as he jumps. "So anyway, men decided to ignore what they know about God and chose to do the wrong thing, which made Him angry. The next verses in that Romans passage make it even clearer. Listen. 'For since the creation of the world his invisible attributes are clearly seen, being understood by the things that are made…' That shows that we should honor him through our appreciation of nature and such. We should be in awe of what he created." I climb to my knees, move closer to the wall, and run my fingers over the splintery etched wood in front of me. "And look at this part. '…so they are without excuse.' "

Alex leans forward, squinting. He traces his fingers over my letters. "I see that. And here's why. 'Because although they knew God, they did not glorify Him as God…' "

"You're getting it." I pat his shoulder. "Do you understand what happened? You let church become about you and what you wanted to feel or gain from it. Instead, it should be about praising and honoring God."

His cheeks flush. "I did that. I always complained about the details affecting my comfort, like the temperature or how much room I had to sit. Do you think God could forgive me?"

"He forgave Paul, right? The apostle who used to persecute Christians? Paul called himself chief of sinners. But God used him throughout his ministry. So yes, he can forgive you, too. But you have to become a Christian first."

"I'd like to study it more, but how?" Alex braces himself against the beam and stands. "There are no churches in the Alliance, other than Adrian's orchestrated meetings and ceremonies."

"Oh, there are churches. Trust me." I accept his outstretched hand and let him pull me to my feet. "Hidden in every corner of the West Virginia hills. And yes, there are some things you need from a church. But if you want to keep visiting, I can teach you what I know. You don't have to be in a church to offer praise to God."

"Really?" His eyes twinkle. "How?"

"How about a simple song?"

Three hours later, he rushes to the door. "I've enjoyed our visit so, but we've lost terrible track of time. Thank you, Callie."

"I'll pray for you, Alex."

"Do. And pray for yourself."

He pulls the door behind him, and tears fill my eyes.

I drop to my knees and clutch the rail of my cot. "Thank you, God, for this unexpected opportunity to minister to Alex. Please keep him safe and bring him peace. I will press on, and proclaim Your truth to anyone who will listen." My breath rattles out. "As always, I pray for deliverance so I can further serve Your purpose on this Earth, but perhaps You had a different deliverance in mind."

I glance at the soggy bread Alex left me. It swims in a bland pool of cold broth. "Please, help me to accept Your will. Ever Your servant, Callie."

Alex pokes his face back in. "Amen." As he closes the door and the lock clicks, my heart soars. *Though I walk through the valley of the shadow of death, I will fear no evil...* God is with me.

# Chapter Seven

## ETHAN

**THE PINK FLANNEL BLANKET** falls from Amber's empty bed. I might choke that girl. If I can find her... How could she do this to Martin?

Rain thunders against the roof of our squatter home. I stalk across the hardwood floor down the long hall to the room where Martin sleeps. As I pass a claw foot marble-and-brass table backing up against the olive green walls, my knuckles brush a dainty lamp. It teeters, forcing me to unclench my fist as I steady it.

Oh, for a bit of electricity... and some heat. How our luck has changed since Mr. Mueller left us in Northwood. We've passed through seven communities now and are no closer to finding Callie than we first were.

With every new house, Martin insists we be cautious, borrowing only what we need to survive. This time, I think he gave up. Soon as we moved in, Amber took over the former owner's entire stock of outdated cosmetics and roamed the secluded neighborhood with some street rat she found. Bet that's where she's gone.

"Amber's not here." I grip Martin's shoulders, rousing him from a deep sleep. "She left pillows in her bed, and there's no sign of her anywhere."

"Gone?" He scoots up, bumping his crown on the headboard. "Like she ran away?"

"Looks as if. I can't believe she'd run off in this storm."

He rubs his temple. "She's snuck out with that long-haired squatter in that house on the corner. I'd lay money on it. We could go get her."

"With this lightning?" I groan. "I mean, I thought that, too. I'm sure she's up to nothing good, but we'd have to walk a half mile uphill in that mess. Let's wait it out."

Outside, wind rattles the shutters and dust swirls around like blustering snow. Dried leaves blow past and rain pelts the dirty, double-paned windows. Thunder claps, followed by electrical bolts that span the entire skyline.

He throws off his frayed quilt and swings his feet over the edge of the mattress. "Storm woke you, I guess?"

"Thought I heard cats fighting outside. Went out back to scare them off, and found her window open." Running a hand through my disheveled hair, I fall into a stiff paisley armchair. A plastic dart gun juts from beneath the cushion.

The former occupants of the house left behind several tablets and laptops. Toys litter every corner—expensive-looking dolls and huge sets of Legos. Laundry piles the corners of every bedroom, and crusty food still lays in wrappers on some of the bedside tables. And now, remnants of Amber are strewn about—makeup brushes, nail polish, and tons and tons of her stringy hair.

In the few weeks since Mr. Mueller left us, we've survived on what bits of edible food remain in abandoned houses, inching our way past road signs to Monongahela. From what we've gathered, the Alliance now spans the state of West Virginia, and part of Ohio and Virginia. Most citizens are concentrated in Charleston, a tiny fraction of the followers Adrian amassed, and we've heard the rest are imprisoned in the Monongahela schools. It's a joke to even call it a country.

Martin stumbles down the hall to the bedroom Amber claimed. He flings the door open and storms in, knocking the pillows to the beige carpet as I come in behind him.

"Her pack's gone." I nod to the closet where hangers lay strewn on the floor. "And I think she's taken some of the clothes, too."

Martin's lips form a sideways pucker. He turns to the window. "So she has run away, then."

"Looks like it." Tracing my fingers across the dresser trim, I brush the dust to the Berber carpet. At my feet lies a note scrawled in eyeliner. "Here you go. 'Left for Mexico with Bae. See you on the other side.'"

The words spring from my lips like poison darts.

"No sense chasing her." Martin clutches his heart and sits on her bed. "'For these things I weep; my eye, my eye overflows with water; because the comforter, who should restore my life, is far from me. My children are desolate because the enemy prevailed.'"

"I don't know that one."

"Lamentations. Ethan, for years I've dedicated my life to study and devotion to the Bible and the ways of Christ. I shouldn't think this way. I've studied the book of Job. But still, how is it, that being such a faithful servant, I find myself in continual assault? I thought if we resisted the devil, he'd flee. He presses harder." He crosses his wrists behind his head, landing on her pillow.

All the sermons I've ever heard explaining grief away could do nothing to fix this broken man, clinging so tight to the Book he'd loved for years. None of my feeble words would suffice. "I'm sorry." But I'm not. All I have left to feel for Amber now is hate, and Christians aren't supposed to feel that.

I sit cross-legged on the floor and fold crumpled clothes into a pile. After a few minutes, he joins me, and we clean the room in silence until no traces of Amber remain.

Martin and I pick up toys and declutter the other bedrooms until late afternoon. Therapy, I guess. Somewhere around six, we pause for a meager dinner of a small handful of blackberries.

"Did you know you can grow these indoors?" He takes a bite of the rare treat and a quick smile flashes across his face. "I traded them for some of my whittled creatures. We could build an operation like that. Make a garden… if we don't find Callie."

"We'll find her." Is he giving up? My face muscles contort in anticipation of the bitterness. As I close my lips over a small berry, the juice oozes between my teeth. Some sugar or ice cream would be nice about now. "But we're not planning to be in the Alliance that much longer, remember?"

"Ahh…these are tart. I so loved blackberries as a kid." He holds one a couple inches in front of his face, waits a few seconds, and shoves it in his mouth. His lips pucker, and he grins. "When I was ten, my mom took us to this orchard about ten miles past Lexington. We spent hours picking baskets of berries and apples. That night, she taught me how to can them. I still remember the sweet smell, and all those jars of jams and jellies filling our pantry shelves." His bitter laugh jolts him. "Better than anything you can buy in America these days. I'd guarantee you that."

"I'll bet." I pick a seed from my teeth and suck the juice from my finger.

"Blackberry was my favorite. We made this cobbler together out of cheap biscuit dough and churned butter. I smelled it baking and cooling for over an hour, and then Dad called me out to the garage to help him with something." He twirls a string from the cushion and tugs it so hard it snaps. "Changing a water pump, I think. He'd been working on that old car all day."

A sappy smile spans Martin's cheeks. "We walked in greasy and smelly, and Dad's eyes lit up like a Christmas tree. He danced Mom around the kitchen and kissed her right there in front of me. I felt like the luckiest kid in the world." As he licks his lips, his chest heaves. "I can still taste it. The best cobbler I've ever put in my mouth. Better than Angela Harding's, even."

I chuckle. "That's hard to imagine. I always tried to be first in line at the church dinners so I could get some of her cobbler."

A shadow crosses his face. "The next day, Mom acted strange. She kept counting the jars, insisting we'd made more than what sat on the shelves. Swore Dad stole them and sold them off to some of his friends." His lip twitches, and he lifts his right hand to scratch his nose. Seconds pass without him speaking, then he faces me. "She made me come in and count them for her. Some were missing. Listened to her freak out on Dad and accuse him of lying. He called her mad, and she stormed off to the garden."

A huge crack of thunder sends us jumping. Martin stands, and rushes to the window. "We need to move on after this storm passes. We'll be in the middle of winter soon, and the snow will cost us even more time. If Callie's still alive…"

"She is. But I understand you being discouraged. You'd think we'd have caught at least one break by now. Keep praying. We'll find her." I pluck another berry from the bunch, tearing it free from its wispy stem. Across the room, a picture hanging beside the window features a guy about my age in Army fatigues. "This family had a son in the military. Wonder what happened to them."

"I wonder that in all these homes. Hate being a squatter. It goes against everything I believe in." Martin shuffles back to his leather armchair. "So, anyway, Mom stormed off to the garden." He kicks the Oriental rug back a few inches as he slides to sit. The footrest springs up, and he grapples for the arm, knocking the fabric covering it to the floor.

I reach behind an end table for the fabric, leaning over a basket of newspapers. The top one is dated from last July. Gripping the stiff, yellowed paper with my other hand, I raise up and toss Martin the fabric. "You were saying…"

"Right." He covers the chair arm and leans back again. "When Mom came back from the garden, she acted very strange. Fell to her knees, and begged his forgiveness. Told him she'd never stop paying for all her mistakes and apologized for accusing him when she deserved all the blame herself."

The paper falls to my lap. In the front page picture, a line of traffic stretches for miles along I-77. "Why do you think she acted so weird?"

"Adrian. It had to be." He flings his right hand against the leather seat. "Once he learned she was his mother, he bullied her all those years. I'm sure of it. Stole food, tormented her in the garden, which was her sanctuary… And then, he found out I loved Ella back in high school and pursued her with a fury. We even broke up a couple of years over it during college. Ella told me the whole story when we were at Adrian's mansion. How he'd pressured her into sex and she became pregnant at twenty and hid away until after she'd had the baby. Mom helped her put the girl up for adoption. We got married a couple years later and Amber was born eleven months after that."

"I'm surprised Adrian let you talk to her."

"I think he wanted us to talk. He wanted me to know the whole story so I could feel the pain." He yawns wide enough to expose his tonsils, blinks several times, and takes a deep breath. "The more I think about it, there was this old, abandoned barn a few miles down the road from us, on this property where the old man who owned it died. Mom would never let me walk that way. Said there was a pedophile living in one of the houses and she didn't want me to run into him. I wonder sometimes… She lied about so many things, Ethan. The longer I live, the more I see that."

The juice from my blackberry drips off my fingers to the old paper. "Hard to believe things could change so much in such a short time. And even harder to believe America hasn't swept in and taken back over since the Alliance has lost so much ground."

"Who's to say they haven't?" Martin stretches his long feet over the end of the chair. "We're going to have to find some new rebel contacts. Not your buddy Davey's variety."

Puckering, I chew around the seeds and swallow the tart berry. "So, why do you think she did it? Give Adrian away, I mean. And what about your dad? Did he know?"

Martin shrugs. "Why do people do anything? Dad was overseas with the Navy, so she was alone when I was born. He never knew there were two babies, I guess. Maybe she didn't think she could raise us both without Dad. Adrian claims he was raised by some middle-aged couple who treated him badly. It doesn't make sense for her to give a baby to someone like that. But the burning question on my mind is why did she choose me? Why not him?"

"I've looked into those eyes, Martin. The color changes with his mood, but they always reflect evil. Don't you think she knew?"

"Maybe." He unwinds the string from his finger and lets it fall to the floor.

I walk the berry container over to the sink and rinse it out with some of the water we'd collected in a makeshift rain barrel. "We're losing daylight." Martin pushes the footrest back under the chair and moves to the kitchen. "Think we should go ahead and get some sleep. We'll leave in the morning."

Hours later, a bright flash jolts me awake. I race to the front porch, and Martin's footsteps pound behind me. Six houses down, flames lick the edge of an exposed garage, lighting the sky like sunrise.

We hurry closer, leaving the door gaping behind us, and almost stumble into two bulky, dark-headed men coming from between the two houses next door to ours.

"Sorry." One extends his hand and steadies Martin. "Didn't see you guys."

The taller one lifts his palm toward the flames. "Too big a fire for lightning. And no explosion, unless the thunder covered the sound. But the storm died down hours ago." He points to an open window on the second floor, where flames dance around the ledge and lap at a torn red fabric hanging from the edge of the sill. "Didn't realize anyone was staying in that house. Wonder if they're alright."

As we inch closer to the billowing fire, his profile becomes clearer. Cleft chin, stubborn angle... pointed nose.

Is it even possible? Have we finally ran across some luck? I skip a couple steps to catch up. "Don't I know you?"

He draws his left hand to his lips and strokes his hint of a mustache. "Ethan, right? From Virginia?"

"From Kentucky. And you're Luke." Wait. He's not tall enough to be Luke. "No, you're Brandon. Your brother was Luke. Your dad, Larry, helped me and Callie cross the border. There were four of you."

"Yep." A voice behind me booms. "But right now, it's me and Drew. Tristan and Luke are in Charleston, smuggling people across the border. Every now and then, they meet us here with supplies and we distribute them to trapped Alliance citizens."

I can't believe we've found these guys. If anyone can help us find Callie, they can. Incredible luck or providence? Maybe a bit of both.

Martin's engrossed in the flames. I step from the street to the sidewalk in front of the burning house. "Do you see anyone?"

"No, and I didn't hear any screams." Brandon points to a camo backpack on the ground behind me. "Drew, get me those thermal glasses."

Drew shuffles through the pack then hands Brandon a pair of binoculars. "Didn't bring them. These may work."

A few minutes later, they've canvassed the entire home, while Martin stands transfixed with me by the mailbox. Years ago, Callie told me he had occasional panic episodes. Could that be what's going on? What do I even do? Help him sit?

As I ease him to the sidewalk, a handful of other small groups straggle closer from different directions. Guess everybody was scared to come out of hiding. They watch us from a distance in somber reverence.

"Meth heads." Brandon comes out from behind a neighboring home holding several empty boxes of cough medicine. "Think they accidentally started the fire. Wonder how they managed to get their hands on this."

Can't answer that, but I have a good idea who was involved.

Brandon kneels next to Martin. "You okay, man? Can we get you anything?"

"We heard about Callie." Drew crouches next to Brandon and pats Martin's shoulder. "I'm so sorry."

Brandon nods. "Broke our hearts to hear of her passing."

"She's not dead." Martin shoots to his feet, shaking his head. "They faked her death and kidnapped her."

Drew clears his throat. "I know you'd like to—"

"Have you heard of ASP?" I move between them, grabbing Martin's wrist before he can sling his clenched fist. Not that he would. "The rebel organization behind the bombings?"

"We know of them." Brandon's jaw twitches.

"I've been working with them the past few months. They sort of… um… captured me, I guess, and set me to working on their missions to get people out of the country." My grip loosens, and Martin wrestles free.

"James Caudill was supposed to help us get to America." Martin's clenched fists drop to his side. "Apparently this ASP group stepped in and bombed the arena where Callie was speaking. We never had a chance to escape."

Brandon reaches into his pocket and pulls out a hand-drawn map. "They used to help us with extractions. We backed away from them before when they started bombing everything." He points on the map. "Our operations are somewhat exclusive of each other. You can see they concentrate in these northern Alliance areas, and we focus more on the south. They do their own extractions, but with less humane means. Our goal is to get the most people out with the least amount of casualties."

"Well, I've been working on their extraction teams." I steal another glance at the map. Big blue checkmarks cover about a third of the marked locations. "I'd love to work with yours. To keep looking for Callie."

Brandon folds the map back up and pockets it. "Tristan and Luke were supposed to be making a run to Monongahela with their team. The stormy weather's slowed them down. Can't get into the prisons there. Way too much security. But there are pockets of people in little abandoned neighborhoods who are trying to get out. Hard to do these days without being able to buy gasoline. We've had to rely on the trains for transport, and that's assuming the engineer can be bribed."

"Tell me about it." I wiggle my toes in my worn sneakers, where the sole hangs halfway loose from the rest of the shoe. Before the Alliance, I'd had about ten pairs, strewn all over my bedroom. Wonder if they're still scattered. If I could go back and put them away for Mom one more time...

"Have you heard any news of Callie at all?"

"No. Before I left, ASP got word that Adrian was holding Martin's wife, Ella, in one of the military schools." My voice drops further. "Maybe even the one where they first sent Callie. So I was thinking she might be in one of the schools."

A cloud of smoke wafts toward us and Brandon waves it away. "Well, we can try to get you to Monongahela. Meet us on the porch of our house in the morning." He points to an older red brick home backing up to a thick line of trees.

"We'll be there." Martin folds his arms across his chest and starts back to our squatter house. But he stands straighter and holds his head higher.

And so do I. For the first time in months, we have hope.

# Chapter Eight

## CALLIE

**BOLDNESS** can bring either destruction or gain. Dad used to say that all the time, and I never understood until today. Maintaining our prison church is a huge risk, and yet my pulse throbs from the excitement. What started with Alex has grown—a small group of guards, and now they've decided to let all of the prisoners meet in a common area for 'recreation.' Adrian even approved it, because he thought it might condition them to be workers. Goodness knows the Alliance does not need more prisoners who can work like slaves.

If anyone told me years ago that I'd be starting a Bible study for twenty-some adults before my nineteenth birthday, I'd have laughed in their faces. Now? It's natural. Comfortable. Not scary at all.

Alex orchestrated things with brilliance. We meet following one of Adrian's visits, after the last of his extra security detail has departed for the capital, and the handful of cafeteria workers and custodians have returned to their families. In four weeks, he's shared what I taught him with all the other guards, and they've all been in to see me. One even managed to smuggle us a few copies of the real Bible, and each have admired my etchings. They claim my memory is miraculous, and I can't convince them it took hours of hard work. Though I've tried hard to set the record straight, a couple believe I'm a prophet.

Today, I hope to help them understand I'm a mere servant, as they can be.

While waiting for Alex's six-knock Adrian signal, I sit cross-legged on my cot. A page from the Alliance Bible rests in my lap, folded into the shape of a butterfly. Who knew my ninth-grade obsession with Origami would come in handy one day? Beside me, hundreds more sit in a haphazard pile, each of them bearing the verse I'd written with my daily dose of black bean juice and a nail. John 3:16. A verse that Adrian may have cut from the Bible, but it still remains etched in many minds.

When Alex knocks, I sit straighter and paste on a smile.

True to his wonky nature, Adrian bounces in with his entourage. Three officers, with twinzie curly hair and frayed uniforms. Perhaps the Alliance doesn't have the money to buy them new ones?

I sit stoic while they perform their normal room inspection. They miss the small Holy Bible atop a high beam in the corner and ignore my butterflies. At this point, they seem so bored with me I could smuggle in an elephant.

"What's this?" Adrian marches over to me and snatches the page from my lap. "Your Alliance Bible?" He sneers and turns to the officers. "Leave us." When he faces me again, his face is gnarled in a triumphant smirk. "Thought you were a Christian, Callie."

"I don't need your poor excuse for a Bible, with its altered text and missing verses." I point to the etched table then to my forehead. "Not when I have most of it up here."

He examines the butterfly, wrinkling his nose as the dried, crusty bean juice crumbles to the bed. "I suppose you haven't changed your mind."

"Not at all." I offer him another. "Do you know that verse, John 3:16?"

The officers have clustered. Bobbing his head toward the door, he glares at them, and they trickle out of the room.

"Well, do you?"

He snorts. "Everyone knows that one. For God so loved the world... He gave his only begotten son... to die, Callie. He killed his child. Surely you can't justify worshiping a God who'd kill his only son."

"Are you planning to kill your only daughter?"

Another snort. "You think you're the only one? I have many, many daughters. Some are more faithful than others."

I open my mouth wide and pat my fingers over my mouth. "Oh, Adrian. Have you never read First Peter? 'Blessed be the God and

Father of our Lord Jesus Christ! According to his great mercy, he has caused us to be born again to a living hope through the resurrection of Jesus Christ—"

"Blasphemy!"

"You blaspheme!" I shake my head. "Do you not fear eternal punishment for your self-worship? Have you not heard stories of men and women who blasphemed God? Take Jezebel, for example. Eaten by dogs. And Sisera. A woman drove a tent peg into his brain while he slept. You don't expect to live forever. What will you do when God requires your soul?"

He shrugs. "Burn in hell, I guess. Oh, judgmental Callie. I've grown tired of your condemning attitude already."

As he turns toward the door, I sweep my arm over the pile of butterflies, scattering them on the floor. "John 3:17. 'For God did not send his Son to condemn the world—' "

"Exactly." He jerks the knob. "Say goodbye to your little Bible table. We'll burn it next week when we move you to your new prison. Maybe this time we'll put you in a room with no furniture. Think of it as a Christmas present."

"Looking forward to it." I jump as the door slams. He meets my eyes through the window. He's moving me? Why is he moving me? What will happen to my Bible study? I mean, I guess Alex can carry it on, but I'd hoped…

And where is he moving me? To Charleston, I hope, because Alex has told me a lot of the prisoners there have escaped. If Ethan's trying to find me, that's where he'd look. There or Monongahela. But I'm sure Adrian's figured that in to the equation.

That man kills my every joy. Well, God should be my joy, but Adrian kills my every earthly joy. Still, I don't understand. Why would God want me to stop now, when I've gained so much ground with these men?

A while later, Alex taps his characteristic Adrian knock again and opens my door a crack. "We must postpone. Pray, Callie."

I rush to the door, but he's already closed it behind him, and the lock clicks. My heart sinks. Something's wrong. Has Adrian found us out? We've taught all the other prisoners to keep our mission quiet, but what if one of them turned us in? What am I praying for?

Before I can bow my head, footsteps thunder in the hall outside my door, and a girl's screams echo behind them. My lock turns again, and I hold my breath. *Please, Lord, watch over us all.*

As my door creaks open, light filters in, spotlighting a familiar face framed by tawny hair. Court! The girl who's haunted my dreams ever since the shooting. She *is* real. I cross my arms tight over my chest. I knew she was real.

She bucks and kicks at the four men who hold her.

Past them, Adrian leers. "We found a street rat hanging out by the prison gates. Thought you'd want company." He tugs at one of his greasy curls and it springs up next to his temple. "You've been missing your sister, right?"

I grunt. "Where is Amber, by the way?"

His maniacal laugh echoes in my chamber. "Not Amber. Another sister. Bet you didn't know you weren't the only candidate for First Daughter. Shame this one had to go and fail, too."

He shoves her into the room next to me, and she swings her long fingernails toward his face.

He ducks back then looks past her to me. "Enjoy her company, dearie. Everyone loves a good atheist."

His laughter deepens as the door closes and the footsteps intensify then fade.

She turns on me, her bloodied face dotted with a spray of freckles, like mine and Amber's. "He told me you sit in here spewing your God stuff all day, every day. Well, let me get this straight right off. I don't want to hear it. Not any of it."

I snort. "Do you think you can come in here and boss me around? If you want to stop me, you're going to have to kill me, because I'm going to continue quoting the Bible until I draw my last breath."

"Tempting thought." She licks her finger and wipes away some of the blood crusted around her nose. "Should have let you die when I had the chance."

"Who are you?" I stand as tall as my bum knee will let me. "What did he mean?"

"We've met before. Don't you remember?"

"Court." I spit the word like poison. "The girl who kidnapped me and got caught."

"The girl who was set up to take the fall."

Her deep blue eyes darken like Adrian's. I'm more convinced than ever. "You are my sister."

"It's as he said." She half-limps, half-saunters over to the table and traces my etchings. "My grandma is your grandma, though she never acknowledged me or him. Adrian's my father. My mother— some woman he met in college. So I guess that makes us sisters. In the half-way biological sense."

"Adrian is not my father. He lied about that." I sit cross-legged on the floor and resume scratching letters into the table leg. "So I guess that makes us cousins. If that."

She leans closer to the table and squints at the tiny letters. "What is all this? Scriptures? How on earth can you remain faithful to a God who'd abandon you in a hole like this?"

I shrug. "I'm not so special that God needs to swoop down here and save me. Believing brings me comfort and peace."

"False hope." Court sits on the edge of my cot. "One bed, I see."

"I'll take the floor." Stifling my smirk, I wait until her shock passes. I mean, why would I be nice to her? But I've got the kill-'em-with-kindness act down. Still, no harm in having fun. "I'm used to the centipedes and rats. They'll terrify you."

"Rats?"

A laugh escapes before I can stop it. "Big ones with gnashing teeth. The kind that make you pray before you sleep. Even an atheist."

Court raises her blood-clumped eyebrow and swallows. "Well, thanks I guess. What's the grub like here?"

I point to a centipede. "You like grubs? I'm sure we can find some if we dig. The concrete isn't too thick here. Maybe after a while, we can dig ourselves a tunnel like that guy in the prison movie. Of course, you'd have to crawl through the sewers and all."

"You're so gross."

For a few minutes, she sits quietly while I scratch letters into the table leg. Then, she leaps to her feet. "I know what I can do. Got another nail? I can remove these letters one by one."

"Suit yourself." I bite back the harsh words at the tip of my tongue, and toss her my crooked nail. If she scratches them letter by letter, she'll have to read them. "I've got it all memorized anyway. In fact, think I'll nap a bit before bedtime. That way I won't have to sleep so long on that old, disgusting floor."

I hobble over to the cot and she moves to the table, digging into my words. Turning my back to her, I close my eyes and blink away the tears that are sure to come.

It's not my tears that flow. Her cries fill the room. They creep under the door and down the long hall—wails that I'm sure cut into Alex's very soul. Humming, I sit up and wrap my arms around my knees.

The music seems to soothe her. Her wails become soft sobs, and she stops pressing the nail into the wood.

"What's the song?"

" 'Nearer, Still Nearer'. It's an old one."

"Oh. A Christian song. Nice." She spits vitriol with the words.

"I don't know how to make this easier, but if there's something you can think of, I'll try it."

She tosses her head, her stringy hair spilling over her shoulders. "I don't need your help."

"Everybody needs something. Besides, didn't you save my life?"

Laughter ripples from her. She clutches her ribs and winces. "That's a good one. You were hallucinating hard core when we overtook the medic. Whatever they slipped into your IV had you dancing with fireflies on the moon."

"But I remember…" I frown. "You, and some guy. The ambulance driver. And an officer."

"No officer." She scratches on. "Well not until they caught us, anyway. But the 'some guy' was my stepbrother, and who knows what they've done to him. They took you off in a helicopter and let me walk away."

The fog lifts from my memory. "The bombs in the arena. You set them off. Why?"

"Not me. Davey Brinkle arranged it. Because Adrian has to be stopped." She smirked, wiping her eyes with the back of her hand. "I'd think you'd want that as much as I do."

"Oh, I do." My knee aches, and I stretch my legs. I'm sure I want it more. "But I don't want him dead. Adrian needs mental health treatment. Drug rehab, for one, and maybe something for schizophrenia? He needs help." I swallow. "He needs God."

"Help. And God?" She flicks a dismissive wave over her left shoulder. "How could you say that? After all Adrian's done to you, how can you hold on to the idea that some divine being is out there acting on his behalf? Or on your behalf? Or, that our slimeball of a father somehow deserves a second chance?"

"Because God is bigger than me." I stand, and move closer to the door. Alex is shuffling outside, but it sounds like one set of feet. Can he hear us through the cracks? Is Adrian with him? "Tell me about Davey."

"He's a genius. Tall, dark, handsome, and brilliant. Like this one time, he outsmarted Adrian's goons by..." She's almost beaming. Did she love this guy? She must've.

"What's Davey's end game?"

"Destroy Adrian." She separates a section of hair from the top of her head and twists it into a tight braid. "Get the glory and the fame. Impress the US government as a hero in the War on Terror. Because Adrian, as you know, is a home-grown terrorist."

"So this Davey guy is working with the US military?"

"No. He's working with this organization that his father sort-of runs." She laughs. "But Davey answers to no one but Davey. His strategy is to attack the Alliance from within."

Right. By bombing arenas and killing citizens. Sounds like Davey's as much a terrorist as Adrian. "And you guys were going to kidnap me."

"Your whole family. Amber, Martin..." A sardonic grin spread across her face. "Ethan..."

Cold chills wash over me. "How do you—"

"Oh, Callie. Your whole life has been blasted on CNN for months. But for Davey, it started up on that mountain when your boyfriend declared his love for the world to see."

That stupid Twitter post. I wring my hands. Why had we been so stupid? One carefree moment, and everything was destroyed. "I'm not sure how that—"

"Following the infamous post, Davey formulated a plan. He'd use you to draw Adrian out so to enact public punishment for Adrian's crimes against humanity. He hoped to convince your boyfriend to join his team to save you rather than kidnaping him. But he didn't plan on Adrian having your sister and drawing you back into the Alliance. When he heard Adrian was throwing you a huge debut party, he decided it was time to get his agenda on center stage."

"Did he get to them? Dad and Ethan, I mean? And Amber?"

"He intercepted them on the way to that train." She laughs, then a shadow crosses her face. "So easy to play. We all were. He tipped the officers so I'd be caught with you in the ambulance, and now I'm the rebel behind the cause. Davey knows Adrian would never kill me. Then, he took off to play militia man with your boyfriend."

My knee buckles, and jolts of pain shoot through it as I grab the doorknob to steady myself. "So Ethan's alive?"

I cover my lips with trembling hands. Why did I say that? Now she knows she's reached me.

"Last I heard, Ethan was in Davey's van headed to our facility. Of course, I was captured after that, so I don't know what happened next. Adrian let me go so the officers could surround me with their big-boy guns. But I do know that the brilliance of what Davey's done—he's pitted the whole Alliance against each other. He's created a civil war, and he needed foot soldiers. Or bargaining chips."

"So why were you here, then? Why were you outside the gate?"

"I escaped capture from a nearby facility and came to save you. Believe it or not." Something squeaks outside the door, and she grips the leg of the table, pulling herself up to stand. "What is that?"

"Food, if you can call it that." I move away from the door and nod to the rickety chair. "You can sit at the table. Hope you like bland black beans. That's all we get these days."

"Look at us. Two sorry princesses forced back to peasants. How far have we fallen from our heritage?"

"Christ is my heritage." I return to the cot. "I don't need to be a princess. I'm a daughter of the King."

She snorts. "Callie, you're delusional."

# Chapter Nine

## ETHAN

**TWO WEEKS** after the fire, Martin and I leave Northwood with Drew and Brandon by train after they send word by letter to their brothers. Armed with directions from one of their contacts, we hike for a couple days then take shelter in an abandoned home, an empty monstrosity sitting atop a tree-covered hill about forty-five miles from the heart of the Monongahela forest.

Six huge brick pillars prop three arched entries, and the place has more windows than a shopping mall. Would be nice to have electricity, but we can't be picky. If Callie had been able to come along, we might have found our own little paradise, because someone's managed to work up an irrigation system, and even start a garden a couple houses down from us. We could live here forever without Adrian ever knowing, like settlers.

Brandon bobs his head toward a dirt path, and I follow him through the trees. "When I spoke with our buddy, I asked about Callie. He told me I should bring you to this place because there's an old school down the hill that Adrian visits weekly. His entire entourage accompanies him." He tosses me an apple from his pack, grabs one for himself, and sneezes. "I need a break anyway. Feel like I'm coming down with something. Or, could be all that coal dust from riding on the trains. I'm sure we'll all pay for this one day."

"I'd say you're right. Like they did in the old days." From the beginning, the Alliance reverted back to lax mining regulations and lowered its expectations for best safety and health practices. Freedom from the over-presence of government, Adrian called it. Now that the American government is paying attention, rumor has it the Alliance is facing serious fines for emissions. No telling what the citizens are breathing.

Brandon takes a huge bite from an apple, the juice squirting around his mouth. He chews, swallows, and takes another bite, then wipes his face with his sleeve. "Good stuff."

"It is." I sink my teeth into my own apple.

His shoulders slump. "But I don't think we're going to be able to make many more runs like this, for food or otherwise. The officers are starting to monitor traffic like crazy in Charleston. Asking people to trade out their cars for black sedans. Forcing them to get perms and tattoos to prove their loyalty. It's scary. Like Hitler or something. If you don't drive a sedan, you're not one of his followers. If you do drive a sedan, you can buy as much gasoline as you want. But you have to sign over a bunch of stuff to get one, and we haven't been true Alliance citizens for so long we don't have any of the documents."

"That's so stupid." I step over a large root. "Why the sedans?"

"Something about them being formulated to use a special kind of gasoline and that's all we'll have available now." Brandon pushes a low-hanging branch aside and twists it free from its tree. He lets it fall to the ground. "This is our calling. We agreed to it. We can't quit because things get tough. We have to work harder to blend. But I hate it."

"Yeah. There has to be an easier way."

We reach the overlook, and my breath catches. Below us, the school spreads across a small span of properties, its varying floors jutting at different heights. Air conditioning units sit along the roof, alongside bald spots where the shingles have come loose. "Do you think she could really be there?"

"If Adrian is making a two-hour drive once a week to visit someone, it has to be a person of distinct interest. And based on what ASP told you, her mother is at a different school. If he'd keep one of them at a school, maybe he'd keep the other at a school? Wouldn't he want them close?"

"I guess so." If only she's there. All my fantasies of saving her could pan out. Sweeping in and carrying her out of a dingy basement, or now, maybe a modified classroom. Kissing away the scars from her gunshot wounds, and bruises from Adrian's abuse. She'll be frail, but beautiful. She's lost more weight, no doubt, because Adrian has a bad habit of starving prisoners. And now that the Alliance is short on food... I shudder. "If we do find Callie, what happens once we break her out?"

Brandon tosses the core of the apple over the ledge. "You know about the subsistence farms, right? They border the Alliance, and if we're lucky, we can get close enough to the American military and have them take her out through one of the river routes. You and Martin, too."

Martin approaches, carrying a bag of peanuts. He submerges his hand and comes out with a fistful of salt-covered shells. One, he crushes in his other palm, letting the shell pieces fall to the sandstone below us. "When can we go get Callie?"

Drew comes up behind him. "We'll do some surveillance from here and on the ground, but we'll wait for Tristan and Luke to bring a team before we make our move. With Adrian's presence and the added security, it will be tough. And, we haven't done a prison extraction in a while."

"Maybe we can be back in America by Christmas." Martin pops two shelled peanuts into his mouth.

Brandon coughs into his elbow. "Maybe."

My baseball cards come to mind, and I can't stop a sappy smile from taking over my face. If I sold them, I could get Callie a ring for Christmas.

A grimace replaces the smile. Amber would be furious if I proposed to her sister. Wonder if she ever made it out of the Alliance, or if she got herself caught. Adrian would have no qualms in killing her now. He's got Callie and Ella, so he doesn't need her anymore. Us, either, for that matter. I flick my gaze to the plaster ceiling, uttering a wordless prayer. Have to keep in mind that any day could be the last, and that my purpose on this earth is God's.

Drew holds out a sack, his arms sagging from its weight. "I found weapons." He glances at me. "Abandoned house down the street had a whole shed full of ammo. Surprised we were the first to find it. I took six guns and left instructions on how they can get compensation. Trust you know how to use a Beretta?"

I snort. "I have Alliance Officer Training, thank you very much. I can take out a grown man with pressure points if I have to. I hate taking someone else's guns."

Brandon snickers and takes a step away from me, and Drew ribs him in the side. "Hopefully Tristan and Luke will get our message and they'll be here soon."

An hour later, Martin, Brandon, and Drew have gone inside to rest. I should go, too, but I can't leave the overlook. Not knowing Callie might be down there suffering.

Cold air cuts to my bones. Remnants of the bright fall leaves cling to their branches, and the deep West Virginia valleys boast tiny rays of hope, though there's beautiful devastation. As we pass abandoned buildings and forgotten streets, my heart aches for them. West Virginia has always known poverty. Must be why so many pockets of people survive. They're used to living off little and sustaining themselves with whatever they can find.

How spoiled have I been to grow up in a middle class family and have everything at my fingertips? Doing without for so long has made me realize that there's very little I need. Even my smart phone, which had almost turned into an appendage, has been far from my mind for months.

I tug at my collar. My "borrowed" T-shirt irritates my neck, or maybe it's my guilt. How could I not see myself as much a sinner during my days of drinking and partying? How could I have pursued my own self-gratification at the expense of my faith? Bringing my folded hands to my lips, I squeeze my eyes shut. *Dear Lord, I come to You ashamed, with my greed and pride.*

I swallow, and saliva catches in my chest. *Please, forgive my covetous, materialistic nature. Forgive me for all the things I've taken along this journey that have belonged to others, either knowingly or indirectly from things Brandon and Drew might have secured us. If I find a way, I will repay the families. The Alliance is a terrible monster. It brings out the worst in all of us. But I promise, if you'll provide me the opportunity, I will help to take it down. If that's Your will...*

*And please, Lord, help me be the man Callie deserves. I pray that we can someday settle peacefully in a Christian home, like my parents gave me.*

A tear squeezes from my eye, and I rub it, as though I could push it back in. It's been so long since I've given deep thought to my faith and allowed myself to miss my parents. But now, I have much to be grateful for. Callie lives. We know where she is, and we have the resources and connections to free her.

This time, we're taking her home.

# Chapter Ten

## CALLIE

**FIFTEEN DAYS IN**, and Court still thinks she can break me from my faith. I've had enough of her nagging. But today, amidst the cracks of whips and screams of random prisoners from outside the windows, she's quiet.

Shouts ring out from down the hall. Footsteps come closer and then retreat.

"It's bad today." Her raspy whisper fades.

"When Adrian's coming, they do inspections. Inspections are always bad." Scuffles across the ceiling give me chills. "Alex once told me the floor upstairs from us only holds new prisoners. So the guards are always finding stuff they've smuggled in, and no one stays in those rooms more than a couple weeks."

She sits on her hands on the cot and rocks side to side. "At some point, he's probably going to kill one or both of us."

"I know." My voice catches. "It seems late for a visit. Look how dark it is out there."

Her frame shrinks as she brings her legs up to the cot and wraps her arms around her knees. "Aren't you scared?"

Am I scared? Numb, maybe. All my greatest fears have already come to pass. Losing my parents, being shot, losing Ethan after finding him again... what else could this man possibly take from me? What more could he do to hurt me? "I try to not be scared."

She tilts her head, and her tawny hair spills over her shoulder. A tiny pout juts from her lips. "You know, I watched you grow up from a distance. Every now and then, we'd meet with her. Try to convince her to let us into her life. We'd find you at Grandma's house and wait down the street until you left. I watched you and Amber play, and wanted to join you so badly. But dear, sweet Grandma didn't want that. She made us come when no one else was around and only let me stay for a few minutes. And she was always so hateful."

"I wish I'd known about you." I gather my own hair into a fist, twist it into a bun, and secure it with my nail. "I wish I'd known about Adrian—all of it."

"If Grandma acknowledged me, she'd have to acknowledge all her mistakes."

"Yeah." Dust from my etching lays piled at my feet. I brush it aside and scoot around the table to where Court has scratched away my words.

Tears fill my eyes as my hand glides over her marks. If only I could get through to her. Help her see that God is a big part of how I manage my fear. Give her something to hold on to.

Her accusations toward Grandma break my heart. It's hard to picture her as hateful when she treated me so kind. But then again, how could I ever trust the woman who hid such deep, horrible secrets? Dad being a twin, and her giving up the second baby because she only wanted one? Knowing about Mom's affair and not telling Dad? Maybe his rage has some merit, even if manifested in lunacy. "I'm sorry you had such a hard life."

The screams die down, and her soft sobs become audible. She sniffles and wipes her eyes with her sleeve. "Callie, I'm glad we met."

"Me, too. I wish I'd known you existed before the Alliance. Maybe we could have found a way to be friends. Maybe I could have helped you." Doubtful, but there's no way to know.

"If you ever get out of here, find the key. Use the locket, and find the key."

The key? Grandma's locket? What's she talking about. "What do you mean?"

She shakes her head. "You can figure it out. You need to know. Find the key."

Alex taps the door six times, his signal that Adrian's on his way. Ten minutes at most.

"And, Callie?" Court clears her throat and comes to sit beside me on the floor.

"What?" I try to hide the edge in my voice.

She smiles. Like we're the best of friends, hanging out. Something's up.

"I want to sing that song when he comes. You know, the one about being nearer to God."

"Why would you want to do that?" My scoff echoes in our empty room. "You don't believe in God, so you'd be lying."

"Maybe I'm starting to. After all, you're not living in fear." She pokes her bottom lip into a pout, looking more like Amber than ever. "It would help me feel less scared if we sing to him."

I close my eyes. Why not? It's something I haven't done in a while, and something he hates. Seeing Court singing would drive him bonkers. "Okay. 'Nearer, Still Nearer', right?"

"That's the one."

She launches into the first verse with a quiet voice so pure it gives me chills, every word memorized. She *has* been listening. When she looks up, tears cover her cheeks, and the ice in my heart cracks a bit. Maybe I've reached her after all.

Three knocks, and we fall silent, each taking our Adrian stances. I sit cross-legged on the floor etching the last corner of the table. She lays on the cot, posed as though in a coffin.

Several more minutes pass, and Adrian's shrieking laughter slips between the cracks, grating my nerves like screeching brakes. The door opens, and he bounces in like a kindergartner. He must be doing uppers today.

"Hello, ladies." He saunters in and stands between us.

We remain stationary, locked in our poses.

"I thought you'd have killed each other by now." Leaning down, he peers into my face and scrunches his nose. "Still etching out that God-talk? Thought Court would have broken you from that by now."

"Come on, Callie, let's show him our new act." Court clears her throat and sits up. "A one, two, and a one, two, three…"

I blink. This is her show, not mine.

Adrian claps his hands. "I love it. Callie has turned to stone."

"Oh, fine. I'll start it." Court stands and fills her lungs. "Nearer, still nearer…"

I moisten my lips, and close my eyes as the harmony encompasses my soul. "…close to Thy heart."

As we sing, a scowl settles on Adrian's face.

"…nothing I bring, naught as an offering to Jesus my King." Court draws out the last note, kneeling on the floor like she's praying. I should have never gone along with this.

"So beautiful. And yet, so disgusting." Adrian's mouth contorts he lunges for her, shoving her toward the table.

A scream catches in my throat as her legs buckle beneath her, and she strikes her head on the corner of the table where she's destroyed my letters. She rolls, and lands head first on the concrete floor. The centipedes scuttle as blood trickles from her nose and right ear.

"My darling." Adrian drops beside her and slaps her face with frantic waves. "Sweet Court. Please. Wake up."

I hold my breath, focusing my gaze on the table leg. Has he killed her? My tear ducts moisten and I blink in fury. I will not cry. Not now, in front of him.

He crawls to face me, his dilated pupils looking monstrous against his bulging eyes. Beads of sweat dot his forehead, and his snarl deepens. "You did this to her. You killed my daughter."

I scoot away as he grapples for my neck. The officers rush in to us, and several pull him back before he makes contact.

Alex checks Court's pulse while they drag Adrian out of the room. I chew the skin off my lip, digging my nail into the concrete.

A tear slips down his cheek as he hoists her over his shoulder and closes the door behind him.

I sit for a while, my gaze fixed on the small pool of blood. So much I don't understand. Why did Court have to die before I could save her?

A couple hours later, Alex gives his safe knock, and slips into the room. "Adrian has decided to move you to a new location. He's taking you to the facility where they're rehabilitating your mother."

"You need to run. Adrian always kills the people who guarded or helped me. At least that's what he tells me."

The right side of Alex's lip curls into a slight frown. "I need a lot of things. Prayer, more than anything. But right now, you have visitors."

He moves to the door, opening it wider. James Caudill stands before me, decked out in full gold-trimmed Alliance red, surrounded by at least six other officers. I'm comforted by his presence, but how could he possibly help me now?

His white hair, stiffened from spray or gel, frames his furrowed brow. Wrinkle lines edge his lips, and his hollow eyes seem to look right through me.

Alex reaches for my hand with his own quivering one. "Miss Callie, it's been a blessing to serve as your guard."

"Enough of that." One of the other officers shuffles past James and drags Alex out of the room by the shoulders.

I gasp, covering my mouth as my heart engulfs him in the full embrace we cannot share.

James withdraws a syringe from his coat pocket, and fills it with a milky substance from a glass vial. "If you fight us, he dies."

His voice, so chilling. But his eyes full of regret. This is what Adrian wants. He has to. Gritting my teeth, I raise my right sleeve.

"I need you to lie flat on the gurney." James waves to an officer standing outside the threshold, and they roll in a wheeled cart, complete with arm and leg restraints.

Two officers rush behind me and scoop me up to the canvas stretcher. I lunge against them then freeze as James's words sink in. He's saving my life right now. Finding a way to stall until he can get me to a safer place.

They drop me to the canvas. *Dear Lord, I know that You are in control, and whatever happens in this situation is within Your plan. Please be with Alex. Be with me, and Ethan, and if Court has any other family to mourn her, please watch over them as well.*

The needle jabs into my arm and an exploding pain seeps through my veins. *Lord, protect James, and Dad, and Ethan… and, help us fight Adrian. Help us fight…*

# Chapter Eleven

## ETHAN

**A FLASH OF LIGHT** jolts me from fitful sleep. Sunrise. Rock scrapes my cheek as I turn it, my stiff neck barely cooperating. I've fallen asleep on the overlook.

A chill washes over me. I could have rolled off or anything. With a drawn-out groan, I grapple for the rangefinder binoculars. Something's going on at the school.

As I adjust the focus on the lenses, several cars come into clearer view. But no vans. Guess they've moved all the prisoners already?

People swarm them like tiny dots, scurrying between the school and cars carrying what looks to be boxes of files. For some reason, they're moving everything out. And probably everyone. If Callie is there, she won't be much longer.

I run back to the house and to wake Martin, Brandon, and Drew, and find a beat-up Chevy parked in front of the house. The brothers must finally be here.

Inside, a tall, bulky man whose profile matches Brandon waves from the kitchen. He holds an aluminum saucepan over a couple of tea lights beside two empty water bottles. "Ethan."

"Tristan, right?"

"No, Luke." He grins. "Tristan passed out. He was up driving all night. I'm making us some instant coffee."

"I'll wake the others." As I pass through the living room, I snag the backpack Mr. Mueller gave me, which contains my scant possessions. "They need to see what's going on outside."

Grim-faced, he lowers the pan. "What is it?"

After I fill him in on what we saw at the school overnight, he shakes his head. "We keep seeing this. Moving prisoners and closing the facilities."

"It looked like genocide to me." I take a spotted banana from the counter, peel it, and down it in seconds. "Tell me, where is the American Army? We can stand up to international bullies whenever it's convenient, but what are they doing to stop the homegrown ones?"

"Oh, they're trying." Luke circles the pan over the small flame. "But there are so many of these small make-shift prisons that it's taking some time. The real problem here is that no one's in charge of anything. It's a free-for-all." He yawns. "If it gives you any comfort, I don't think the bodies you saw being tossed into vans were dead prisoners. They give them sedatives so they don't need as many guards or vehicles to move them. What's mostly happening is as the Alliance is shrinking, the prisoners are being moved out of areas that are being reclaimed by the US. The reasoning, I guess, being that as long as there are prisoners in the way, the US won't come in with a heavy military hand. They're cowering. It's disgusting."

"Oh." I guess that's better than killing them all, but what lowlife creeps would resort to that?

Within a few minutes, the four brothers stand in front of a balcony window, their faces glowing from the beautiful red-and-purple streaked sunrise.

I clear my throat. "Morning fellas."

They all turn at once, stair steps of dark-headed men, each bearing the stubborn profile of their father. Tristan, oldest and tallest, makes up two of Brandon, the youngest. Drew stands out with his ever-present smirk and the slight tint of auburn in his air. All four of them together? A formidable mixture of rugged and brawn.

Luke breaks away first. "Guess we need to get down that hill. I'll go scope out some of the side roads and see if we can find a distant angle to approach the school."

"That big park that backs up to it might work." I hold up my left palm and trace a circle with my finger through the air next to my thumb. "There's a lot over here that's almost completely surrounded by trees, and a back entrance that doesn't get anywhere close to the school."

Brandon faces me and Martin. "I'll scout the security. Act like I'm a local and ask about finding work if I run into any of them."

"I'll go with you, if that's okay. If Callie's there, I want to be close to her." With my Swiss army knife, I scrape a notch in the time counter Martin whittled for me, and the shavings settle to my feet.

"We don't need to get too close." Tristan scratches his chin and lets out a long, wide yawn. "We've pulled the trigger too fast before. It never ends well. We're lucky to have escaped several of those times."

"I know you're right." The dull ache in my heart intensifies. "But the thoughts of her possibly being down there in all that mess…"

Martin grips a thick branch from a nearby sycamore and snaps it away from the tree. "Adrian might do something to Callie before we get a chance to save her. He may have already moved her."

I squint into the binoculars. "Look at all those cars. Isn't that one the car Adrian always travels in? Why would he visit a prison after they've moved all the prisoners out? Unless, maybe Callie was there and still is. Not that he's more than a figurehead, but one might question how he has time to run a country and still harass prisoners all over the country."

Behind us, Drew kicks at sandstone pebbles, sending them scattering. "I don't know that he is running the country, not even as a figurehead anymore. Seems like he's strung out a lot these days from the reports we've had lately."

"I agree." Luke rifles through his backpack then hands Martin a stack of photographs. "Friend of mine managed to take a few pictures from the capital a couple of weeks ago. Brought them by and gave me copies. It looked like Alliance bigwigs were having important meetings without Adrian. My guess is they're thinking about rejoining with America. Richies don't like to live on broth and dry bread."

"Some of them aren't." A bitter chuckle sticks in my throat. I can't imagine Davey's father living on broth and bread. "If that's really Adrian, it does make a good case for Callie being here. Although maybe it's not the best time for scouting the facility."

Luke's pictures show several men exiting a side door to some government building. Three wear suits, and four are dressed in fatigues. "Who are these people? American military?"

"I think so." Luke points to a smoking building in the top corner of one of the photos. "And I'm pretty sure that's the work of ASP. If my friend's not mistaken, the Alliance has paid members of the American military to help end their attacks, and the president went along with it to have a military presence in the Alliance. We might as well go ahead and start calling ourselves Americans again."

"Never stopped." Martin scowls over the cliff toward the dirt road where the entourage makes slow progress toward the facility. "I can't watch this anymore. Makes me want to throttle Adrian. I can't wait any longer. We have to get her out."

He stalks back toward the cabin, and I check the view once more. Another caravan pulls up to the school. Several officers in full red Alliance gear exit the cars and line up in a row by the entrance. Wonder why the formality?

One, with stark white hair, glances up at the hill. Could that be James Caudill?

He raises his face toward our rock. Can he see us? Surely not. From the distance, we must look like ants, but then again, Luke insists on wearing a neon orange coat. Maybe he looks like a bright tree. Either way, I don't see Adrian driving up the crumbling, steep and narrow road to get up here. And if he does, bring it. We have weapons.

The officers disappear into the building and return after a few minutes, dragging four men by their ears into the parking lot. Guess they still haven't cleared out all the prisoners. A man who resembles Adrian prances in front of them like a peacock then passes each of the officers some type of brown stick. No, wait. He's giving them whips. Please, tell me they're not for Callie.

Luke drops the pictures back into his bag and darts toward the path. "Ethan, you ready?"

"Wait a minute." A glob of saliva and phlegm builds in the back of my throat, and I swallow it. "Something else is up."

He takes the binoculars, watches a second, and passes them back to me as the officers rip the shirts from the men and strike their backs. "They're punishing the guards. They must have revolted and been caught."

Though I'm too far away to hear the screams, each hit drives a jolt through me. But one comforting thought prevails. If there *was* a revolt and Callie *was* at this prison, I'm sure she'd have been behind it. Maybe Adrian hasn't broken her spirit.

I scramble to my feet, bracing myself against a small tree clinging to the edge of the cliff with its feeble roots. Focusing my binoculars on the white-haired man's face, I squeeze the thin trunk so hard the bark digs into my palm. So methodical. So intense with the whipping. And so unlike a Christian if it is James. Is it possible he was playing us when he promised to get us out of the country? Was his claim to faith a farce?

We pile into the diesel-rigged pickup and make our way down the steep hill to the woods to the park behind the school-turned-prison. Carrying our packs in case we don't get back to the truck, we hike closer, following a dried up riverbed until we come into sight of the facility. As we inch forward, garbled shouts become chilling words, and we reach a clear view of Adrian ripping a leather-bound book to shreds.

"Your cockiness astounds me." His shrieking voice goes even higher in pitch as he leans nearer to a scrawny man dressed in a guard uniform. "Did you think we wouldn't find it? Did you think I wouldn't know?"

"I'm sorry, Lord Lamb." The man falls to his knees and grasps Adrian's feet, exposing his back to the whips.

His flesh blurs to red as the grass rustles beside me.

Martin clenches his fists, his fixed gaze narrowed, and his kind face twisted in the kind of snarl you might find on a murderer.

"Who brought the American Bibles in?" Adrian waggles a finger in front of the other cowering men. "Who is responsible for this heresy?"

"Bibles." Luke shares a look with Martin. "Other rebels are close by."

Martin's breath grows louder, and his nostrils flare like a bull's. "If I could wrap my hands around that man's neck..."

"Wait." Luke's hand grips Martin's shoulder. "Don't do anything rash."

The officers cuff the bleeding guards, inject them with something, and throw them into the windowless rear of a van, then Adrian disappears inside the school.

My heart aches for Callie, if she's really there. Who knows what she's having to endure, or if he's drugging or abusing her.

So many times, I've imagined sweeping into what must be her cold, damp chamber and taking her into my arms. She'll be gaunt, like most of the other Alliance citizens, with sunken cheeks and hollow eyes. Bruised, but not her face. The dye will have faded from her hair, which will hang in the brittle and wispy strands that come from malnutrition. But she'll still be beautiful.

Her deep brown eyes will shine when she sees me, from tears she's held in. She'll stagger toward me in disbelief, falling into my arms as I scoop her up and carry her away. Sappy, I know, but it's the dream that keeps me going. But right now, I need to focus on reality.

We inch forward, lining up beside a thicket of evergreen bushes separating us from the school. I part the thick, bristles and leaves enough to see, then wince at how near we are to the officers. And, I was right. James is among them. Him and his stark-white hair.

They all enter the building, except James and one other man, who stand at attention in front of the entrance. After a long pause, James looks over both shoulders. "I can't keep doing runs like this. Hard to hold up the charade."

"I know." The other officer coughs into his elbow, a thick, hacking cough that's more like bronchitis. "And to walk right into the kitchen catching men reading the Bible? Didn't they know he was coming?" The man wheezes as he draws in a breath. "Although he hasn't made us go into the kitchen the last several visits."

Martin teeters. He grabs the weak branches of a bush, knocking a few loose twigs to the ground.

"What's that?" The coughing officer takes a step in our direction.

"An animal." James stares our way for a few painful seconds. His face flickers then he shrugs. Did he see us, and he's covering? "Look. Right there. The squirrel. There are raccoons all over this place. And birds… every time I guard here, I get spooked by some kind of animal."

Martin's chest falls as he lets out a silent blast of air from puckered lips.

"An animal." The other man's brows shoot up.

"I'll go check it out if it makes you feel better." James adjusts the strap of his rifle and the other guy falls back into place.

We can't move. If he walks much farther, he'll see us, and if we move he'll hear us. Question is, can we count him as friend or enemy this time? From the way he was talking, definitely friend. But, it's hard to know for sure.

He brushes against the needles of a towering blue spruce and a red squirrel jumps several branches, darting past him and across the school yard. Laughing, he scans the woods behind us, his gaze staying over our heads.

Somehow, he misses Luke's neon jacket and returns to his post. "See? So many critters out here. If it wasn't a prison, it would be kind of nice. Good place for hunting."

We sit twenty more minutes in painful silence while the other officer launches into a hunting tale. James shifts his weight from foot to foot, and the other officer coughs so hard he ends up bent double.

"I need a drink." The man nods to one of the cars. "Think there's anything left in those coolers?"

"Probably." James yawns. "I'm surprised he's been in that long. There can't be that many more prisoners left to move." He flicks a leaf from his padded shoulder. "And since we've already moved his daughter… But then again, he's probably grieving her."

Grieving her? Callie?

My heart stops. It can't be. But, if they moved her…

Something thumps against the glass entrance door and James jumps back as someone shoves it open from the inside. A balding man lands cheek first against the pavement, and I wince as he slides. That's going to burn, for sure.

A young officer with narrowed eyes wearing a springy perm like Tristan and Luke's dives after the man. If we could get inside that building…

As the scuffle continues, Martin bobs his head the way we came. We steal back to the path.

"What now?" Luke's whisper carries a chill.

"Wait and follow." Martin's voice catches. "Ethan?"

"I guess so." Although part of me wants to at least try to talk to James. "Either way, we need to do something soon, because the sky's clouding over. It'll storm again. Maybe we could go back to Callie's first school where they are supposed to be holding Ella. If he's keeping her there, maybe he'd move Callie there, too."

"Maybe." Shoving his hands in his pocket, Luke stalks along the path.

Shouts draw us back to our watch point, and we sit for a few more minutes. Adrian runs out of the building waving his hands like a maniac, followed by a slew of officers dragging another man in cuffs. Shame we couldn't help. Should we have at least tried?

I push to my feet, anger bubbling in my chest. Raindrops pelt the ground beside me and smack into my scull. Focusing on a tumultuous cloud, I grit my teeth. *God, please. We have to find a way to save her. To save all of them. This torture can't go on forever.*

Thunder rumbles in answer, sending chills along my spine. As my skin prickles, I jump back as a bolt of lightning strikes the tree I'd balanced against earlier.

The words of Exodus 3:14 rush back to me, when God said to Moses, "I AM WHO I AM." A pang strikes my chest. God worked through Moses to end the oppression of the Israelites by Pharaoh. We aren't praying enough or trusting enough. And we aren't accepting His will.

Martin faces me. "God never promised there would be no suffering." His voice lacks conviction and carries defeat.

One of the first passages Callie and I memorized together comes to mind, from the last chapter of Job.

I draw in a deep breath. "I know that You can do everything, And that no purpose of Yours can be withheld from You. You asked, 'Who is this who hides counsel without knowledge?' Therefore I have uttered what I did not understand, things too wonderful for me, which I did not know. Listen, please, and let me speak; You said, 'I will question you, and you shall answer. I have heard of You by the hearing of the ear, but now my eye sees You. Therefore I abhor myself, and repent in dust and ashes."

Kneeling, I grasp a handful of sandstone dust and let it fall between my fingers. Tears cling to my eyelids. God blessed the last days of Job more than the beginning. A long life, beautiful children and grandchildren… God's promises are new every morning. I have to trust Him.

When we return to the truck, Brandon and Luke climb in to the extended cab, and Drew bounds up onto the bed.

Martin hesitates. He adjusts his backpack and turns to the trail. "I'm not going with you."

"What?" I furrow my brow. "We have to stay together. Where are you going? I'll—"

"No." He stands taller. "I'm going to find James. You stay with the brothers. One of us will have an easier time than a group. And when I find him, I won't be alone."

Drew shakes his head. "Martin, I don't think that's the best idea."

"Of all of us, he has the most hiking experience." Tristan rests his hand on the tailgate. "And the best survival skills."

"And I have money, food, and water." Martin pats the front zipper pouch of his bag. "If I can't get to James, I can hopefully find the rebels who've distributed the Bibles."

"What if you find Callie and we don't have any way to get in touch with each other?" My pulse races. This is such a bad idea. "Let me come with you." I reach into the bed for my backpack.

"No. You guys move on to Monongahela where they're holding Ella. Ethan, let the brothers help you go home and you can appeal to the American government to help find Callie. I'll make my way there when I can, hopefully with her and her mother. If something happens to me, you can make another attempt. If we all go down trying together, then she has no hope. We have to split up if we're going to gain any ground."

I grimace. "How would I know if something happens to you? Martin, this is a terrible idea."

"Have faith." He shuffles away, and I stand speechless. No words would have changed his mind but should I go after him?

"Let him go. He's right. Splitting up is hard, but he has a better chance of getting to her on his own than the four of us do. If he can find her, he can get word to us and we'll get her out. I gave him a list of all our contact points." Tristan plants a light hand on my shoulder. "Good luck, Martin." His voice fades in the cool, brisk air.

Martin faces us once more, his expression a mixture of resignation and grit. "Pray for me."

My heart heavy, I climb into the truck bed next to Drew. I should be going with him. This is so wrong on so many levels. Hopefully he knows what he's doing.

# Chapter Twelve

## CALLIE

**A GRAY HAZE** morphs into dingy concrete.

"Callie?"

Mom. I must be hallucinating again. Rolling toward the wall, I pull the coarse, musty blanket over my eyes. Wait. Wasn't I restrained? Definitely hallucinating.

"Callie, wake up."

There she is again. Sitting, I reach for a murky water pitcher on a table to my left. Maybe if I dump it over my head, reality will return.

Mid-reach, I freeze. There is no murky water.

The frail woman on the other side of my prison bars grips the wheels on her chair and rolls closer. Deep, dark circles punctuate her gaunt face, and bits of clotted blood hang from her full, chapped lips.

I study the circles. Bruises? Maybe not. Regardless they frame eyes filled with more anguish than I've ever seen. Slipping my feet over the edge of the bed, I find the concrete floor and brace myself to stand.

"Mom?"

She nods, tears streaming her cheeks.

I fall to my knees, engulfed in breathless gasps. Wrapping my palms around the splintery legs of my cot, I pull myself up again. "But how?"

She lifts her blouse, revealing a red, blotchy scar that matches my own. "The bullets all pierced my body, but missed vital organs."

Licking my cracked lips, I kneel on the floor beside her, reaching through the bars to touch her and leaning my head on the cool iron. I sit for what feels like an hour as the haze slowly lifts from my mind. She feels real. She is real.

Tears wash over my cheeks. "You're paralyzed."

"The legs down. You're dehydrated." She brushes my brittle hair from my eyes. "Did they give you food and drink in your last prison?"

"Something like that. It was disgusting. Like food from a third world country."

Sniffling, Mom turns her chair sideways rests her temple against the bars. "The Alliance is more or less a third world country. Adrian has run it into the ground."

"Why doesn't he kill us?"

She gives a harsh laugh. "We're already dead. What good would that do? At least with us alive, he can take solace in our torture."

"Do you know Court?"

Another bitter laugh. "You could say that."

My jaw drops. "She's yours, isn't she? You're her mother, too, and she lied to me."

Mom rolls her wheelchair to the other side of her cell and faces the wall.

"It's true!" I fling my arms to my side. "What else have I not been told? Has any small piece of my life held even a shred of truth?"

"When I was sixteen."

Blood rushes my face and neck, and venom boils in my veins. "He killed her, you know. Shoved her into a table so hard it cracked her head open."

"No." Her chair pivots and comes to rest in the center of the room.

"She tried to kidnap me and he caught her. Let her go, and captured her again. We've been in a cell together until her death."

"I don't believe you." Her icy words bring a chill to the entire room. But her eyes say otherwise.

A creaking noise draws my attention to the small window on the right wall of my cell. I tilt my head, then take shaky steps over, shivering at the air coming from a small crack.

Mom rolls her wheelchair to the corner and cries as I trace my fingers along the base of the window, finding a jagged metal hook in its center. I push, and the gap widens, letting the cold, January air blast through.

A folded paper pokes through, and someone jerks the window closed from the outside. I stand on my tiptoes and peer out the dirty glass, finding a sparse line of trees standing between me and a deep gulley. Who could have dropped the paper? And how did they get to me? There must be at least a 300 or 400-foot drop, and from the sliver I can see, it's a pretty straight shot to the bottom.

I snatch the paper from the sill and move to my cot, leaning against the concrete wall beside it. Should I open it now, or wait?

Mom might stir up a stink about it and draw attention. But it could be important.

With slow, calculated motion, I untuck the folds, careful to make no noise. The handwriting slants left with closed, abrupt loops hard-pressed on the page.

*We will get you out of here. Keep the faith.*

Who wrote this? Dad? It looks like his handwriting. Is that even possible? Are we unguarded?

The narrow hall in front of my cell stretches past Mom's. I press my face against the bars. A solitary camera spies from the far end. No lights, so it may not even be working. I must have the corner cell, because this end of the hall stops at me.

I hide the note under my poor excuse for a pillow and return to the window, this time giving it as hefty a shove as I can manage in my weakened state. It protests with a loud creak, but slides open wide enough for me to poke my head outside.

Gripping the sill, I raise myself to full tiptoes and stretch my spine to see the length of the building. As I suspected, I have the corner room. A three-foot path separates the building from the gulley, and it's more of a steep hill than a straight shot down.

A heavyset woman wobbles toward the far, east end, steadying herself with a familiar wooden cane. Her close-cropped hair tapers at the base of her neck, and hope bubbles up inside me. Is it possible? Reva? My old schoolmaster? Am I back at my old school?

Clouds gather along the horizon. The water tower, off in the distance. The same one I saw when I first arrived in West Virginia, when I first laid eyes on the Monongahela forest and enrolled in the Alliance academy. In a sense, Adrian has brought me home.

"Are you out of your mind?"

I turn. Mom grips the bars between us. "Close that window or we'll both freeze tonight. It's cold enough without a draft." She attempts a huff, her chest quivering with shaky breaths. "Besides. We're due any minute for our exercise and restroom break. The guards will have both our heads if they see you've tried to escape."

"The window is closed." Escape. I snort. Like either one of us could fit out that window. But I pull it closed and sit on my cot, wrapping my hands around my knees.

"See, here they come now." She hisses as a door creaks in the distance.

"Break time, ladies." A deep male voice echoes and the hall fills with shuffling. Two men pause by our cell and escort us out to a commons area, where about thirty other women wait in line for a small restroom. A handful stand. The others are like mom, bound to chairs. At the end of the line, a tall, thin redhead helps each woman into the tiny room.

As we grow closer, the woman's face becomes more familiar. Reva who'd used that dreadful cane on the students to discipline us, but showed me kindness. Was it possible she could help save me?

Three days pass, same as they did back then. Long hours broken by restroom breaks, pitiful attempts at feeding us, and time spent missing Ethan and waiting for nothing to happen. In this concrete cell, I can do no etching. But I can't sit here and wallow anymore.

I slide a glance to Mom and clear my throat. She lies on her cot, waiting for someone to come and help her sit since they left her wheelchair too far from her reach.

"Hear my prayer, O Lord, Give ear to my supplications. In your faithfulness answer me, and in Your righteousness."

"Oh, Callie." She rolls to face me. "My sweet Callie. All this, and you still hold on to God when all others will give up."

"Do not enter into judgment with Your servant, For in Your sight, no one living is righteous."

"Which one is that one?" She lifts her torso with her weakened arms.

"Psalm 143. Remember when Dad helped me memorize it, and we had to spend a half hour explaining to Amber what supplications were?"

"Keep going." She inches closer to the wall, and pushes her body until she's sitting.

"For the enemy has persecuted my soul; He has crushed my life to the ground; He has made me dwell in darkness, like those who have long been dead." My lips quiver. "Therefore my spirit is overwhelmed within me; my heart within me is distressed."

"Hasn't he, though?" She blinks, so slow. Is she falling asleep? Hope she won't tip over. If they'd let us in the same cell...

Her chest heaves. "Do you remember more?"

"The middle is kind of fuzzy." I frown. "I remember there's a line, 'My soul longs for You like a thirsty land.'"

"Yes. And the part about delivering us from enemies."

The hall door creaks, and I jump to my feet. I race to the iron bars and grip them with both hands. "Deliver me, O Lord, from my enemies; In You I take shelter. Teach me to do Your will. For You are my God; Your Spirit is good. Lead me in the land of—"

"Callie."

Dad.

I stumble backward as Mom topples sideways. Can Dad be here? In this prison? And free?

Well, someone who looks like Dad, with a six-inch beard and camo-streaked face.

Reva hurries up behind him and unlocks our cells. "You have fifteen minutes. Maybe less. When I say time, you leave."

He rushes to Mom's side and helps her stand in his arms.

"Martin." Her voice tapers into a whisper. "I'm so sorry. I've sinned so much, against you, and God, and Callie, and...I know you could never forgive me, but if there's any chance..."

My breath catches. She's asking his forgiveness?

"I made mistakes, too. I worked too many hours." He cups her chin. "I was married to my job. I was never committed to you. Or to the girls, for that matter."

To hear him say those words… Of course, they didn't have a perfect marriage. But, who does? He did try to be a good dad. Didn't he? I mean, he taught me to love God and to be a faithful Christian. He made sure I memorized Scripture and developed my own faith. Maybe he wasn't the guy who took me to ballgames and shuffled me around the fairgrounds, but he gave me so much more. I step forward. "You—"

"No." Mom grips his shirt with both hands. "I wasn't faithful, Martin. Not to you, and not to the girls. I was weak, and I strayed." She gasps through her tears. "So many times."

His stern face softens. "I wasn't easy to live with. All the pressure I put on you to be perfect, when I should have shown you love…" His voice catches and he reaches for her, sobs erupting from both their throats.

As they embrace, I clutch my collar. Never in a million years would I have thought this could happen. *Thank you, Lord.* Mysterious ways.

He draws back and waves me over. "And Callie. So brave."

"How did you find us?" I squeeze his and Mom's shoulders. "How did you even get in here? And where's Ethan and Amber?"

"Ethan is safe. He's with four brothers who are helping him get to America. Amber ran away with some man who promised to take her to Mexico." His jaw twitches as Mom gasps. "This woman," he nods to Reva, "had the benevolence to write to me after you left this school the first time. She said she'd discovered one of my pamphlets and found the church address there. Somehow, she found someone to smuggle the letter out and have it mailed. So, when we came back to look for your mother, I started with her. It was our good fortune to find her, but also to discover you'd been brought here. Reva's been working with me and one of the officers the last few days to come up with a plan."

"That was good fortune." Mom sniffles. "Can you help me to my chair?"

"I will. And we're going to get you out." He straightens. "In a week or two. We still need to work out a couple of logistics with the wheelchair and some other details. But I've met a man who poses as a guard. He assures me he can help."

"Leave me," Mom says, and at the same time, "You have to save Reva and Nina," bursts from my lips.

Reva shakes her head. "You don't go on about me, now."

I back away from Mom and Dad and throw up my hands. "Every guard or hospital worker who knows I'm alive either ends up dead or cast into prison."

Reva shrugs. "I'm already in prison, dearie. And dead to the life I once knew."

"That's why I need to take care of the other details. Keep Reva out of it as much as we can." Dad carries Mom to her wheelchair and sets her in the seat. He slides his hand to her temple, brushing her hair with his fingers. "I will kill that man for what he's done to our family. With my bare hands, if needed."

"Mr. Noland." Reva's keys fall to the floor, and she stoops to pick them up. "I've read your articles. Such kind words. You are not a murderer."

He scoffs. "It's not murder. It's vengeance."

"Vengeance is mine, saith the Lord." She shoves the keys in her apron pocket.

"It is His." Dad grasps my hand. "Callie, this is for God's glory. If I kill Adrian Lamb, then the Alliance will fall."

I run my fingers through my tangled hair. "Adrian is nothing more than a puppet. All he does is visit prisons and taunts people. He doesn't run this country. You think no one will step up and take his place? He had over a million followers when this nonsense first started. Sure, he's lost some of them, but he has supporters. Plenty of supporters."

"Nothing will change my mind." Dad steps into the hall. "Our time is almost up. I love you, Callie. And Ella, I am trying to forgive you. I will save you both."

Mom rolls the wheelchair to his side. "I—"

Several cells down, a door screeches then slams against the wall. Dad and Reva's faces turn ashen, and she raises both hands over her head.

"Well, well, well." Adrian's chipper voice echoes a high-pitched shrill throughout my chamber and into my veins. "How's that for a reunion? Strategized, planned, executed." He laughs. "And I do mean executed."

Metal flashes in front of me. Dad clasps his hands over his heart then falls to his knees. Not one, but three blades stick out of his chest. Small circles of blood stain his shirt, and he holds his right hand in front of his face. As he tumbles to the rough concrete floor, his tears fall with him.

# Chapter Thirteen

## ETHAN

**THOUGH I'VE LONG GIVEN UP HOPE** of Martin's return, I use what's left of a dried-up Sharpie to leave him a note on a piece of cardboard. Not like he'd ever find it. I doubt any of Adrian's goons would ever venture close to our squatter house, but I keep my note cryptic anyway. Can't be too careful. Next, I follow Drew and Brandon to the five-columned concrete porch. Since we arrived in Monongahela, memories have assaulted me, and I'm feeling far off my game.

Every tiny detail of this place reminds me of Callie, from the snow-covered sycamore trees to the abundance of fruity lotion the previous lady of the house left behind. Even the wispy dark hairs clinging to a soft pink brush in one of the bedrooms. So many things.

When we first arrived, I took a bottle of the lotion for my backpack, and left a few dollars in its place. A huge sacrifice of my minuscule cash, but it's almost like carrying Callie with me.

We're standing on a porch built like her old house, with a wrought-iron railing and chipped gray paint on the concrete. Identical even down to the swing. Pangs come from all sides as images of me making out with her sister flash through my mind. I should have been kissing Callie on that porch. Well, no. I should have been respectful and appropriate like a Christian. Man, I need to get back in church. I don't even think like a Christian anymore.

I walk over to the swing, catching the rusty chain in my fingers. As I sit, I drag the vinyl seat back with my feet and let it fall forward, swaying in the cool morning air.

Drew hurries to the driveway, where Tristan has pulled up in his newest car conquest, one of the coveted black sedans that says we're legit Alliance citizens. He whispers and gestures to Tristan through the window then stalks back to the porch. He's not happy to be going to Charleston, but he might as well get used to it. He seldom gets a say in their plans. Poor guy. Always outvoted.

Tristan and Luke are more brazen than usual after securing not one, but now two of black sedans, and a ton of gasoline. They siphoned it from abandoned cars. And they've brought new clothes, shoes, and climbing gear. Even guns. I don't ask anymore. Think I'd rather not know where things come from.

They returned three days ago, with no word of Martin or Callie, and said they'd secured me a meeting with a man from the CIA who can help us. And now, they're off again, heading who knows where while we make our way to Charleston. I still don't understand why they can't let me in their inner circle.

After loading the car back up, they wave to us and peel out of the driveway again, spinning the gravel under their wheels.

"Are you sure about this?" Drew tosses a bag of food into the backseat. "I'd hate you to live a life of regret."

"Sure as I'll ever be." I adjust the strap of my backpack and tighten the buckle. "I think we're at a standstill. Tristan is right. If we're going to save Callie, we need to get help from the American government. Martin may not even be alive at this point. I can't keep waiting to hear from him."

Brandon hands me a worn leather wallet and a curly black wig attached to a baseball cap. "Three fake ID's in there. I suggest you leave one in the wallet and hide the others. From a distance, no one will know you're wearing a wig. You'll need to stay back from the officers whenever you can. Hopefully we won't have to get out of the car."

"Okay." I don the cap and stuff my too-long brown hair underneath the black curls. They feel real, like they were made of human hair. Shivers course my spine, and the backpack strap slips off my shoulder. "It seems so surreal every time I think about how the Alliance could have formed. I know the intellectual answers, but what happened to America? How did Adrian Lamb come into power?

How did he convince so many people to walk away from their country—their heritage?"

Pushing his glasses up the bridge of his nose, Brandon clears his throat. "Well… since you asked—"

"Not again." Drew punches him in the shoulder.

"What?" My snickers draw a mock-serious glare.

"Well, you've studied Hitler and the holocaust, right? Know how he managed to take over Austria? Not by weapons, and not by force. He took them over by promises. And that's what Adrian did. He made promises. Weirdo that he is, that lunatic has a way with words, and people buy into them hook, line, and sinker." Brandon straightens his pants leg over his boot. "Looks like it might start snowing any minute. We'd better hurry."

"Yeah." Drew bounds down the steps toward the car and pops open the trunk. Twelve five-gallon tanks full of gasoline. Not that would matter in a worst-case scenario, but he stuffs a fireproof blanket over them and tucks it between them and the back seat.

"You two can have the front." Brandon opens the back door on the passenger side and slides across the faded leather. "I'm planning to sleep all the way there."

"Well, if the gasoline blows, you go first." Drew laughs, but it's strained.

I grip the front passenger handle and take five deep breaths. "Maybe we should pray first. Wouldn't hurt to have God on our side."

Brandon sits up and pops out of the car. "Dude. You are so right." He takes mine and Drew's hands and bows his head. "Dear Lord, we thank you for our many blessings, including this gasoline and car. We pray that you help us get Ethan to the train and that we make the connection with our pals. And please, please, bless us with a safe trip. No trouble or explosions."

He follows his loud swallow with a pause. "And keep us safe in this weather. We are ever thankful and grateful to be your servants. In Jesus' name, amen."

My chest catches. "Amen."

"Amen." Drew walks around to the driver's side. "Now let's jet."

Our short drive to civilization ends when we merge into the line of black sedans heading toward Charleston. It's like something in a sci-fi novel, passing all the windows with Adrian-permed twinzies, all of whom appear more frightened than friend. Most alarming is that there are no children. None. Did Adrian succeed at putting them all in residential schools?

"I told you," Brandon grips the back of my seat, "it's like Hitler. Austria had astounding unemployment rates, and he promised jobs. And then, he delivered those jobs. The people of West Virginia were so happy to work again they never saw it coming when Adrian stuffed them in his little Alliance boxes and treated them like puppets. And now, he's handing out cars and gasoline like candy to regain support."

"It is like Hitler, I guess." Like the newspaper Callie and I read before Adrian had her snatched away. Propaganda. Feeding on fears.

"And then, he started in with the education and youth. Trapped them in schools where they heard what he wanted them to learn." Drew leans forward, frowning as he glances in the rearview mirror. "The cars behind us turned their lights on. Must be a motorcade coming." He switches his on too, and slows with the rest of the traffic.

"I guess the next thing was the food." I pat the pocket of my backpack, feeling for the last of the fruit we'd managed to secure. "Hitler made them use something like food stamps, right? I think I remember studying that." Mrs. Adams, my tenth grade World Civilization teacher's face comes to mind, snarled and twisted as she waggled her finger at our class of disengaged students.

"One day this will all come back to haunt you," she said. "You'll regret not learning history so you don't repeat the mistakes of your forefathers." Guess she was right.

So many things I wish I could do over. Listening in school, loving Callie... but maybe, if we can work with the US military, we might be able to get her home and have a fresh start. If she still wants me, that is. After Adrian's endless torture, she may not have a hint of a feeling left for me.

Tiny snowflakes dance around the car, melting as soon as they hit the ground. Drew must be focused on them, too, because we hit a huge pothole. Brandon winces as the car jostles.

"Sorry, bro." Drew tightens his grip on the steering wheel. "We could tune in to Alliance radio." His sneer is evident in his voice.

"I'd rather listen to Martin snore."

We all laugh, but worry lines crinkle across my brow. I hope Martin's okay.

"Think he's found her?" Drew passes them and signals, moving into the lane in front of them.

"I sure hope so." I—"

"Drew!" Brandon lifts his palms as the car behind us taps our bumper and lays on the horn. "Are you trying to get us killed?"

"No." Drew's jaw twitches. "Be quiet. I'm trying to concentrate."

Horn still blaring, the car creeps closer again. So close I can count the driver's nose hairs in the rearview mirror. The man glares with hateful eyes and speeds into us again. I didn't expect to see so many cars on the road.

"Dude! I'm sorry!" Drew taps the gas pedal, coming too close to the car in front of us. He catches a break in the traffic and shifts left one lane.

The other driver follows, closing the distance between us once more.

"You're going to have to take the exit." Brandon points to the sign as snow falls in earnest. Thick, quarter-sized flakes cling to the road and grass. "Catch him off guard and dart through the other cars at the last second."

"If I can." Drew scans every mirror. "Ethan, watch for the break for me."

As the exit draws nearer, I hold my breath. Come on, cars. Spread apart. Give us an opening. When we almost pass it, the rear car slows, almost like Moses parting the red sea. "Now."

Drew jerks the wheel and whips between the two cars, crossing into the exit lane amidst a symphony of horns. He speeds down the ramp, slamming the brake as he reaches the bottom.

The tires strike a patch of snow, sending the car into a tailspin.

"The gasoline! We have to get out!" Brandon fumbles for his lock, and I unbuckle my seatbelt as Drew fights for control.

As the car spirals toward the embankment, I unlatch the handle and dive out, landing hard in the crisp, snowy grass at the side of the road. My cheek burns and my shoulder aches from the impact, but as I roll into it, the momentum fades.

Brandon strikes ground a few feet away, much worse than my landing. He scrambles to stand while Drew keeps steering, gripping his elbow with a deep wince.

I brace myself for the explosion, scanning the roadside for shelter against the blast.

"He's not going to make it." Brandon limps over to me as the car does a 180 and comes to an abrupt halt.

He clutches my shoulder tight enough to pierce the skin, letting out a long whoosh of air. Drew waves us to the car, grinning, though his blanched face shines through the windshield.

"He did make it." My whole body shaking, I lumber back to the car, leaving footprints along the pristine, white road. "Thank God. And thank God there weren't any cars on this road. And that the crazy guy didn't follow us off the exit."

"Whew." Brandon slips as he reaches for the car door. He lifts his gaze to the clouds. "Lord, please bless us with safety for the rest of our journey."

As I buckle, I meet Drew's grin. "Showoff."

He laughs. "How many times did I beat you guys racing on the farm? I've got this." But his voice quivers.

Once Brandon and I fasten our belts, Drew merges back onto the Interstate. Our somber reflections look like statues. The snow continues falling in huge flakes, surrounding us with the purest white scenery. The Alliance's drab, neglected buildings stand proud with their beautiful coating. If only God could cause a snow of peace to rain down on them.

My resolve strengthened, I lean close to the window. My warm breath leaves a hint of condensation on the glass, and I trace out the word hope.

Beside me, a man glances at my letters and smiles. He blows on his own window and traces his own word. *Pray.*

Nodding, I rub the window clean with my sleeve.

Two hours later, we exit the freeway again, joining the flock of black sedans waiting to enter the capital. The gas light comes on as we wait at the light on the off ramp, and Drew grins. "Told you. This baby would hold enough to get us here. Now, we need to make our way to the trains."

He darts through a few city blocks and makes a couple sharp turns as the gas light blinks its warning. The indicator light shifts to three flat lines as he whips into a driveway and fishes through the console for a garage door opener.

Once parked, he closes the door behind him, leaving us with only the light from a small ceiling-height window. Brandon and I fumble through the dark garage to the door leading into a one-story brick house with a two-car garage while he empties one of the five-gallon tanks into the car.

"Wait. Help me get all these out of the trunk." He nods to the trunk. Brandon rushes to it, lifts one of the tanks out, and sets it by the wall.

I grab another, and we put them in a line. Even the smell of gasoline brings Callie's face to my mind—the time I let her pump gas in my Mustang, and she spewed the stuff all over us. Her horrified expression made her even more beautiful. With the memory so crisp and clear, why didn't I notice that beauty at the time?

Soon as I find a pen and paper, I'm going to write all these memories down. One day I'll tell her how much she's meant to me from the day we met until now. I hope I still mean the same to her.

Brandon and Drew enter the house and land on the cushy sectional as I pace from room to room. All three beds are made, and the mirrors shine like they were polished yesterday. Not a hint of dust covers the floor or furniture, and the ceiling is void of cobwebs. Someone lives here, and takes great effort in keeping the place up.

In the kitchen, three boxes rest on the table. More weapons, passports, and—dare I hope? Peanut M&M's, Reese's Cups, Twix bars, and Snickers.

"Help yourself," Drew calls from the kitchen. "Our uncle Bobby left all that for us here."

"Sweet." I rip into one of the yellow packs with my teeth, letting the M&M's spill into my mouth. As the candy shell crunches open and the warm chocolate melts against my tongue, I settle into one of the kitchen chairs.

There was a time I'd have eaten ten of these little bags in one sitting. Often, I'd sneak a couple out of my college roommate's stash. Who'd have ever thought I'd consider something so normal a luxury? The Alliance has crushed my every joy.

But no more. As soon as I get to America, I'm going to clean out my savings and find a way to take Adrian Lamb down.

# Chapter Fourteen

## CALLIE

**SECONDS AFTER DAD HITS THE GROUND,** I register Mom's screams, and perhaps my own. I race past Adrian to Dad, and land beside him.

"I'm so sorry, Callie. So sorry." He slides lower, resting his head in my lap as Adrian saunters over and slaps his shoulder.

"Hello, brother." His snicker sends surges of rage through my every vein. "I suppose you've figured out by now that your new officer friend is loyal to the alliance. So trusting, you are. Like my beautiful daughter."

"You are not my father." When I lift my gaze, his face blurs to a blob. "I hate you."

"I've done it." His laugh severs the nerves in my spine. "I've broken her. You hear that, Martin? She hates me. And last I checked, that was sin, you self-righteous pig." He waves to the hallway. "Get the medics in here. I'm not ready for him to die."

Well, at least there's a hint of comfort. But can they save Dad? And what torture will Adrian make him endure before killing him?

"Now you, on the other hand..." He tips up my face with his clammy finger. "Now that I've broken you, what reason do I have to keep you around?"

"So kill me, already." I straighten, but my knees wobble as a jolt of pain shoots through the scarred one.

"I will never give you the satisfaction." He snatches my arm and drags me backwards past the cells as Mom wails in the background. Two officers cuff a silent, brooding Reva. As we stumble along, he kicks my bum knee and shoves me into the iron bars so hard my bottom teeth sink into my gums.

When we walk out to the commons area, he drags me down two flights of stairs to the lobby, a stone-walled room trimmed with dark oak molding. My teeth ache from gritting, and my eyes sting from tears that refuse to fall.

Arches surround the high ceiling, and huge columns extend from the dusty tile floor. Light floods the room from several thick-silled windows, the oak stained a couple shades lighter than the upstairs. A stone-and-wrought-iron railing divides the balcony into three wings, and from its edge, seven officers stand, holding their arms behind their back as in tribute.

Adrian thrusts his hand out, palm down, and arm raised to a slight angle. Like Hitler.

I lurch free from Adrian and raise my fist to them. "How can you stand there and watch him abuse so many innocent people? Do you not know that this man tortures at his whim? That he's responsible for genocide?"

Adrian swings to restrain me, and a nearby officer prods my shoulder with the end of his rifle. "She's lost it now. Should we sedate her?"

"And he's a pillhead. I mean fiending for drugs. You all know that."

A hulking hand grips my neck, and presses his thumbs against my skin.

"Why do you follow him?" Thinking back to my Alliance training, I jab my elbow backward, hoping for the officer's face.

He grunts, and drops me to the floor. My eyes water as my jaw makes contact with the cool concrete, slipping out of alignment. I try to crawl forward a couple feet, stopping when a boot presses into my back. An officer jerks my right arm behind me, twisting until my left arm slides from beneath me, pinning my shoulder to the floor. He steps on my hand and tugs harder, and I clench my teeth. I will not scream. I will not cry. I will not yield.

But Adrian's right. I already have. Why doesn't he kill me? It's what I deserve.

The officer drags me to my feet and shoves me over the threshold into the bright sunlight. Warmth covers us, and snow drips from the familiar maples and sycamores that sheltered my prior escape.

We pile into Adrian's tricked-out van. They shackle me like I'm some kind of mass murderer. I can't help but chuckle. How nonsensical. These people—his followers—they're idiots. Why do they buy into his cause? Even with all that self-defense training they made us learn at the Alliance schools, I'm powerless and weak. But at least they give me a window seat.

After driving a couple miles, Adrian closes the window dividers that separate us from the officers. I keep my face toward the glass. We pass the old cafeteria and dormitory buildings from when I first arrived. Students trickle into the main entrance, as though nothing has changed.

Adrian laughs. "Would you like to start over?"

I reward him with my silence.

He withdraws a folded paper from his shirt pocket. "I'm giving a speech in a couple hours. Would you like to hear it?"

No. I tug at a fraying thread at the edge of the gold cord trimming the black leather seat.

"Greetings, my beloved citizens. It is with great relief that I announce the capture of Martin Noland, the rebel soldier who has threatened the Alliance livelihood since its inception. This man bears the responsibility of poisoning the mind of my wife and daughters, and stripping our country of its very security. As my wife sat in a nursing facility, paralyzed from the waist down, this man plotted to break in and attack. We caught him in the very act, and this terrorist is now in an Alliance prison, awaiting the fate that our tribunal will award him. This man will pay for the death of my beloved Callie." He clears his throat. "What do you think so far?"

"Wordy. Too many uses of very." I shrug. "And full of lies. I mean, didn't you already tell them all Mom was dead?"

"Oops. Better change that." Adrian sneers. "What was it Hitler once said? 'Make the lie big, make it simple, keep saying it, and they'll eventually believe it.' Isn't that the truth?"

"Hitler's a fitting comparison. Have you drawn up plans for your gas chambers, or would that be too humane for you?" I rest my head against the seat. "I don't think I need to hear any more of your speech. It's the same old nonsense."

"That was the pertinent part anyway." He folds the paper in half and presses the crease. "You know, our next mission is to find that scrawny little boyfriend of yours and extinguish him. I'd planned on letting him go until he decided to join forces with the terrorists that bombed your debut." Blowing a quick blast of air over his upper lip, he puffs the lower one in to a pout. "Want to know what's going to happen to your precious mom and dad?"

I remain stoic.

"Your parents will end their lives in slow, painful misery, as you will. In fact, I've got a mind to move all three of you back to Charleston."

"Why Charleston?" And why did I say that? So much for feigning disinterest. But I am curious. "Why did you decide to establish the Alliance there?"

He extends his interlocked hands and faces his palms outward, stretching until his knuckles crack. "I suppose we've got plenty of time. I should tell you the entire story of how the Alliance came to be. It's quite fascinating."

I flare my nostrils. "I'm sure." This interview session might be painful, but it's less painful than spending who knows how long sitting in silence together.

"It all started with this little Facebook group. There were five of us, fed up with America's continual string of imbecile leaders. Our venting sessions turned into activism, and activism turned into inspiration for our leadership plan."

Makes perfect sense. Let's build a country based on political rants. "Did any of you have experience in government?"

He crossed his pointer fingers. "Cade Franklin taught political science at a prominent university. He studied law at Harvard and practiced for seventeen years before becoming a professor." Tapping four fingers together, he grinned. "Mitch Loggins worked on Wall Street. He's a brilliant economist. How's that for you? The best and the brightest."

I snort. "How do you fit in?"

He folds his speech and tucks it back into his pocket. "I won debate and mock trial every year I entered. State and national levels. Then, I started running the competitions. They sent me the invite to their group. We grew from there."

"So, what did you do? Post something and make it go viral?"

He fishes in his other pocket for his ever-present bottle of pills. "No. We started having these town hall meetings. I traveled all over to speak at them. This little Iowa community here, that little Texas community there. Before we knew it, we were 1.4 million strong."

"What about the chemical spill? You know, the one that poisoned several children and forced everyone to move out of West Virginia."

"Pure brilliance." Popping the cap, he lifts the bottle to the light and peeks into it. He frowns then turns it up and swallows several pills. "The man responsible discovered a toxin with an easy antidote. All we had to do was spray the treatment over all our bodies of water, stir it up a bit, and it dissipated into safe compounds. It's an energetically favored reaction, you know. He orchestrated the spill and was hailed a hero when he cleaned it up. Well, most of it anyway. Some of the plants nearby the waterways are still affected, but we're handling it."

Pure terrorism. I press my tight-clenched fist against the top of my restraint. "What about the people who became sick or died from it? What about the children?"

"Necessary losses for the greater good."

"You're a psychopath."

He chuckles. "And you're a sinner. I've broken you, Callie. And here, I thought it would be so easy."

"Do you understand so little of Christianity?" I almost feel sorry for the guy. "I am saved by the grace of a perfect God, not by my own perfection. There's not a Christian alive who doesn't sin every day and need repentance and forgiveness."

"Anyhoo." He recaps the bottle and slips it back into his pocket. "I would think you might wonder what will happen next to you."

My jaw clenches before I can stop it. "I can do all things—"

"Through Christ. Blah, blah, blah." He spits at my feet. "There's a warehouse, two blocks away from my mansion. It's where I keep all my little pets. I should have sent you there in the first place."

"Why didn't you?"

"Secrecy." His mouth twists into a frumpy gnarl. "Stupid rebels hovered around the building like bees. And I put an end to them. We couldn't have word get out that you survived being shot, now could we? In fact, that's why I've had to move you in the first place. Word spread among the prison , and I…" He gives several shakes of his head as he raised his chin.

"You had them all killed, didn't you?" I narrow my gaze. "Murderer."

He snickers. "You got me."

"And the Monongahela prison, too."

"Every last one. Including that hefty woman who helped my obnoxious twin break into that prison."

Reva, gone. If he's telling the truth, anyway. So senseless.

"So, why not kill me? Wouldn't that be easier?"

He touches my cheek with cold, clammy fingers. "Oh, sweet daughter." A shadow crosses his face. "I've already suffered so many loses. I would hate to lose you, too."

I paste on a smile, but my insides churn. Too bad, because he can't lose someone who's never belonged to him in the first place.

# Chapter Fifteen

## ETHAN

**ANOTHER HELICOPTER.** Brandon, Drew, and I connected with the American Army a couple hours after arriving in Charleston, and they insisted on flying us across the border in a huge military chopper so we could talk away from all the chaos. If not for the circumstances, I'd have been stoked.

The catch? If I leave, I can't go back.

A tiny piece of me cringes as the West Virginia countryside disappears behind us. Am I doing the right thing leaving the Alliance? Could I have found another way to get to Callie if I'd stayed? Brandon and Drew have decided to enlist in the Army and help from the other side. Maybe I should, too. But what if I get deployed somewhere and I can't get to Callie?

Thoughts of her sweet singing drown the roar of the chopper. Out the window, masses of trees and overgrown weeds surround eerie, abandoned neighborhoods. The city below resembles something from a science fiction movie with its carless driveways and empty streets. Did I live through all this? Did any of us?

"Think it's time for all the loyalists to admit the Alliance is one big failure, don't you?" Brandon nudges Aaron, the Army guy beside him. "Can't see this farce going on much longer."

"Yeah." Aaron grunts and shifts his weight in the hard, plastic seat. "My understanding is plans are already underway to close in and shut things down. You're lucky to be getting out today. It'll be a hardcore battle with some of those vigilante crazies." He faces me. "But don't worry about Callie. Soldiers are combing the country for her. We'll bring her home, too. You can count on that."

"Maybe it won't be such a battle." Drew rethreads the straps of his backpack and tightens them. "I know some of those crazies. They'll do about anything for cold, hard cash."

"Or chocolate." A bag of Peanut M&M's rustles in my pocket. "Do you think they'll move everyone out and let the previous landowners go back home? Reelect the state officials and such?"

"Hope so." Aaron bends down and tightens the laces on his boots. "Borders will be reinstated, and they'll run on a low-staffed local government for a while. President Cooper started calling the states by name again and avoiding the use of the word Alliance. They have plans in place for a couple new elections. Some of the former government officials are on standby to resume their roles as interim, but anyone with Alliance loyalist ties will be ineligible."

"Oh, look. There's the refinery. Guess that's where Adrian has been buying his gasoline." I wave my hand over the pipes and stacks against the skyline. "That place is a beast. I've never seen it from the air before."

"Largest inland port in the US, I think." Aaron fiddles with the Velcro on his pocket. "They had a huge battle over who got to keep control, and the US government protected it with thousands of soldiers. Wish I could have been there. Would have been fascinating to see how the place works."

My grin seeps out before I can stop it. "I studied it in school. They heat the oil to different temperatures so they can distill all its components. Next, they purify it and put in the additives, and whammo—you have gasoline. Very, very cool."

"Smarty pants." Drew kicks the toe of my shoe then scoots back against his seat. "What's amazing to me is that the place remained untouched by all this."

He's right. Across the West Virginia border, the landscape explodes into a flurry of activity. Cars dart in and out of streets, and people walk around on sidewalks like ants. We pass a school where bright jackets polka dot the monkey bars and slides. Life and livelihood. Everything will be fine. As long as Callie comes home.

We land in a remote Kentucky field next to a line of pickup trucks and tractors. Aaron leads us to a waiting SUV, and they drive us into town, along busy city streets to a bricked office building that looks to be some kind of makeshift border patrol.

I pause beside the thick, oak door and smooth my too-long hair down. Aaron nudges me forward, and a suited bald man in thin-framed glasses nods to me from behind a white plastic table. As I take the seat across from him, Aaron, Drew, and Brandon disappear down the hall.

"Ethan Thomas?" He scrawls across a boxy form with the thinnest ink pen I've ever seen.

My heart races. "Yes, sir."

"Welcome. Please, have a seat. I'm Mr. Reed." The man removes his glasses and folds in the frames. He steeples his fingers and rests his wrists on the table between us. "We need to ask you some questions, and then we'll process your citizenship form."

"Of course." The slightest tear builds in the corner of my left eye, and tension spreads through my veins to the tips of my toes and fingers. Am I going to be in trouble for anything? What if they don't let me stay? If only my parents could be here. I could always call Michael Harding, a lawyer and friend from church back home. I'm not going to drag him all the way to Washington, D.C. unless I have to. But, will I have to? After all I've been through, especially Davey Brinkle and his nonsense, is full, reinstated citizenship a guarantee?

"We are recording this, Mr. Thomas." Mr. Reed picks up his pen and makes another note on the form. "Please tell the complete truth. Do not leave out any details. Everything you reveal can help us understand the scope of what's going on in the Alliance." He reaches into a satchel that rests on the ground beside him and pulls out a clipboard with a thick stack of papers.

Is that whole stack for me? This could take all day.

"First, we need to know exactly when you first left America. When did you become an Alliance citizen?" He turns the form over and takes the first page from the stack.

Apparently they are all for me. "Two years ago, in August. I took the dual citizenship option, so I'm technically still an American citizen."

"Why did you go?"

"The girl I loved was kidnapped. My parents were killed in an accident, and she was all I had left. I had to go after her."

"Your girlfriend's name?" Mr. Reed doesn't even flinch as he asks. Like he didn't hear me say my parents died.

"Callie Noland." I swallow. "A couple days after the presidential assassination, men from the Alliance arrived with guns and kidnapped her. I had to go after her."

"Do you know any of their names?"

Like an elephant. "Agent Kevin Wiseman. A real creep. Eventually, Callie's dad and I did find her. We got her back into America, but Wiseman lured us back in."

"Agent Kevin Wiseman." Mr. Reed taps his pen against his lips. "Why did they want her in the Alliance so badly?"

"Well, Adrian Lamb thought she was his daughter. He's actually her dad's twin brother. So, he's her uncle. It's one of those unbelievably twisted family stories. But he had a decades-long affair with her mother, and for a while, we all believed that Callie could be his daughter."

"I see. How did Wiseman lure you back?"

"He followed us. We lost him for a while, but he knew we'd try to cross at Cumberland Gap. He had people watching for us. And then, some girl tweeted our picture. Callie and I were at one of the lookout points, and when we got down to the rest area, Wiseman was waiting for us." My stomach lurches as I think of Amber's bloodied face. "He had pictures of her sister. Adrian had kidnapped her, too, and beat her to a bloody pulp. We met Adrian to negotiate her release, and Callie offered to go back to him in exchange for her sister's freedom."

Tiny dots of ink splatter the page under his words. "And at that point, were you still serving as an officer?"

"No. I wanted to get home with Callie and go back to a normal life. As normal as I could without my parents around. You know, the accident."

"What kind of accident?"

"Car. Dad crossed over into the other lane. He hit an oncoming semi."

"I'm sorry." Mr. Reed face remains stony. Guess he has to be that way when he's questioning someone. "So after you went back with Adrian…"

"He was going to make Callie do this big debutante-style event. She had to publicly claim herself as his First Daughter and give her undying support to the Alliance. We'd arranged with James Caudill, one of the Rebels, to take a helicopter to America. We were allowed to leave the arena, but we never made the helipad. There were bombs. Explosions inside and outside the arena."

"Did Callie make the public claim?"

Mr. Reed's eyes say he already knows this answer. But I have to relive the videos Davey showed me anyway. "She decried the Alliance and told the citizens who attended the event that they needed to abandon its Bible and follow the true one. She basically called Adrian a liar in front of the whole crowd, and he shot her."

"What did you do?"

"At first, Martin, Amber, and I kept running. We didn't know she got shot until later. Then we got separated. This guy, Davey Brinkle, pulled me into a van. He parked there under the guise of saving people, but really, he was recruiting for his organization, which I'm pretty sure was behind the bombing. I think they waited for me. They'd planned to kidnap Callie, too, but Adrian captured her back."

"What organization?"

"The Allied Security Patriots. A secret society, he called them, and apparently notorious in the states for pranks and such at several Ivy League colleges."

"I've heard of ASP, yes. We consider it more of a terrorist organization these days."

"That's pretty much the truth, although I think we did… *they* did help a lot of citizens escape the Alliance."

The questioning continues for three more hours. Why did I stay with ASP? How did Davey operate? Who were the board members? How many operatives did ASP seem to have? A lot of questions I didn't know, because Davey kept me isolated in our small team. When Mr. Reed finally gets to the last page, I rest my folded hands in front of me on the table. "So can you tell me anything about Callie? Do you know how they'll find her?"

"I'm sorry." He shakes his head. "That's not my department."

When we finish, Aaron walks me out to the parking lot. He opens the driver's side door of a black Chevy extended cab, reaches out, and slides my bag off my shoulder. "Just so you know, I'm on one of the teams looking for your girlfriend. With assault rifles. I'm dropping you off in Mt. Sterling, but then I have to report back. Think you can find your way home from there?"

"Yeah. I know someone to call."

An hour later, Aaron leaves me on the front sidewalk of the Mt. Sterling WalMart parking lot with a handful of cash for a cab, standing under a canopy of rain.

A family of four hops over puddles hand-in-hand in matching raincoats as they cross to the entrance. Like Mom made us do when I was little. Man, I miss her. A small tear breaks loose, rolling down my cheek, and I step out of their way into the deluge.

An oncoming Lincoln shudders to a halt. From behind the windshield, an older couple gapes and the man rolls down his window.

"Sir, you okay?" The wrinkles in his brow deepen as he leans out. Thick raindrops pelt his age-spotted forehead.

I didn't even see them. "I escaped the Alliance." The words replay in my head. Escaping the Alliance. "Think I'm more than okay. If I can find my way home."

"Where's home?" He wipes raindrops from the window seal with a wadded tissue.

"Union City. But first, I need to get to Stanton, to my grandfather's bank. I have an account there."

The man smiles. "We're from Stanton. Get in."

Can I trust them? Will they drop me at the bank and wait to rob me? Across from the man, the lady grips her armrest. She must be thinking the same thing. It is ridiculous society has come to this. My lips curl into a genuine smile. "Thank you, sir. I'm blessed by your kindness."

His wife's shoulders relax as I slide into the back seat and buckle my belt. Their Lincoln smells like a blend of old spice and musk, like my grandparents' car once did, and I stifle my chuckle. "I appreciate the ride. I have no idea what's waiting for me when I get home."

"You haven't heard from your parents?" The lady lifts her round-lens glasses and peeks at me through the visor mirror.

"Both my parents are dead. Car accident, right as the Alliance formed." My voice catches, and I clear my throat. "I haven't been home in months."

"Oh, that's too bad." She clamps her husband's arm. "Byron, isn't that too bad?"

He darts a glance over the back seat. "Isn't what too bad, Evelyn?"

"Boy lost both his parents." She drops her glasses back to the bridge of her nose and presses against the seat. "What will you do?"

I trace my fingers over grooves in the seat. "A man from church promised to watch over my house. So I'm sure it's fine." My lungs ache. Should have known coming home would trigger all the emotions I've avoided for so long. "I didn't expect to find a normal America. When I left, people were rioting in the streets."

Byron adjusts the heater to a way higher temperature than my preference. "Those disturbances didn't last too long." He tilts the air vents so they blow in my face. "Mostly they stayed in the big cities."

"Gotcha." I rest my head against the window and close my eyes.

After a few minutes, beads of sweat pop out on my forehead, and the stifling air makes me dizzy.

"Sure is getting quiet in this car." Byron flips on the radio, blasting an upbeat blend of banjo and violin. Some man belts a high note, and I wince as Byron strains to sing along.

"Home, sweet home…" Evelyn joins in, and by the time we reach Clay City, I've been treated to an entire concert.

Pivoting in her seat, Evelyn grips the headrest with her wrinkled hands and fake fingernails. "I was the lead singer in all our high school plays. Can you imagine?"

"I can imagine." When I pat her hand, she blushes. "Bet everyone loved you."

"They did." Byron snickers. "Poor girl had so many suitors her dad had to chase them all away with his rifle. But not me. He liked me. Different times back then, let me tell you. Nothing like this 'hashtag ridiculous' world of today."

He said hashtag. Biting back my snort, I bend over and pull the tongue out of my tennis shoes.

As we drive along, we meet clear blue skies and the occasional passing car. Several drivers are on cell phones. Business as usual in America. Not a hint of evidence the Alliance ever existed.

At the bank, I hug Byron and Evelyn goodbye. I linger outside a few minutes, digging through my backpack for my driver's license. It expired a month ago. Hope that doesn't affect anything.

Inside the concrete building, professionals bustle in a choreographed dance that feels too fancy for such a small town. A woman carries a stack of files past and plants them on the desk in a glass-walled office. A man whistles as he crosses the bank lobby to the teller station.

"Can I help you, sugar?" A white-haired lady with high cheekbones and a model's posture plants her three-inch heel beside my worn sneakers. I must look a total fright.

"My name is Ethan Thomas. I…" The blue carpet swirls at my feet. "My great-grandparents were customers of this bank. And my grandfather. I have a safety deposit box, and…"

She pats my shoulder. "Why don't you come into Mr. Lawson's office, and we'll get you all straightened out?"

"Sure." Her swanky perfume overtakes the air around me, and I cough.

"Would you like some water?" She drags me to a bottled dispenser and fills two plastic cups. "Here. Take one."

As she sips from the other, I follow her into a corner office.

The jovial Mr. Lawson sits behind a mahogany desk, the phone receiver to his mouth.

"I'm telling you, Bill, we're going to be bringing in the green within the month." He winks at me. "Have a customer. I'll call you back tomorrow and give you the update."

As he docks the phone with his right hand, he extends his left one. My palm becomes buried in his thick, chunky fingers, and he squeezes my hand like a python. "What can I do for you, son?"

"Well, I escaped the Alliance, and I want to start over."

He scans them, and passes them across the desk at me. "I suppose you'd like to clear out your account?"

"Yes, sir." I set my driver's license in front of him. "Like I said, I want… no, I need to start over." I *need* to find Callie. And then, we can start over together. "My baseball card collection will help. If I can sell it, that is."

He turns to his computer and taps several strokes on his keyboard. After a few clicks, his brow lifts, and he leans forward, squinting at the screen. "Are you sure you want to sell the cards?"

"Have to do something." I rest my folded hands on the slick Plexiglas covering his desk then reach for my water. The clean, refreshing taste hangs on my tongue. Man, I've missed America. "Can't live off the air."

"So, you're not aware that you have a savings account with our bank containing sixty-five thousand dollars?"

Water spews across my papers. "Sixty-five?"

"Thousand. Yes. In a joint account belonging to you and Harland Thomas. Your grandfather, right?"

"Yes. He passed away several years ago." I hold my palm over my chest, though I doubt anything could still my pounding heart. Sixty-five thousand dollars. When? How? Why didn't anyone tell me?

Closing my eyes, I inhale deep and exhale slow. Talk about providence. Stealing a glance at his screen, I rub my tired, aching neck. "Do you think I could borrow your phone to call someone from Richmond? Is that okay?"

He nods. "Here. Do you know the number?"

"Yeah. 859-624…"

He presses the numbers on the keypad, beeps of different tones sound. Haven't heard anything like that in years. When he sets the phone to speaker, I hold my breath as it rings. What if Michael and Angela were killed? Or what if they lost their home and had to move? They were Mom and Dad's closest friends. If not for them, and Martin, I don't know who else I could have called.

"Yes?" Angela Harding's sugary voice holds a nervous edge.

"Ma'am? I have an Ethan Thomas here, wishing to speak to you." Mr. Lawson nudges the handset toward me. Loud clunking noises transmit from her end of the line.

"Angela? You OK?" My breath blasts through as he switches back to the handset.

She laughs. "Oh, Ethan. I dropped the phone. It's so exciting to hear from you. We've been so worried."

"I'm in Stanton. Think someone from church could come get me? I don't think they have any kind of rental place here."

Mr. Lawson shakes his head.

"Let me get Michael. He's in the garage checking the oil in my car. You know how he is. My crazy husband never stops." She forgets to move the speaker when she yells his name. Wincing, I hold the receiver away. Two full minutes later, she sighs loud in my ear. "He's coming. Said he can be there in about an hour."

As I end the call, Mr. Lawson scoots his chair forward. "Well, son, what do you want to do?"

"I want to get the cards and all the money from this account. Would that be a problem?"

Mr. Lawson's forehead scrunches, and his face reddens around his collar. "Well, that's a lot of money to withdraw at once. You realize you'll have to pay taxes on it."

"But I don't live here." My heart stops. Taxes? What on earth am I going to do about taxes?

He laughs. "Don't worry. They won't take it all. I'll see what I can do for you."

Forty-five minutes later, I'm stuffing a wad of cash into my backpack and carrying two large metal tins filled with baseball cards. I lug the monstrosity to the bank entrance as Michael pulls up in his Ford F150.

"Pleasure doing business with you, son." Mr. Lawson wallops my back and sends me jolting forward.

"Thank you, sir." I reach in for another python handshake. "I'm ready for a new start."

Mr. Lawson leans close to my ear. "Two words of advice for you. Finish college. Anyone so close should get the job done."

"I will…" Wow. I hadn't thought about college in ages. And how did he even know? But I have to find Callie first.

Michael leaps out of his truck and embraces me. "Your Mustang is waiting in your parents' garage." He grins. "I've enjoyed driving it around the neighborhood and keeping up with the maintenance. Couldn't wait for you to get home, though."

"Thank goodness." My breath catches as he squeezes me, and I gasp for more. "What about the house?"

"Trust fund has taken care of your mortgage payments, and Angela and I've handled the electric and water. We decided to leave them turned on in case you came back. Kept the heat down, and with the low usage, it hasn't cost that much."

"I'll pay it all back to you. Figure it up."

"No need for that." Michael shakes his head, lets me go, and hurries to the driver's side of the truck. "You know Angela is dredging chicken as we speak. I'd imagine the whole church is going to be waiting for you."

"I'd say so." Catching a glimpse of my wry grin in the visor mirror, I lower my chin. "Wish I was bringing Callie home with me."

"Oh, Ethan. I'm so sorry about that. When Angela and I heard she'd died—"

"She's not dead." The words burst from my chest like the bullets that pierced her side.

"Not dead?" He drops the keys and scrambles along the floorboard for them.

"She's trapped somewhere in a prison. Martin went after her, and the Army's trying to find her. But there's nothing I can do. At least not from here."

"Oh, there's one thing." Michael's cheeks widen in a full-dimple smile. If not for the guy's graying hair, someone might take him for thirty. "As long as there's hope, we can pray. And if she's alive, you know there's hope."

Right. Hope. And when I get back across that border, it's Adrian who'll need to pray.

# Chapter Sixteen

## CALLIE

**FURY AND TENSION** surround me as Adrian's motorcade approaches a long, dingy building that might have once been white. His and the driver's shadows are visible through the tinted glass separating our seats, and each is in a hunched posture. Something's gone awry.

Adrian's head jerks up and down toward the driver, and the car whips into the left lane. Three swerving turns, and we approach a different building from the rear, without the motorcade. Paint peels from its façade, advertising some kind of farming warehouse. The old wood-and-brick structure leans to the left, and parts of its tin roof peel away.

Is this the best he's got? And why separate from everyone?

Six gray garage doors line the back of the building, and one opens as we draw nearer. The driver eases the car between the doors and parks in the middle of a concrete expanse. Pallets containing dozens of black barrels sit in a corner, and several white columns support the upper floor.

Adrian leaps from the car and makes a call on his cell phone.

I press my lips together. There's no service in the Alliance. And yet... so many things he's lied about. The technology never went away. Bet he took over the providers and dared them to offer any Alliance citizens service.

Whoever he's talking to escalates his anger. He paces the dismal gray floor to the point he'll wear a groove in it.

The driver watches him a few minutes then exits the car. He wrinkles his nose, gags, and covers his face.

Tugging against my restraints, I tilt my head toward my own door. With some effort, I'm able to grip the handle with my teeth and pop it open a crack. Frigid air swarms me like we've driven into a freezer, and the stench gags me. What are they keeping in here? Spoiled meat? Or... please, no... I stretch my right foot and tap the door, widening the gap, and choke back bile.

"What do you mean there's no gasoline shipment?" Adrian's tone deepens to chilling. "I instructed—"

His pacing quickens. "You do whatever it takes to..." Pause. "Whatever it takes. Whoever you have to blackmail. Get the job done."

As soon as he ends the call, it rings again. "This had better be important."

Through the open car door, the gray floor turns a light, dingy blue. Blood spatters it everywhere. Tremors assault me, convulsing shivers that pulse like electricity. With my chin, I inch my shirt over my mouth and breathe into the cotton. My eyes travel to the barrels. No...

"You have got to be kidding me. I want him found. Right now. Martin Noland is the utmost threat to our national security, and—"

Dad? Escaped? Dare I hope it?

His face grows redder and redder. "None of them? Am I supposed to believe that not even one of the officers guarding him could be trusted? They've all defected?"

He unsnaps his pocket and takes out his pill bottle. As he turns it up, at least five or six of the little white capsules spill into his throat. Maybe more. How can the man's poor liver take it?

As he listens, hope rises in my heart. If Dad's escaped, maybe James came through for us after all. Maybe he's still coming back for me.

"I will not let that happen." Adrian jabs the phone with his pointer finger, then pivots, his face gnarling as he meets the gaze of the driver. "What are you doing? I told you to wait in the car."

"Lord Lamb, I—"

Adrian lunges, catching the base of the man's chin between his finger and thumb. With his left hand, he whips some kind of gun from his pocket and shoots a dart into the man's neck.

I shiver.

A few seconds later, the man has dropped to the floor his arms and legs convulsing like a dead snake. With considerable straining, Adrian drags him across the warehouse to the black barrels, and pries the top from one. Ugh. Why did I have to be right? Does he intend to imprison me with dead bodies?

The air gushes from my lungs. Or, are his intentions far worse?

Heart pounding, I rub my wrists raw, reaching for the door. Though pain shoots through every square inch of my arm, I catch hold of it with a good lunge and manage to pull it closed. Who knows what Adrian would do if he finds out I was listening in. Then again, who knows what he'll do with me now.

He hoists the incapacitated driver and plants him feet first in the barrel.

My breath catches. Though the man's head pokes out the top a couple inches, Adrian shoves the lid on, crunching him in tighter. I pound my skull against the headrest.

"Dear God, please..." What can I even pray for this man? Or for me? There's not a hint of anyone in sight. Adrian's words come back to me. His pets.

Dry heaves take over my body. Thank goodness Adrian hasn't bothered to feed me.

He storms back to the car and snatches my door open. As I hack and cough, he slams his palm into my shoulder. "I'm going to undo your wrists now." His words are like ice. "You have two choices. Walk straight to that room, or be stuffed into a barrel like your friend over there."

Right. I hold still while he undoes my restraints. With silent breaths, I force air into and out my nostrils. "How many bodies?"

He quirks his brow.

"How many? Did you murder all of them?"

Laughter ripples his chest as he drags me from the car. "Murder? Punishment, Callie. Appropriate corporal punishment."

"Then why stuff them in barrels? Why not bury them?"

"The barrels are their burial chambers. We're running behind."

I plant my worn leather shoes on the warehouse floor and smirk. "You know this can't go on forever, right? Someone out there is going to put a stop to your terrorism. America has invaded countries much greater than the Alliance and won. What makes you think you can—?"

His left hand strikes my cheek, turning my neck so far the joints crack. "Politicians in America are crooked as they come. All I have to do is toss green their way, and I can have as much protection as I want. That's what the Alliance was built on. Blackmail and bribes."

"Could it be you're running out of green?" My smirk intensifies. "Let's see. What was it? Sixteen original states filed for secession, right? And within mere months, you were down to six?" A bitter laugh catches in my throat. "And that was last May. What is it, almost January or February now? March? I can't imagine things haven't collapsed further since then."

He fumbles in his front pocket and retrieves his pill bottle. His eyes wild, he twists off the cap and lifts the bottle to his mouth. After swallowing who knows how many more of the pills, he jerks me by the arm and drags me toward the room.

Does he even know he double-dipped from the bottle? Maybe he'll overdose. A calm washes over me. He's near-finished, and he knows it. No way would the American government stand for this. It would have taken some time to get a new administration under foot and to do the research and planning necessary to put an end to his reign. But the Alliance is crumbling.

A familiar ache throbs in my knee. I'm crumbling, too. I catch a hint of our reflection in a glass window to the side of the room where he leads me. Two ghosts walking through a void.

An involuntary wince replaces my smirk, and his face softens. "I can give you something for that pain."

"I'd rather die from the pain than accept drugs from you." I meet my hollowed eyes. Who is that girl speaking? She sounds nothing like the one he snatched from Kentucky, the one who lay around pining as her sister stole away her true love. He's right. He has broken me in so many ways. I close my eyes and inhale. "No thank you."

When he drags open the heavy steel door and shoves me into the sparse concrete room, my feet stumble over something. A gasp explodes from my chest as a bone rolls across the floor. Maybe a tibia. Human, for sure. Wish I'd kept it together, though. His satisfied smirk makes my skin crawl.

He kicks the bone out of the way like it's nothing.

A small cot rests in the far right corner, with a wool blanket folded in the center of it. Beside it, a square card table sits lopsided, like it might collapse any second. Atop the table, a brush laced with fine blonde hairs teeters on its edge. Blood covers every wall.

"What is this place? A human butcher shop?"

"I'll have it washed down for you tomorrow. Or sometime." He shrugs. "We weren't expecting to have to move you on such short notice. We'll be bringing in other prisoners soon." Bitter laughter contorts his face. "Dead or alive."

I shuffle to the cot and sit while he drags the table from the room.

"Can't have you etching the plastic and steel." He sneers. "If you even still believe in that stuff. Do you still think your God loves you?"

"I will always believe." He cannot take that away from me. No way. " 'If God is for us, who can ever be against us? Since he…' um... " The words fail me. Again. Have all those sedation drugs in the hospital destroyed my memory?

A pang strikes my heart. " 'And I am… convinced that…' " Why? Why now, can't I remember? " 'Neither death nor life, neither angels nor demons, neither our fears for today nor our worries for tomorrow…' " Yes, that's it. " 'Not even the powers of hell can separate us from God's love.' "

"You poor, misguided dear." He leans against the door frame and cocks his head. "Do you remember your grandmother's garden? The butterfly bushes and the monarchs?" His voice drops to almost a whisper.

My pang deepens. "I do."

"The hummingbird feeders, too. She spent hours out there, whispering secrets to her tiny winged creatures as I hovered in the shadows." He taps his shoe against the threshold. "Well, aren't you going to ask? What secrets?"

"What secrets?"

"Her abandoned son, of course. How much she regretted the decision to give him up. How she wished she could have afforded to raise two babies... Why she chose Martin over me."

"And why did she choose Dad?"

He huffs. "His chubby dimples. My hollowed eyes. Said I was so scrawny she figured I'd suffer from poor health."

Hollow like mine. "I'm sorry that happened." What did he expect me to say?

"One day, I got brave." He swallows, his Adam's apple protruding even further than its normal jutting. "I revealed myself to her and waited for her reaction. She knew who I was, and demanded I stay out of her life."

He takes out his pill bottle again and tosses it back and forth between his palms. He's going to overdose right here in front of me. "So, I did. I went back to the so-called family who beat me and starved me, and I swore I'd amount to more." Uncapping the bottle, he grimaces. "Did I tell you I have my pilot's license? And I'm a black belt in karate, skilled archer, a master of many different fine arts... none of it was good enough for her."

More bile bubbles in my throat, and I fidget to stifle it.

He drops to his knees, swallows a couple, and caps it again. I can't imagine taking pills with no water, but he doesn't even flinch, like he's immune to his gag reflex. Must be, for this room to not affect him. He stuffs the bottle in his pocket. "When I came to her the last time, she told me she wished I'd never been born. So, I snuck up behind her one morning and injected her with a chemical that triggered her heart attack."

My own heart stops, and again I fight to keep my features stony. He killed my grandma. And though I've watched him kill in cold blood so many times, it's still hard to believe. Grandma loved everyone. If he'd given her time, she might have accepted him.

His chilling laugh holds a hint of a quiver. "The small-town, redneck coroner didn't even question it. Told your grandpa she was the classic textbook case of a heavy smoker with clogged arteries. And I watched Martin sob like a baby. With utter satisfaction, of course."

He steps out of the room then pokes his head back in. "You are right, Callie. The Alliance falters. I've failed as a leader, because of my family distractions. The American military goes where they wish on Alliance soil and threatens our liberty. But rest assured, we will rise again. We are smaller, yes, but our core is stronger. The men who helped me found this nation still strive for the same principles we fought for from the beginning. Freedom from the oppression of a government that encourages injustice and irresponsibility. A return to the ceremonial, royalty-based leadership of our forefathers…"

I shake my head. Is he insane or did he miss out on reality in school?

As the door inches closed, four words crush my heart. I have to say them, mean them even, and follow the same example Dad gave me with Mom. "Adrian, I forgive you."

The room dims.

His footsteps retreat, but approach again. As the door creaks open, I stand tall, facing it.

"Really?" His voice is childlike.

"I do. I forgive you, Adrian. I hope you find peace, as I have." I toss my brittle hair over my shoulder. "If you ever want me to tell you how, I'd be glad to share my faith. I'll be praying for you."

"Silence!"

The door slams so hard it must shake the entire building. This time, he secures the lock and I settle into the stale air. At least the stench fades a tiny bit when the door's closed.

Light streams in from a high window, and I press my back against the wall, wrapping myself in the wool blanket. There. I have at least one thing to be thankful for. "Thank you, God, for blessing me with this cover."

Hollow, with no remaining tears, I drop to the dry-rotted foam pillow and stretch my legs. Can't think about who may have laid in the same spot in the past, or the spatters of their blood surrounding me. When my eyes close, Ethan's face appears. My happy place.

I remember a time when we visited Mr. Whitman, a man from church, in the hospital, a week after he'd had a stint put in. We'd gone caroling to all the other elderlies and shut-ins, and decided that his time in the hospital would not keep us away.

Ethan came in wearing a full-on Santa suit, his beardless baby face gleaming from behind a cotton beard. Mr. Whitman laughed so hard he set all his monitors beeping, and they came in and asked us to leave. But before we did, Ethan led us in "Have Yourself a Merry Little Christmas." Even the nurses joined in.

I can still picture him standing across the room from me, meeting my eyes as Amber clung to his side. "From now on," he sang, "our troubles would be out of light."

Of course, the whole room laughed at his malaprop. But in our devotional that night, he turned that thought into gold. Yes, we may have troubles, but if we stay with God, there's no fuel for the Devil's fire. And when our troubles have no light, they fade away into the darkness.

I sit cross-legged on the cot, and raise my pointer finger. "This little light of mine, I'm going to let it shine…"

My voice comes out purer and clearer than it has in a long time. Tears stream my cheeks, and I sing on with my deepest resolve.

The choking stench of decaying bodies hangs in the air, keeping my thoughts grounded in reality. Still, I must be thankful I'm not one of them. Perhaps God has a purpose for me yet.

# Chapter Seventeen

## ETHAN

**WALKING INTO MY PARENTS' HOUSE** feels like opening a time capsule. It's hard to think of the place as mine anymore since I lived at the college most of the time before the Alliance formed.

A thick layer of dust covers the living room floor and all Mom's swanky candlesticks and vases, triggering several sneezes. Footprints track behind me, almost like snow. She would hate this. I make my way to the laundry room and open the cleaning supply cabinet.

Rusted metal cans and faded plastic bottles sit in a faced row, like the store shelves—glass cleaner, then furniture polish, then toilet bowl cleaner. As she'd prefer. I grab the furniture polish and remove its cap. A little squirt in my hand, and the orange scent fills the room. Smells like Mom.

After finding some towels in the guest bathroom linen closet, I damp-mop the laminate floor and vacuum the couches, my heart aching with every step. So many times Mom asked me to help, and I always did it with complaint. Now, I want to do her proud. But first, I'm going to figure out how to get to Callie.

I know going back is stupid and risky, but leaving the Alliance was a horrible mistake. There's nothing to do here but sit and wait. I can't even help the military because of my ASP ties, even though they didn't officially charge me with anything.

Michael bangs on the door and bursts in, carrying a handful of bags. "Brought your supper."

"Thanks." But how could I think of eating? I take half the bags and set them on the kitchen counter and he follows with the rest.

"Listen. You're going to need help getting back on your feet. I want you to come work with me at the construction firm. I'll teach you the carpentry, the management—if you like it, it could all be yours one day, Ethan." He takes ham and cheese from one of the bags and puts it in the fridge. "With all my law obligations, it's hard to manage both, and you know I don't have any children to pass it on to."

I spin on my heels to face him. "I'm going back for her."

Michael reaches for my hand, and I jerk it away.

"You can't go back for her, Ethan. They've closed the borders and forbidden US civilians from traveling into the Alliance." He sits on one of the counter stools and scrolls through the Internet browser on his phone. "See? They're arresting anyone who tries to get into the country."

"But you don't understand. She's starving. And Adrian could—"

"Ethan." He leans forward. "Don't know if I ever told you this, but I was the first to happen upon the scene of your parents' accident. Promised your dad I'd take care of you. His dying wish. I can't let you go after her. You have to trust God and the American military to rescue her, or be content if that's not His will. They are trying."

I turn away, tears building in the corners of my eyes. Of course Dad would want Michael to take care of me. But how can I stand by and return to life as normal when Callie's in such grave danger?

"Ethan, you have to stay put. Get yourself together and give Callie something to come home to."

"I'll think about it."

"Give it a few days. Let me make some calls." Michael shoves his cell in his pocket. "I'd love to retire over the next couple of years. At least from the law firm. And I need your help. Besides, Mary Whitman has planned you a welcome home party. You can't disappoint her, you know."

My chest heaves.

"Promise me you won't go running off and do something stupid. Promise me, Ethan."

"I'll stay put, for now. But if Callie's not home in three days, I'm going to find a way." I snap a banana from its bunch, peel it, and devour it. "Thanks for the food."

"Two weeks."

"Five days."

133

He walks to the door and grips the knob. "Nine days. For your dad."

My lungs deflate. Why did he have to go and bring Dad into it? "Maybe."

"See you tomorrow. Nine sharp." The screen slams shut behind him.

Gotta love Michael. He knows I don't need the money, but maybe he's right about me needing to work. I have to do something to keep these crazy thoughts reined in. Back to cleaning.

Once the living room is polished to Mom's standard, I head out to the garage. My Mustang sits under a plastic cover on the spotless concrete floor. Dad's SUV rests next to it, sad and dusty. I'll end up selling one of them, but for now, I sit in his driver's seat and fill my lungs with his sporty smell.

Dull smudges on the leather of the steering wheel show me where he placed his fingers while driving. I rest my own hands over the spots, gripping the wheel like I'd clung to his hand at the funeral. What a jerk I'd been, wasting away my life with beer and parties, when we'd had so little time. And rushing to find Callie, I really haven't had time to mourn him.

There's no sign my brothers or sisters ever returned to this place, which surprises me. Of course, they all have their own homes and families in other places. We'd fought over me keeping the SUV, but he'd made everything clear in the will. They all got money, and I got the house and car. With us estranged, I wonder if they even know I left the country.

So many mysteries to figure out. Like the $65,000. Who knows when it was deposited, or why I was never told. Maybe… that tweet of me and Callie went viral. If one of my siblings knew I had been in the Alliance, maybe they decided I needed their share of the inheritance more than they did. I should look for Dad's rolodex and see if I can find their numbers.

Tomorrow, I'll head to the bank, make my deposit, and pick up a new cell phone. And get new car tags. Oh, and new tennis shoes to replace these threadbare ones.

The ray of light streaming in the garage dips lower. Michael kept the Mustang much cleaner than I left it. The pink nail polish Amber spilled on the console is gone, and the leather seats shine like new.

I open the glove box and pull out the paperwork. Michael's even taken care of my car tags. So scratch that off the list. I can't put into words how much I owe him, although I think he does a lot of it out of guilt. He's always hated he wasn't able to do more to stop Adrian from kidnaping Callie. And it's kind of sweet of him to treat me like a son.

Ah… Callie. I reach across the seat, draping my arm over her imaginary body. So many times, she'd sat in this very spot, and I hadn't appreciated her. I hadn't listened to what weighed on my heart. I don't even deserve her return.

Dragging myself back into the house, I stagger through the dimming light to my bedroom. Oh, wait. A flip of the light switch floods the room. "Electricity, I've missed you."

My bitter laughter echoes in the empty house.

After adjusting the thermostat to a reasonable temperature, I explore the bedrooms, tracing my fingers over the nicks in our homemade bunk beds and clutching the crocheted blankets to my chest. It's a wonder all six of us kids never killed each other living in such small quarters. Three to a room was painful when I was little. But now, the house feels empty and huge.

When I come to the last room, the one that belonged to me, my heart catches at the door. My old-school rock-n-roll posters have curled on the ends, and like the other rooms, dust covers every surface. Otherwise, the room is unchanged. My college laundry sits in a basket, folded. The last thing Mom did before she and Dad set out in the car that fateful night.

I walk over and pick up my denim jacket from the top of the pile. It smells flower fresh, which triggers more laughter. Callie always told me I smelled like spring. Now I know why.

On my bookshelf sits a number of scrapbooks, one for each year of my life up to high school. I take the senior one, and spread it open on my bed.

A cloud of dust spreads around me as I flop to the mattress, setting my eyes to watering. Callie's sweet, innocent smile greets me from every page. As I move through pages from April to June of that year, her smiles fade. More and more pictures feature me with Amber, and a few have her watching after us, looking like her puppy's died. Had I been so blind to her love? I knew she had a crush on me, but this... so much deeper than a crush.

In one picture, she's sitting cross-legged on the floor, a pile of tissues next to her lap. The photographer has caught the moment I reach her to see what might be wrong, and there, frozen in space and time, is the most angelic face I've ever seen. Pure joy and happiness, wrought on by me, who did not deserve it. Oh, how I long to see that face again.

Wait. That night. The night I started dating Amber and crushed her heart into a million pieces. She'd lied, even with her features.

In every picture following, her face is somber, with dulled eyes and halfhearted grins. Her shoulders slump, her feet drag—not a single picture of the brilliant smile I've come to love.

I did that. I chose the wrong girl. And I have to find Callie. To make things right.

The doorbell rings, and I race down the stairs. Angela Harding lets herself in with a key. Several other church ladies walk in behind her, each overburdened with cleaning supplies and condiments.

"Thought we'd get you settled," she says. "I doubt you'd want to eat two-year-old canned food or ketchup."

Not necessary, since I'm leaving tomorrow afternoon to scope out the Alliance border. But I can't tell Angela that.

They pile bag after bag on the kitchen counter—all my favorite things. Chocolate-iced yellow cake covered in Peanut M&M's, pork chops, shrimp, and steak. There are vegetables galore and fruit trays. Milk, juice, coffee, and all the staples.

I grin at Angela. "You know I don't drink coffee."

She winks. "Yeah, but Michael and I do. We expect regular invites. Maybe you could even host the youth Bible study in that big basement of yours."

"Maybe..."

They spread over the kitchen like ants on a spilled soda, scrubbing every corner down to the seal of the fridge. After they finish in that room, they divide and conquer the bedrooms, and by ten-thirty, the house looks perfect.

"Thanks." I lean against the door jamb, holding one of Angela's baskets. All the other women have already left. "I appreciate you guys coming over and doing this."

"We're glad to." She takes the basket from my hands and walks out to the porch. "You know, Ethan, you're welcome at our house anytime. But we respect that you want to make a go of living by yourself. If Callie…"

I step onto the porch in my socks, landing in a small puddle of water. "She will come back. I feel that with all my heart. The American government is already there. They're going to sweep in and take the Alliance states over again, and they'll free all the prisoners and help them find their families. That's going to happen." And if it doesn't, I'm going to find another way.

"We've been praying night and day."

"Thanks."

After she leaves, I head into the den and flip on the television for the first time in ages. I'll have to pick up cable again, but for now, I get about ten network channels. Very snowy and static-filled, but I can at least get an idea of some news.

My eyes grow heavy as I wait for eleven-o'clock. I get lost in the plot of some crime show, but doze before they catch the criminal. But right at the turn of the hour, I jolt out of my seat at the image on the screen. James's white hair pokes out from beneath an army helmet, in an action shot of him leaping from a helicopter. The screen cuts to national correspondent Donald Blazer, who might be as old as the Earth.

"In a moment, we will take you inside the former Alliance capital building, where extremist leader Adrian Lamb abused his amassed power and ordered the senseless killings of many American people, under the guise of striving for a better nation. This building now houses the movement fighting against him, and the so-called Lord Lamb is ruling from an unknown location. Sources tell us that Lamb cannot get in proximity of the building, as the rebel movement has taken over the area."

Blazer sips from a glass of water. "The conflict has divided historical Charleston right down the middle and threatens to shatter the Alliance into bits and pieces. We have reason to believe that Lamb's closest advisors are now working with the American military in an effort to jump ship and reverse the secessions. There's hope yet for a reunited America."

My heart aches. Why does Callie have to be in Charleston of all places?

"Tonight, we're excited to have several guest commentators. First, let us welcome Colonel James Caudill, who has proven instrumental in providing the American military with the intelligence needed to put a stop to this terroristic threatening and... well, people, let's call it what it is. Genocide."

Wait. James? The James I know? The one who almost got me killed and couldn't save Callie? Anger bubbles through my veins. It feels so good to know the American military had our back all along. But why didn't James tell me? I guess he couldn't tell anyone. But we were close...

Blazer casts a dismal frown to the camera then looks up as a pretty anchor hands him a single white page. "This just in, ladies and gentlemen. As the American military combs the West Virginia countryside for Adrian Lamb, civil war has erupted in the Alliance streets. Officials are looking for this man," Davey Brinkle's picture pops up on the screen, "who's said to be the leader of an organization called ASP. That's the Allied Security Patriots."

"Right." I point at the screen. "You guys go get that loser. Annihilate him."

With a grimace, Blazer lets the page fall to his teleprompter. "The so-called patriots have taken their fighting door-to-door in a guerrilla-style warfare, and as rumor has it, they're seeking to control the country. Before you close your eyes this evening, say a prayer for our servicemen, as they, too, are falling under attack from vigilante soldiers who do not understand the rules of war and answer only to themselves."

And Callie. Callie may be under attack, too. Why did I promise to stay put? Maybe I should go back anyway. I have the resources now.

Blazer leans forward. "Let's keep alive the hope that Adrian Lamb, and all his co-conspirators, will be captured and brought to justice before we lose more of our sons and daughters."

"Yes, let's." I flip off the television and head to my bedroom. I need to take some time to truly meditate on the situation. Consult God for guidance. As I crawl under the covers and settle for a long night of prayer, branches strike my window, and rain pelts the glass. Another storm. I lost Callie on a stormy day. Perhaps this one will bring her home.

The next morning, the sun shines through the window from a brilliant blue sky. After a long, hot shower, I set out for the bank and deposit my money in a new account, opting to keep the baseball cards at home. I might go through them all and see which ones are most valuable. Maybe I'll keep them instead of selling them. Too many Dad memories to let go of.

After some hassle, I renew my driver's license then head out to the college to see what I can do about finishing my degree. It feels wrong to make future plans, but Michael insisted. Said if I didn't go, he'd drag me there. Two hours later, I'm registered for summer classes and carrying my second new ID. I can always withdraw if things don't work out.

I make two more stops, to the cable company and the AT&T store. By the end of the day, I'm starting to feel like myself again, but emptier.

As I'm leaving the strip mall with my new phone, one more sign catches my eye. Deb's Jewelers. Wouldn't hurt to at least look.

The tall, sleek Asian girl at the counter flashes me a bright smile as soon as I walk into the store. She smooths her hair and rushes over. "Bet I know what you're here for."

"To look." I stop at the first glass cabinet and study the diamond-studded rings.

"A special girl, no?" She lifts her frames from her eyes and chews the handle. "You have a long history." Leaning closer, she wrinkles her nose. "A troubled history, right?"

A tall, thin mirror on an earring display sitting atop the counter shows my face betraying me. "You could say that."

"But some pleasantry in that history. And… she's not with you right now. You guys are separated, but you're hoping for a future."

My brow quirks. Who is this girl? Did she recognize me from the Twitter post? Did she read my mind? "Yes. We are apart, but by circumstance. If we could be together, she'd be with me right now, looking for the perfect ring."

"You will have your future." She flips her hair over her shoulder and reaches into a distant glass case. "Oh, I know the perfect ring. This one."

Trying not to gasp at the nineteen-hundred dollar price tag, I let her slip the ring over my pinky. "It's not gold."

"Oh, it's gold." She chuckles. "Rose gold. Fourteen karats. And those three stones… for your past, your present, and your future."

"It is pretty. Big stones, though. But I like how the gold wraps around them."

She snags my collar. "And, it's your lucky day, because it's sixty percent off. Sixty! How could you ever beat that price?"

"So what, about five fifty?"

"Something like that." She lifts out a velvety black box. "Five twenty-five. So, you in?"

I close my eyes, everything I love about Callie rushing to the forefront of my mind. How awesome would it be to surprise her with a ring the moment I see her?

When I open them, the girl's face is about two inches from mine. "So…"

"Okay."

Box in hand, I skip along a few steps back to the car. Cranking the radio, I sing along to Ed Sheeran and daydream about a different life.

A bolt of lightning strikes something in the skyline and static interrupts the broadcast. Shame on me for allowing myself to feel normal. Tomorrow, I'm going to make some calls. I need to find a way to reach James Caudill. Surely, with his pull, he can get me to Callie.

# Chapter Eighteen

## CALLIE

**BRIEF PAIN SEARS MY CHEEK**, and I press my face against the dry-rotted pillow. The brimstone scent conjures images of campfires and roasting marshmallows with Ethan, and for a moment, grogginess pulls me back into dreams.

Another sharp jolt scorches my shoulder. As I sputter and cough, my eyes open to swelling embers and a cloud of smoke above my head. My prison cell glows an eerie orange, and flames lick through the foam ceiling.

My chest tightens as I stifle a gasp, clamping my lips to hold my breath. A fire? Was it set on purpose? I throw my wool blanket aside and dive away from dropping ash. My gaze lands first on the high windows lining the wall above me, far out of reach. Next, I spin to the thick steel door to my left, bracing for pain when I touch the metal. It's locked, as I knew it would be, but at least it's cool. Tears sting my eyes, and I cover my mouth and nose with my shirt collar. *Please, Lord. If this is your will, help me yield to it.*

An overhead beam crackles. A chunk falls to my bed, igniting the sheets. Shudders pulse through my body. I crawl to the blanket and pull it to the floor. Maybe if I roll it tight around me… Or would it make things worse?

I edge back to the door, ball up under the blanket, and sing in a shaky voice. "Amazing grace, how sweet the sound, that saved—"

The lock clicks, and the door handle turns. My shoulders stiffen, and I stand as a crack forms between the door and the frame. Screams and shouts from the open room outside my cell give me hope. Someone is setting us free. Maybe one of the guards has shown compassion. Clutching the blanket so tight the fibers dig into my fingers, I wait for my savior to burst into the room.

Feet shuffle, and a low cough punctuates the popping and cracking.

Why haven't they come in yet? Should I go out? Will they relock the door if I don't?

I ease it open wider, drawing in fresher air, if I can call it that. The smoke obscures the constant mustiness I've endured since Adrian snatched me from my beloved sycamores and forced me into Alliance custody. The influx of light reveals ash spots on my blanket. If I'd slept any longer… Chills shoot down my spine.

Maybe… dare I hope Ethan could be here? For so long I've dreamed he'd come save me like he promised. But Ethan would have burst in and embraced me. Wouldn't he?

"Thank you." My shaky whisper vanishes in the void as I widen the door to its full span. "Now, who are you? Friend or foe?"

Dim sunbeams stream from the ceiling windows into an empty room with cracking mortar and stray crates and boxes. Rough patches mar the dulled concrete floor, but no embers. A handful of disoriented prisoners dash in uncertain paths, but still no savior. And no clear escape path. A salty tear rolls over my lips, and I shove it away with the back of my hand. If Adrian's watching, and this is some kind of twisted game, no way will I let him see me cry.

Six red garage doors line the far wall. One rises, and I duck behind a pallet of crates, then creep past forklifts toward a smaller, nearby door. Someone wouldn't free all the prisoners only to give us away. Would they?

Following skid marks from the rubber tires, I edge closer as the opening garage exposes two pairs of Kevlar-covered legs in Alliance red. The other prisoners charge them, fleeing the flames now crackling behind us. A spray of rifle fire sweeps the opening. The frontline prisoners' bodies jerk. Others scramble backward.

I shield myself with the blanket like it could render me invisible, still seeing no sign of a savior. Hope this person is a friend.

But what if they're not? I reach for the knob on the side door, praying my jagged breath doesn't give me away.

A hand clamps my mouth, and another grips my left shoulder. Tremors pulse my spine as I try to turn.

"Wait." The breathy whisper tickles my neck, and the hand drops to my forearm. Two dark-haired men clad in full rescue gear burst through the garage door, their faces obscured by oxygen masks, and rifles propped on their right shoulders. They rush to my cell, and the hand squeezes my arm. "Now!"

A lanky figure, perhaps old enough to be a man, steps in front of me, his face hidden by a knitted ski mask. He bumps the side door with his hips and drags me outside, then eases it closed again. We dash a few feet into rows of rusting café tables and chairs.

His gaze darts to the right and left. "This way."

Across an alley street, we duck into a thicket of thorny bushes. As he clears a path for me, shouts echo from the warehouse and sirens wail in the distance.

"She's not here!"

"Impossible!"

Exiting the thicket, we come to a neighborhood of deteriorating houses. Tiny gravel digs into my bare feet as we flee over a crumbling sidewalk.

He stops, removes his mask, and pulls me onto the cover of a closed-in porch. "My name is Luke. Do you remember me?"

My heart sinks. His hair, curled and gelled, resembles Adrian's, like the men in the warehouse. Is he a loyalist? His face does look familiar, but I can't think of anyone named Luke. "I don't. Sorry."

"My dad, Larry, helped you escape Virginia. And with my brothers, I'm helping you now."

I swallow a shiver. "You look like him."

Luke grins. "Dad?"

"No." Bile sticks in my throat. "Adrian."

A scowl flickers across his face. "We have to pretend to be followers. To secure our freedom."

"So you lie."

"We pretend." He picks the lock on the back door and leads me into the house. Thick dust layers kitchen countertops, and again a musty smell fills my lungs. Water stains the ceiling.

"Here." He grabs a camouflage backpack from a dingy leather couch. "A change of clothes. You can use that restroom, but there's not any running water. Put the hood over your head."

The jeans, mock turtleneck, and oversized hoodie swallow my malnourished frame. A ponytail holder loops around one of the tennis shoe strings, and a brief memory flashes of Mom brushing my hair as we watch the evening news. I can almost hear Dad reading Scripture in the background and Amber huffing as she washes the dishes.

After changing, I join Luke, who peeks out a curtain at the front of the house.

He winks as a black sedan pulls into the drive. "Good timing."

We rush outside, and he opens the back car door. Another Adrian twin waves from the driver's seat. "Hi, Callie."

I chew my lip. He must be Luke's brother. Their eyes are the same perfect shade of hunter green, and they share a pepper of freckles across the bridge of their noses. "Hi."

He chuckles. "I'm Tristan. You don't remember us, do you?"

"I remember seeing you guys in the cave. It's unsettling to see you looking like Adrian."

Luke slides into the front seat. "Yeah, we know."

I crawl in the back.

"Duck down into the floorboards, but brace yourself. This might be kind of a wild ride."

The car jerks into motion, throwing me against the front seat. Tristan whips out of the drive and speeds through the neighborhood streets as I lower myself into the foot space.

"Won't they be searching cars?" Butterflies swarm my stomach like a hurricane.

Tristan signals. "I forgot. You haven't been out in months. In about two minutes, we're going to blend with hundreds of cars like this one. There's only one factory providing cars to the Alliance now, all black sedans. And all the drivers will look alike because Adrian insisted everyone get perms. So, no. I think they'll find searching cars useless."

"That's so ridiculous. Why the perms?"

"Why any of it?" He makes a sharp right turn. "Besides, Adrian hired lackeys to guard you instead of professionals. Those goons are still looking through the burning warehouse trying to find you."

I snort. "I thought Adrian set the fire."

"Nope." Another sharp turn. "We did, as a distraction. But we didn't expect it to spread so fast. Thought the structure was better suited for it. Sorry for scaring you." Tristan twists the steering wheel with stunt-driver expertise that sets my heart pounding. He's still scaring me.

My stomach lurches as Tristan weaves between lanes. When I think I can't take anymore, the car halts.

"Up and out." Luke opens the car door, and I step into a narrow alley between dirty brick buildings.

Tristan tries a number of steel doors as we walk through the alley. At last, one opens, leading us to a long, dim hall. He raises a finger, furrows his brow, and presses his ear against several interior doors.

"Don't you know where we're going?" My whisper almost shouts. "What are you listening for?"

"The hum of machines." He selects a door and raps five times. "We had to make a change of plans."

A short, gray-haired woman sweeps it open. "May I help you?"

"It's me." Luke stands straighter. "I need you to hide someone."

She appraises me, wrinkling her nose when she peeks beneath my hood. "This is another teenager. I'm already having trouble managing the others. What good is she to me?"

"I know this one. She will work hard." He pulls the hood back, uncovering my butterfly tattoo.

Her eyes widen as she studies my face and the color drains from hers. "It can't be."

Luke points to my abdomen. "Show her your scars."

I lift my sweatshirt, exposing the purplish streaks surrounding the sphere where the bullet pierced my side.

She steadies herself against the cracked wall. "Not such an unusual wound. Are you sure it's her?"

Dropping the shirt, I raise my right pant leg to the knee. "Maybe this scar is more unusual?"

Her chest deflates. "Does it hurt you? Will it keep you from standing on your feet?"

I nod. "It's arthritic, I think. I'll need to rest or sit sometimes. But I can still work hard with my hands."

She turns to Luke. "Do you realize the risk? If we are discovered... our whole operation will be compromised."

"You won't be. We'll be back for her as soon as the escape route has been cleared."

A sad smile grazes his face, one that doesn't reach his eyes. "Callie, I have to go. You'll be safe here. Erma will treat you well. Tristan and I will be back in a few days."

I eye the sharp-nosed woman and lick my lips. What can I say? "Okay."

Erma and I stand mute until he passes through the exterior door into the sunlight.

She sighs. "Let's get you changed."

We head to a room with a salon chair and sink. She opens a drawer and removes a basket of curlers. "This will take a couple of hours, so feel free to get some shut-eye when I set the timers."

With a fine-toothed comb, she separates my hair into small sections and wraps them around the rollers.

"You're giving me a perm."

"I'm changing your appearance so no one will recognize you." She frowns. "Though, I'm going to have to leave it longer to hide your butterfly."

"I don't want to hide my butterfly. And I don't want a perm."

She releases a roller, the elastic snap striking my cheek. "Do you want to get caught?"

"No." I chew on my lower lip, blinking away tears. Not fair.

"It's a loose one. It'll relax before you know it." As she finishes the rollers on the back of my head, a nagging thought presses to the forefront of my mind. I survived two gunshots and a fire. I have been an Alliance prisoner for months, and I'm now free... I need to be thankful, not stubborn.

Erma tucks cotton around my forehead and squirts warm liquid over the curlers, then nudges my head against the leather seat. She sets a timer, and my eyes flicker shut. *Dear Lord, please forgive my attitude. I am blessed to be here today, free and hidden.*

The room blurs, and dreams fill my thoughts.

Erma wakes me, this time squirting a cool liquid over my head. A few minutes later, she rinses my hair, pulling springy curls and letting them bounce back. "I suppose we could leave it long for now." She scrunches the hair in her fingers and squeezes excess water. "And maybe we could remove the tattoo if you're ready."

"No. I'm keeping the tattoo. It's a memory of how I overcame a challenging time in my life."

Clucking her tongue, she dabs makeup over my butterfly, then twists my hair into a loose side ponytail that she secures at the base of my neck and pulls toward my collarbone. "I guess this will do."

She spins the chair so I can see the mirror. Eerie how much I look like Adrian with curly hair. But I belong to Dad.

"I understand you are quite the rebel." Her piercing reflection prickles my arm hair. "There will be no talk of rebellion. The Christians have a secret meeting on Sundays, and you may deliver your doctrine to them if you so wish. But never a mention of it on the floor."

"Yes, ma'am."

Her swallow seems to stick, and she clears her throat. "You may find circumstances here shocking. You should know that we emulate all Alliance circumstance and follow those rules. It allows us to operate in secret. Do not risk our exposure by questioning what you do not understand."

"I won't question anything." The pit in my stomach plummets. "Let's go."

She takes me to another room and gives me a gray uniform. Then we head toward a roaring sound. By the time we reach the huge, open room, my ears ache.

"The dishwashing area," she shouts, leading me past steaming steel structures where rows of mason jars drift by on a conveyer belt.

We leave the room and enter another. A line of Adrian-haired women sit at cutting-board tables peeling and chopping vegetables. When the door closes behind us, the noise dies to a dull whir.

"These ladies provide clean, organic food to Alliance citizens using traditional canning means."

"Why?"

"They reduce our exposure to the chemicals we once feared in the plastic liners."

I guess it makes sense.

Erma speaks in my ear, a soft whisper I have to strain to hear. "Though the hours are long and the pay is small, we wire an overtime salary to an account in the United States with your name. Should you ever escape, the money will be waiting for you."

"And if not?" I fumble with the hem of my shirt.

"You will receive your regular salary like everyone else. If you die before returning, the money will be given to someone else who needs to start over when they escape."

She walks me past a line of women peeling carrots with paring knives, to a line of old-school stoves with huge boiling pots with clamped lids. Steam hisses from vents on the top, and some of the pots rattle so hard they might explode. Women move the pots from one burner to another like bees hopping between flowers, easing the rattling to small jiggles. "One day I'll put you with the pressure cookers, but for today, you're going to peel potatoes."

I clench my jaw. Luke said a few days. I'm not going to be here long enough for the pressure cookers. I smile and nod and follow her to the potato counter.

"Meet Harmony." Erma nods to me, and the Adrian lookalikes face me. Teenagers and women, they all wear worry lines on their foreheads and exhaustion in their eyes.

She nudges me toward a stool and hands me a paring knife. The girl next to me peels in one continuous spiral, and I try to mimic her.

For five hours, I peel with no mention of a break. The other girls at the table look toward their potatoes, not venturing a glance in any direction. Though blisters form on my tender hands and aches spread through my fingers, I do the same.

The hands on the wall clock move into the sixth hour, and a bell chimes. All the girls set their potatoes on the counter and stand. They file out of the room one by one, and I fall into the last place in line. We move one at a time through a narrow hallway. The women disappear into a small room and come out with dripping hands. A restroom, I guess. The finished ones walk past and return to the peeling room.

A girl gasps as she passes. She slips in line behind me and plants her lips against to my ear. "Callie? I thought you were dead."

# Chapter Nineteen

## ETHAN

**MY FIRST DAY ON THE JOB** working for Michael, guilt consumes me. Everything is far too normal. My pressed khakis and long-sleeved Polo shirt scratch my skin, and a new pair of tennis shoes traps my toes against the stiff leather. But my heart still aches.

After two hours of Michael showing me the accounting books, he leaves me with the computer and my thoughts.

Which of course go to finding Callie. Several Internet searches reveal nothing but what I already know.

I leave the small TV set on silent CNN all day, but they keep cycling through the same info. The American military inches forward, rescuing Alliance citizens and fighting men who employ ruthless and rudimentary tactics. Wish I could find out how she's doing. Find someone to call…

Why did things have to go down like they did? I wanted to be on that rescue mission. Will she even know that I tried to save her?

When we head out to lunch, I scroll through my Facebook feed on my new cell phone. Hundreds of notifications keep me occupied the entire trip. Birthday wishes, pity over my parents… Callie's profile. Why am I even wasting my time looking at her page? It's not like she's posted anything there.

Boy, Amber has, though. Pictures of her and "Bae" all over Mexico. If Adrian had wanted to get to her, she's made it easy. Seems like he has other worries to consider, though.

On a whim, I type James Caudill into the search box. Twenty-seven people pop up with that name, but not the James I know. Guess I should have known he'd want to lay low.

I try Davey Brinkle. There he is, his bad-boy hair looking so jelly it could pass for plastic. Why did I even fool with that creep? I should have fought my way out of that van, raced back to that arena, and shoved my way through the crowd until I found Callie. Snipers or no snipers, if I'd died, I would have at least died fighting for her.

Now, all I can boast about is running away from the Alliance. Taking the first ride out of the country. I should have demanded to stay. Told the Army I wasn't leaving without her. Why didn't I? Was I scared?

My fingers type Tristan's name into the search box. But wait. What's his last name? Ugh. Social media is getting me nowhere.

Unless...

I log into my Twitter account using the password Callie and I made up together. Hez1k1aH. Thirteenth king of Judah, and not a book in the Bible, which she tricked me into answering wrong. The memory brings a smile to my face. Love that girl so much. She has to come home.

Skipping all the notifications and messages, I tap the screen for the search box. Wonder what hits I'll find for the Alliance.

As I sift through hashtags and posts, I smile even wider. Love it-- #Americastrong, #downwiththeAlliance #stopAdrianLamb. I can use all of those. And, one more...

My finger hovers over the screen a few seconds before typing. *Missing my girl. Callie Noland is ALIVE. Let's #stopAdrianLamb and #bringCalliehome #downwiththeAlliance #AmericaStrong*

She'd hate it, of course. I know exactly what she'd say. "Aren't you the needy one? Aren't you the attention-needy one?" The words chide me as if she's here to utter them. Shrugging, I tap the Tweet button and close the app, but the words still fill my mind. "Nobody should use four hashtags in the same Tweet. It's not cool." Well, if it gets me closer to finding her, I don't care.

Dings sound. I turn the cell on silent then tap the icon again. Twelve notifications. No, sixteen. Twenty-three.

Michael signals, changes lanes, and glances over at me. His forehead wrinkles higher than I've ever noticed. When did his hairline start receding? "Everything okay?"

"I miss her."

"Maybe we could call some of those toll-free numbers on that government website. See if there's anyone who can help you make a connection. They have some family hotlines, and since Callie's so high-profile..."

My phone lights up again. "The Army gave me a number, but last I called they didn't have any new information. And yeah, you could say that she's high profile." I laugh.

"What?"

"I sent out a Tweet on a whim. Announced she was alive. It's getting a lot of hits, but maybe it wasn't such a great idea." My chest heaves. "In fact, with all that's happened, I could have put myself in danger. Or you guys."

Michael's face says he'd like to reprimand me, but he turns his attention back to the road. I'm sure he's thinking of Agent Kevin Wiseman, who would love another opportunity to rough us up.

"I shouldn't have."

No answer.

We pull up to a burger joint, and head in to make our orders. Michael steps between me and the counter. "I'm paying for his."

"No." I try to sidestep him, and he blocks me. "You've done enough for me already."

"My treat."

We both fold our arms. The poor girl behind the register taps her black fingernails on the counter, and my chest heaves. "Fine. He can pay."

He does, and we take the plastic number to the table. As soon as we sit, I meet his hard stare.

"Missed you last night."

Right. Church. Heat warms my neck. "I'm sorry. Meant to go, but it's been so long since I've had access to services that I forgot."

His face softens, but he still leans forward. Michael has always been this amazing, benevolent guy, but he can be pushy sometimes. More than pushy. Still, I owe him so much.

"I will be there Sunday morning. Promise." I pick up the plastic number and turn it over in my hands. If I don't find a lead on Callie. "For Bible class, worship, and evening worship. And I'll even hang out at the building afterward and let Mr. Whitman corner me."

He laughs then sobers. "We've noticed your absence, Ethan. Prayed over you every night."

"Thanks."

Interlocking his fingers, he rests his hands on the table in front of him. "You know, Angela and I have come to think of you as our own son. And I promised your dad. We will be here for you."

"I know. And I appreciate it. By the way, I took care of the college thing. They're going to let me start back classes in August on my same track."

Michael picks up his drink cup and stands. "Angela and I wanted a son. She's cried many, many tears over it. And we never had to worry about expenses like college. It would be our pleasure to cover the cost to help you finish." He scoops our straw trash into his hand and dumps it on the tray, but not before I see his glistening eyes.

At that moment, my flood breaks open, and there's nothing I can do to stop it. Tears pour from my eyes, my body shakes with sobs, and my heart shatters. All the emotions I've stifled for months come back full force.

And there, in the middle of a busy lunch hour, Michael wraps me in his arms and holds me while I cry.

One of his Bible class lessons comes to mind, from a couple months before the Alliance. He'd taught about all these different men who wept in the Bible. Esau weeping over his blessing, Jacob weeping over Rachel, Jacob and Esau weeping when they reconciled… He'd spoken of Joseph weeping in his private room over his brothers, and David weeping for Jonathan. So many different instances, and yet I've always lived by the stigma that real men never cry.

Even Martin cried over Callie, and Ella, and even Amber. Sobbed until he shook. So now, I let my broken heart pour out amidst a myriad of curious eyes.

Michael kneels beside me. " 'The Lord is my shepherd, I shall not want…' " He clears his throat. " 'He makes me to lie down in green pastures.' "

A second voice joins in. " 'He leads me beside the still waters.' "

While I'm still bent over, feet approach. Two more voices join. " 'He restores my soul. He leads me in the paths of righteousness for His name's sake.' "

I lift my chin. A crowd has gathered, and they've all linked arms around me like a cocoon. After a quivery breath, I find my tongue and rake it over my teeth. " 'Yea, though I walk through the valley of the shadow of death, I will fear no evil, for You are with me. Your rod and your staff, they comfort me.' "

A small curly-haired blond girl with a freckled nose pushes her way between their legs. Couldn't be more than six. Maybe even four or five. She takes my hand in hers and squeezes hard, then pulls me to my feet. "Don't be sad, Mister."

With big brown eyes, she leans forward and raises her arms. When I lift her, she kisses my forehead. "All better now." The whole room laughs, and a woman who must be her mom shakes her head as I set her down.

"I know how it ends." She stands straight and tall, catching the skirt of her dress in her hands and twisting. " 'Surely goodness and mercy shall follow me all the days of my life… and I will dwell in the house of the Lord forever.' "

When the crowd finishes, she claps her hands. "You guys did good!"

Laughter fills the restaurant.

A haggard woman with baggy eyes pats Michael's arm. "Thank you for that, sir. You have no idea how much I needed to hear that Psalm tonight."

"Me, either." A balding man drapes his arm over the woman next to him. "My wife and I learned she has cancer this morning."

Michael takes the man's hands in his own. "What are your names? I'll pray for you both."

Before I know what's happened, Michael has an entire list written on a napkin, and he leads a prayer for the whole restaurant. When he finishes, I drop back to my seat as the cashier brings our food.

"That was amazing." She grins big at Michael, revealing several cavities. "Here I've been fighting addiction and debating with myself if I wanted to go to my friend's house, where I know there will be drugs. And I needed strength. I haven't read that Psalm in decades. In fact," she drops her gaze to the floor, "I don't even have a Bible."

Michael returns her grin and reaches to the briefcase at his feet. "You can have mine. It's worn and full of notes, but it should serve you well." He flips the snaps and retrieves the red leather Bible he's carried to church as long as I've known him. "There's a bulletin in the cover with the address to our church. Maybe I'll see you there on Sunday?"

"I'll think about it." She glances over her shoulder. "Oops, got to get back to the line."

Michael holds out the Bible, and she grasps it with a tentative hand.

"Are you sure?" She flips through the onion skin pages and traces her fingers over the words.

"Take it." Michael shakes his head at me. "All that, and I forgot to bless our food."

"I got this one." Bowing my head, I squeeze my eyes shut.

Later, back in Michael's truck, I am still pumped from the experience. "That was incredible. So open and honest, and people were so receptive. It's not every day you—"

"Why isn't it?" He turns the key in the ignition.

"I don't kn—"

"Why can't it be every day?" As he pulls the truck into reverse he looks over his shoulder. "Why can't you find people to pray for and do it? Why can't you quote a comforting scripture to a friend?"

"I can, I suppose."

"Ethan, if the Alliance situation has taught me one thing, it's what a grave danger there is in not sharing our faith with everyone we encounter. There's not a single client I have who doesn't know and respect that I'm a Christian. I will proclaim it from every mountaintop and fight to be sure the world knows. Jesus is my savior. I am redeemed. But I will also show it with my reasonable service, and give God that glory. If we're going to defeat the Devil's soldiers, like the Alliance, we must spread His truth."

I bite my lip and swallow. "Michael, not everyone has your personality, or your money to do benevolent things for people. God doesn't expect us all to proclaim him from the mountaintops. Right?

I mean I'm not shy or anything, but sometimes it's hard to bring up God to people. And when you have a gun to your head? Look at what the last thing I proclaimed from a mountaintop did for me. I lost Callie."

"And he said to them, 'Go into all the world and preach...' unless you have a gun to your head."

"Fine." I rub my temples. "You are right. It's hard to think about being brave. After all that's happened and knowing that Adrian still might have people out there who want to hurt me, how could I? Or to hurt Callie."

"It takes practice is all. And a good mentor."

I muster up the most serious face I can. "Okay. So since you've already taken to nagging me about church, I'll agree to letting you and Angela call me son. On one condition." My smirk escapes before I can stop it.

He chuckles. "If you call me Pa, I'm going to get you down on the floor and wrestle that smile right off your face." His chest bellows with built up laughter as he tries to give me a mock-scolding look.

"You're the one who decided to teach the Pa Kettle math lesson to a bunch of teenagers." I snort. "But you know what, I still remember that class. Xavier and Jordan were mystified by the numbers. Still are today, I bet."

"But not Callie." Michael pulls onto the bypass center lane and merges into the line of traffic. "She piped up and explained why Pa Kettle was wrong, trying to add the tens column as ones, and even figured out my Biblical connection before I had a chance to say it."

"Yeah." My screen lights up again.

"Looks like God's given you a platform, Ethan. What are you going to do with it? Like the little kid song, you can't hide under a bushel."

"What would you do with it?"

He's quiet for a minute, bouncing his left knee. "I suppose I'd do whatever brings God the most glory. Maybe give it thought instead of making spur-of-the-moment posts. Be still, and know..."

"Touché."

"There are some guys who approached me a couple months ago about getting into politics. I've been giving it a thought. We need more Christians in politics." He digs through his pocket, retrieves a white index card, and pushes it across the seat. "By the way, I had your cable hooked back up. Guy's going to be there at four."

"It feels wrong to think about cable while she's missing. I need to be out there, helping them look for her."

"I know. I thought you'd want access to all the news shows and stuff. And Internet, so you can communicate with them by email." Michael whips across a line of oncoming traffic into his parking lot. "There are so many military experts out there looking for her. Trust them, Ethan, and let's make it a good place for her to come home to. I know you've been thinking about trying to cross the border. I saw the pages you were searching. Don't. It's not going to help Callie any if you're hurt or dead. Take some time for true meditation and thought. Seek out what God wants you to do."

He's right. But I still feel like I should be out there fighting for her. "I will." Puffing my cheeks, I pop out of the truck and head back into the office.

Thought... Right. Every time I stop to think, I picture myself trekking the Alliance countryside in search of Callie. But what exactly does God want me to do?

One time, Dad taught this devo on patience. He used me as an example. Said I was the worst, always indulging in self-gratification. Everyone had a good laugh at my expense. Michael commented even then that I needed to be still and reflect on my faith. Guess I still do.

Following work, I drive back to the house, arriving twenty minutes before the appointment with the cable guy. The doorbell rings ten minutes before he's scheduled, and I open the door to a sixtyish man who shuffles into my living room and hands me the paperwork. "Wireless Internet and 200-plus package, right?"

"Yeah." I prop the papers against the wall and sign where he's highlighted then pass them back. "Thanks for coming. You want a drink or something?"

"Got any whiskey?"

I'm pretty sure my eyes pop open wide enough he can see all the way to my brain. "Um... no. I don't drink alcohol. And you can't—"

"Was a joke." He scratches the stubble on his chin and sets his tool bag on Mom's coffee table. "I don't need a drink. At least not right now."

He sets about his business. What can I say to him? It might be a good opportunity for that evangelism like Michael was talking about. Should I ask him if he goes to church?

His hand smacks the corner of the entertainment center, and he blurts out a string of curse words. Guessing that's a negative on the church.

I shove my hands in my pockets and move closer. "So, you ever read the Bible?"

"Cover to cover." He uncoils part of a long coaxial cable and drops the rest on the floor. "Where do you want your box?"

"Over there, I guess. We have one. It's been—"

"Need a new one. That one's ancient. But I can take it away for you." He unhooks the old box and tosses it to the carpet. Bits of plastic fly free, entangling with the Berber fibers. "Piece of junk." More curse words.

Finding my way to Dad's old armchair, I stare out the window as he finishes up his work. Who was I kidding? I'm no evangelist.

When he wraps up, I walk him to the porch. Maybe one more try. "Listen, if you're looking for a good church, I—"

"I'm not." He bounds down the steps toward his truck.

Guess that's that.

Back in the living room, I check my cell again. Notifications still going strong. Spur-of-the-moment or not, I tap the screen. Two hundred new followers? Do my eyes deceive me? What could I write?

Martin always used to say stick with the truth—God's truth. So I turn my gaze to the engraved board hanging over our mantle. Dad got it for Mom as a Christmas gift a couple years ago. Her favorite verse. It's perfect.

I copy and paste it from my Bible app, then frown. Too long. Fine. I'll post part of it.

*Micah 6:8 "...and what does the Lord require of you but to do justice, and to love kindness, and to walk humbly with your God?"*

For the first time, I understand what Michael has been trying to tell me all week. In my obsession over finding Callie, I've forgotten my true purpose. God's true purpose that is.

And now, I understand why He's been stalling me. I can't risk my life until I've taken care of my soul.

*God, I promise. I will be still.*

# Chapter Twenty

## CALLIE

**THE WORDS PLAY** in my mind, again and again. "Callie. I thought you were dead."

I pick up my paring knife and attack another potato, wincing as the juice creeps through the top layer of my skin. It's been a full day since the girl recognized me. She slipped away before I got a look at her face, but I think... or dare I say hope... it could be Maggie, one of my first Alliance friends.

It's impossible to search the workers to find her. Have to keep my eyes on my work. Erma reminds me a bit of Reva, which brings heartache. I've tried hard to focus my thoughts elsewhere, replaying the last six months and trying hard to reconcile what Luke and Tristan told me with what I thought I knew.

If Adrian was right, and the Alliance is about to fall, Erma must live in terrible fear of the fighting that's sure to break out around her. Though she drives us to work faster and faster, rapping our knuckles with a spatula when we slow our pace, she clenches her jaw and looks over her shoulder.

My blisters sting. I want to ask about gloves—shouldn't we be protecting the Alliance citizens from disease? But dare I?

As if reading my mind, someone drops a pair on the counter in front of me. I slip them on. They're too loose, and the rough fabric rubs against my blisters, making them hurt even more. But I press on...

After three more hours, another bell sounds, and they take us to a stuffy cafeteria. Tables are squeezed in so close the girl behind me keeps poking my back as she shovels in whatever gruel they're serving. Yesterday's wasn't terrible. I swirl my spoon through the bowl and dare a taste.

It's good, kind of a cross between the beef stew and vegetable soup my mom used to make for us every winter. When I reach the bottom of the bowl, a woman rolls out a pot and ladles another helping to me and whoever else wants it. The urgency of clicking spoons reminds me to quicken my pace, and when the bell rings again for us to return to our posts, I'm more than satisfied.

When I walk back to my peeling table, the smell of dirt overwhelms me, and dust catches in my throat. A new pile sits in place of the one I'd diminished, stacked even higher than the first.

The thought of cutting another potato makes my stomach churn, but I grab another anyway. Seconds click away in painful increments, and I pass the time reciting Scripture in my head. I should have been doing this all along.

God's word strengthens me, as always, and though the pain still pulses through my blistered hands, a numbing sensation takes over.

The tiny breaks in silence become almost musical. A girl sniffs from two seats down. Another gasps. Random sighs and the thwack, thwack of the chopping knives serve as percussion and build a rhythm for my recitations.

Within an hour, a pyramid of ready potatoes rests in the bowl of water in front of me. Erma nods to me. "Nice job, new girl."

I reach for another potato, but she pulls me aside, nudging me past the rows of busy women and leading me to a small office at the front of the room.

"Sit." She points to a worn leather chair.

I stumble into it. When did my legs get so rubbery? Bad as I hate to admit it, Michael's right. I'm in no shape to scour the countryside.

She unlocks a cabinet and retrieves a basket with a variety of bandages and tubes of salve. "Take off those gloves, and I'll doctor you up."

"Thank you." I slip out of the gloves, exposing angry, raw skin.

"Did you know that except for a handful of political science gurus, the forefathers of the Alliance were all chemists and pharmaceutical experts?" She squeezes a balm from one of the tubes and rubs it on my palm, providing intense relief. "They dedicated their lives to engineering products that would help us achieve better health, faster healing, and less pain. It's a shame they couldn't have done that under the blanket of a united America. It would have taken the FDA decades to approve this stuff. Not everything that has come out of the Alliance is bad."

It makes sense—from the poisoning of the water and having an antidote, to Adrian's continual supply of mind altering drugs. A bunch of disgruntled chemists stand behind everything. Makes me wonder if he's in control at all. "No, I didn't, but I'm grateful to you for treating me."

A smile flashes across her face, but she stiffens. "You'll be amazed—ready to peel again in no time."

Great. "How many more hours will we have to be on the clock?"

"Three-and-a-half hours, then you can go to the cafeteria, bathhouse, and bed. Cameras are in the main rooms, so you know. And no one ever inspects them anymore."

"Okay. Thanks."

I slide my hands back into the gloves and return to the floor, attacking the potatoes with a vengeance. She's right. The balm eases my pain so much that I can work even faster. It becomes a game to see how long it takes me to peel one. After a few minutes, I'm far outpacing the rest of my table.

When the dismissal bell rings, the girl behind me stands and lodges her elbow into my side. "Showoff."

The word ripples through the room.

As the other girls move past, I search their faces, meeting snarls. Which one spoke to me earlier? Who is it that knows my true identity?

A hand brushes my shoulder. A girl, several inches shorter than me, and somewhere around seventeen or eighteen, meets my gaze. My heart stops. Maggie. It is her.

She disappeared from my first Alliance school not long after I'd arrived. I've wondered so many times what happened to her. From the wrinkle lines that crease her brow, my guess is things haven't been easy. A glint of hope twinkles in her eyes, and I wonder how the others might feel if they knew I was still alive. Perhaps there is some way…

Her droopy factory clothes swallow her small frame. Bet she can't be much more than eighty-five pounds. Then again, neither can I. Although, having three reasonable meals a day is sure to help.

I give her a faint smile and she moves on. By the time my table reaches the cafeteria, I've lost her in the crowd. My work group sits, eats another helping of the stew, and then stands in line for the bath house.

A woman paces the hall, handing out clean uniforms and scratchy pajamas. Each woman is given three minutes to shower and change, and then they disappear into another wing of the building.

We inch forward, moving occasional steps along the cracked tile floor and steadying ourselves against the dingy wall. My knee throbs, and I take ginger steps, trying not to put weight on it.

By the time I reach the shower, it's next to impossible to walk into the room. I slide into a stall and disrobe, placing my soiled clothes on a chair outside the curtain. A bottle of cheap shampoo sits on the ledge of the tub. I squirt some into my hand and turn on the water.

Ice cold droplets pierce my back and trickle to my waist. My breath catches, and I step aside, letting the water drip to my right. I lather the shampoo over my body, skipping my curls. Shouldn't wash a new perm. But then again… I attack the curls with a palm full of shampoo. Maybe this will reduce them to soft waves. Erma will be furious, not that I care. After rinsing, I step out of the stall and dress.

Other women do the same around me, though no one dares look at another. A quick pass of a pick through my hair renders it flexible enough to twist it like Erma did, although the makeup has washed free from my tattoo.

If Erma is concerned about its visibility, she shows no sign. She ushers us down another long hall where we split into four rooms.

I pause in the hallway, meeting her eyes. She nods to the front right room, and I follow the other girls inside.

Canvas cots fill the space, with very little walkway between them. Thin blankets sit folded atop each, and beneath them, lumpy pillows. The lead girl walks to the corner of the room, and they all take a seat on one of the cots.

Questions fill my mind. Yesterday, they were all asleep when Erma brought me in. Should I lie down? Do we have to go to sleep right now? Yep, because when the last girl sits, they all unfold their blankets and lay their heads on the pillows. When everyone is horizontal, the dim overhead lights extinguish, and hushed sighs whisper across the room.

I tuck the thin blanket tight around me and recite Scripture in my mind. I can do all things. This is temporary.

For a while, I toss and turn in the cot.

The girl next to me huffs. "Would you be still?" Her whisper drips of hate.

Though my knee aches to the point of bringing tears, I hold it frozen and close my eyes, stifling yawns.

It feels like seconds later when we all stir and the lights come on. We file back into the hallway, where this time we get the standard gray uniforms. After our turns dressing in the bathroom, we make our way back to the peeling counters.

For the next five days, I repeat the cycle, catching Maggie's eye across the room and exchanging slight smiles. Wish I'd hear something from Luke or Tristan. And Ethan. Is he even still thinking about me?

Thought I'd be here a short time, but Erma keeps talking about long-term plans. She'll teach me how to chop and do the pressure cooking. Does she know something I don't?

On the sixth day, following lunch, Erma taps a handful of women on the shoulder. They form a line against the front wall. When she touches my shoulder, I gulp, but join the others.

A heat wave blasts as we're ushered into a side room. Ammonia burns my nostrils. We sift through bins of soiled uniforms, kitchen and bath towels, and other random piles, then throw the fabrics into industrial-sized washers. Next, we move to racks where wrinkled uniforms hang. Overhead, hoses extend from the ceiling to within reach. Following the lead of the girl next to me, I stand on my tiptoes, grab the end, and run the mouth of the steamer over the nearest uniform.

"One hour, ladies." Erma ducks out, and I move to the rack of uniforms. That's not much time.

I've finished the sleeve when a tall girl moves to the center of the room. "Oh, good. We have a new girl. Everybody ready?" She smiles, takes a deep breath, and lifts her hand like a conductor might. "Blest be the tie that binds…"

Church? My heart soars. The other girls join in, and we steam the uniforms along to our praise.

A few minutes later, another girl crosses the room to a cabinet. She retrieves a bottle of grape juice and flat bread. Communion! It's been so long.

My hands tremble as we pray, and even more so when I accept a tiny piece of the bread. I bow my head. *Dear Lord, I feel Your presence in this place. Thank You for these sisters who share your faith, and for Your continued protection. You have again blessed me in ways I do not deserve.*

I bow again when we take the cup. This time, my eyes brim with tears, and when I raise my head, the other girls meet my gaze with concerned stares.

The tall girl pats my shoulder. "Welcome, Mallory. Erma said you were a Christian."

"Yes." I croak the word out, my chest constricting. "But I haven't worshipped with anyone in months."

Several girls swarm me in a tight embrace. The tall girl draws back first, her green eyes twinkling. "I'm Lily." She points to the other girls. "Meet Kara, Ashley, Sheena, and Hope."

I smile, my cheeks warming as they appraise me. "Hi."

"Now, we'll do the lesson." Lily motions to the center of the room, where a frayed white blanket has been spread across the floor."

We sit, forming a circle, and the girls join hands. I take Ashley and Kara's chaffed palms into my own, and squeeze.

Kara leans over, sweat dripping from her chin. "Isn't this awesome?"

"It is," I whisper back. No complaints about the air conditioning here. Poor Mrs. Whitman would be running around fussing about the vapors if our church had met in a place like this.

Lily frowns, pulls an Alliance Bible from her uniform pocket, and passes to me. "Would you like to read? I wish we had a real Bible. This was all we could get our hands on."

I sit straighter. "I can quote from the real Bible if you'd like. I know a lot of Scripture."

Ashley leans forward. "Know? Like memorized?"

"Yep." I grin. "What would you like to hear?"

"Maybe something from Ephesians?" Hope rests her hands in her lap. "I love that one."

"Okay, let me think." I close my eyes for a moment. Got it. "This is Ephesians chapter one, starting at verse fifteen. 'Therefore I also, after I heard of your faith in the Lord Jesus and your love for all the saints, do not cease to give thanks for you, making mention of you in my prayers...' "

Smiles are exchanged around the circle.

"Great," Lily says. "Good verse."

"Oh, I have more." I grin, " '...making mention of you in my prayers: that the God of our Lord Jesus Christ, the Father of glory, may give to you the spirit of wisdom and revelation in the knowledge of him...' " After a few short breaths, I meet Lily's eyes and grin again. " '...the eyes of your understanding being enlightened; that you may know what is the hope of His calling, what are the riches of the glory of His inheritance in the saints, and what is the exceeding greatness of His power toward those who believe, according to the working of his mighty power...' " Another deep breath. Maybe my memory wasn't damaged after all. "Boy, this one's a long sentence."

The girls chuckle.

"Finish it," Ashley says.

" 'Which He worked in Christ when He raised him from the dead and seated Him at his right hand in the heavenly places, far above all principality and power and might and dominion, and every name that is named...not only in this age but also in that which is to come.' " My heart pounds from the excitement. "Including Adrian Lamb."

"Yes." Kara clutches her hands over her heart. "Including Adrian Lamb. How do you remember all that?"

"My dad taught me these memory tricks. Like Romans 6:23." I hold my hand out, palm upturned. " 'The wages of sin is death.' Wages reminds us of money, right?"

The girls nod.

"Okay, so I'm holding my hand out like someone is going to put money in it." I draw my finger across my neck, tilt my head back, and stick out my tongue. "And this one reminds me of death."

Sheena giggles, mimicking my motions. "The wages of sin is death."

"Right." I move my hands like I'm untying a bow. "But the gift of God is eternal life…" With my fingers and thumb, I form a sign language *C*. "in Christ."

"Awesome!" Lily goes through the actions. "You know, there's a deaf girl, Haley, who works with us on the pressure cookers. Maybe I could get her to teach me some real sign language. It would it help us memorize, and we could teach her, too. No one would know what we were doing."

"When? It's not like we ever get to talk." Something dings above me.

The girls rush to their posts, and Lily scrambles to put the juice and bread in the cabinet.

Ashley leans close to my ear. "After lights out, wait thirty minutes, then walk around to the back hall. You can teach me more verses."

We resume steaming, uniform to uniform until they all hang crisp. Erma waits by the door when we exit the room. As I pass her, she grabs my arm and pulls me aside.

"Callie, I have bad news. Luke and Tristan have been captured. They won't be able to come for you."

I massage my temples, blinking away tears. At least Ethan's still out there somewhere. Maybe he'll find me. I refuse to give up hope.

# Chapter Twenty-One

## ETHAN

**TWO WEEKS** after going viral, I spend forty-five minutes in the morning checking my Twitter Feed, acknowledging all the retweets and commenting on the positive feedback. Still from the first post. Insanity among insanities, #bringCalliehome is trending as much as the latest gossip celebrities.

Dozens of people have announced their plans to march into the Alliance and take their homes back the minute the government permits it, and the words they've directed at Adrian are downright crude.

And the spelling… I'm not the best speller, but when someone offers me their gondolenses I have to wonder about the status of America. No wonder the Alliance gained ground.

Friends I haven't spoken with in years have sought me out and sent their prayers. One even offered to set me up a crowdfunding site. They've all wanted to hear about my time in the Alliance. Michael's right. I have an audience. And, I have a story to tell. What could I say to make it meaningful?

I need to learn and study so much more of the Bible before I'm ready to put myself out there. A full year of riotous living robbed me of more than my spirituality. And to think, I could have spent that time dedicated to both God and Callie.

Come to think of it, have I ever repented for those days? Mere hours before Callie was snatched away, I was making out with Amber on their front porch, and went out drinking with friends the very next night. I've matured, yes. Cleaned up my act, sure. But did I ever recommit?

Wonder if I need to go forward at church. Ask for forgiveness and prayer and rededicate myself. It's a shame a Christian can't live in a shell for a while to get themselves back on the same track.

After stumbling to the kitchen and pouring myself a bowl of cereal, I thumb through the mail on the counter. A letter from Eastern Kentucky University juts out, and I drag it free from the pile. Hooking my fingernail under the lip of the envelope, I rip across the top, exposing a bright pink page. All my financial stuff, no doubt.

Guess I need to take care of all that. When I get Callie back, that is.

Two hours later, I walk into Michael's office and plop into the leather seat across from his oak-stained desk. He's built everything in this room. Maybe one day he'll teach me everything he knows.

"Still can't sleep?" He pivots his chair and grabs a mug from the coffee station behind him. Steam rolls from the cup as he pours in the brew and passes it to me. "You look rough."

"It's hard. If I had any word at all, it would make such a difference. This not knowing is killing me. And I want to go after her, Michael. How can I sit here and do nothing?"

"I understand." Michael refills his own cup and lifts it to his lips, swirls of smoke streaming around his baby-smooth face. "Are you praying?"

"All the time. But could I be praying for the wrong things? All I pray is to keep Callie safe and bring her home. I know you're right that I should wait and trust God. But maybe God has other plans for her than returning her to me."

"He could." Michael flips through a stack of checks, signing each, and stamping a date on them. "Are you sleeping?"

"How can I while Callie's still in the Alliance? I can't sleep, I can't eat... No way could I do classes right now. Although, I've been thinking..." I lift my own mug, the warmth radiating through my hands like electric pulses. The herbaceous aroma jumps from my nostrils to my veins, bringing an alertness that I haven't felt for days. "This is good coffee."

"Yep." He takes a sip then turns back to his computer. "You've been thinking..."

"I've been thinking."

He looks up at me. "Okay."

I head back to my office and log into my email. A message in bold text catches my eye, and my heart leaps out of my chest. After scanning its contents to be sure it really says what I think it says, I race back to Michael's office. "I got a message from Aaron, one of the army guys who got me to the states. He says Callie has escaped. They don't know where she is, but she's with rebels and they're trying to get her to America."

"Oh, Ethan." His eyes light up and he practically jumps across his desk to embrace me. "That's incredible news."

"I know. He's supposed to call me the second he has an update."

"Well, you let me know. If we need to leave early to meet her somewhere, I'll have Ann reschedule my appointments."

"Okay. I'm going to go tackle all those lists you left me." Gotta love the guy. My office is covered in Post-it notes: take an inventory of his shop and set up an order, call Mr. Smithers and reschedule, find out if Mrs. Adkins would prefer the laminate flooring or pure hardwood...

Easy enough. I shove them in my pocket and scoot the chair back. Oops, more notes on the floor. Head out to Taylor's office supply store for staples and more Post-it notes. Pick up the lunch Michael had catered for all his workers. I'm convinced he doesn't need me to do this job. But I'm grateful.

When I get into my truck, jingle music blasts through one of those news radio stations Dad always used to listen to, and I suffer through a commercial about prostate cancer.

"More news from the Alliance this morning as families wait in America, holding their breaths for news of their lost children," the host breaks into the fading music. "It's now estimated there are about five hundred students, ages ranging from five to as high as twenty-one, who are trapped in Alliance schools. Their parents, tricked by Adrian Lamb into thinking they'd secured a brighter future for their kids, are outraged, and calling for President Cooper to act."

Cooper. So that's the new guy. Hope he has the sense to fix things. Turning up the volume, I watch Burl and company shuffle back to their truck.

"Our sources say that the Alliance situation has reached critical mass, and full-on civil wars are being fought at street level in every Alliance city. American vigilantes are bursting across the border and complicating the fighting. With President Cooper's controversial gas sanctions and bans on importing goods, our network correspondents tell us that the Alliance days are short-lived. Ground and air strikes may…"

What? Air strikes? They can't do that. Innocent people may die. Who thought that was a good idea? No wonder these vigilante types want to rush the Alliance. In fact, I'm ready to pack up and go back myself, no matter what I promised Michael and Angela.

At Taylor's Office Supply, I stumble through the aisles until I find everything on Michael's list then return to the car and check my phone.

A post on my Facebook feed shows smoldering buildings along the Charleston skyline. Wonder who took them—an insider, or someone else? Were they even recent photos? It's not like Charleston's never had a fire. Either way, I've had about enough. I need to hear from Aaron. I need to know about Callie.

I shove the phone in my pocket and drive back to the office.

A white civic is parked next to my spot with Washington D.C. plates.

On the other side of the glass double doors, James Caudill stands with another man, speaking to Michael with animated gestures. The rebel who was supposed to save us. He's dressed in civilian clothes, and his white hair has been buzzed to a point that ages him at least a decade.

Michael holds the door open for me. "Good, Ethan. You're here."

James engulfs me in a huge embrace, and my body stiffens. Which one of his faces does he plan on tossing me today?

"I was so glad to hear you've made it back to Kentucky." He backs away, his shoulders drooping. "I felt terrible when our plans were compromised. My team was supposed to be waiting for you outside the arena, to intercept you and transport you to the helicopters. We'd never planned to send you to that train, but didn't get an opportunity to tell you otherwise."

"Seriously?" Fury builds in my chest, squelched by my respect for Michael. "I don't understand why you couldn't tell us. If we'd known to look for US military, we might have found them instead of stupid Davey Brinkle."

"It was complicated." His friend stretches out his fingers, cracking his knuckles. "James had to be very careful what he revealed to anyone."

"I bet it was complicated." I scoff and turn to James. "That's why you stood by and watched other officers beat up the citizens without doing anything about it, right? You were playing all three sides. Well, I don't know. Maybe four sides. Adrian, the Rebels, the US, ASP…I bet things do get complicated when you have to keep all those lies straight."

Michael nods to James's partner. "Why don't you come have some coffee with me, and we'll let them talk in the conference room?"

James follows me through the interior doors down a hall into a room with a long, narrow table.

He traces his finger over one of the chairs. "Handcrafted?"

"Yeah. Michael's an awesome carpenter." I back up to the table and lean against it. "You were going to explain all your lies."

"I'd love to learn how to build like that." He sits on the sill of the long glass window. "Ethan, what you need to know is that we're on your side. We're working hard to get Callie home. We've gotten word that Luke and Tristan Patton have broken her out of Adrian's prison, and she's waiting for transport at a Charleston refugee facility disguised as a factory. Of course, Adrian may have the same intel as we do, but we have more resources."

Callie, free? Dare I hope it's true? Maybe the brothers succeeded after all. My heart pounds as I search his face for a hint that he's lying. His sincerity convinces me. Why can't I forgive him? I know I should. And I understand why he kept his secrets. "Can we go get her?"

"The American Army is meeting her at an extraction point." Extending his feet, James flexes them at his ankles. "She's going to be home soon."

"Is it true what they said on the news today? Charleston is like a civil war zone?" The hair on my arms prickles. "Is Callie in danger?" James nods. "Yes and no. It's like a war zone in places, and there's a chance Callie could be affected. It's more like a rioting situation than actual war. Grief-driven people using whatever they can as weapons and standing up against the Alliance. Mix that in with ASP's terroristic threat, and it certainly makes things tricky. But you have to know, we've got this. She's been transported to a safe zone. Marines are all over that countryside, reestablishing law and empowering the citizens to stand up for themselves. I don't think Callie is in danger."

"Then we have to go now." Same phrase he used at the Alliance arena before she was shot. It takes all my strength to suppress my snarl. "How much longer? Will you go back in with me to help save her? Or are you too busy playing TV hero?"

He laughs. "Guess you saw my interview. That was staged to unnerve Adrian. President Cooper wanted him to see that one of his most trusted men was a plant. But about a timeline, truth is, we aren't sure. I was able to pass on enough intelligence that Adrian's interior can be infiltrated, but that man is so wiry. He's gone into hiding, although we do have one steady way to track him."

"The drugs."

"You know it. In fact, rumor has it he's popped so many pills that we wonder if we'll even find him alive. He can't go anywhere without a driver." His jaw twitches. "Hope we do find him alive. I'd love to be the one to catch him and put him in his place. Although, those days are over for me. Now that my cover's been busted, there's no real point in them sending me back. I'm retiring."

"So where did they find Callie? What prison did they break her out of? Monongahela?"

"No." James rests his head against the window. "The last place Adrian moved her wasn't a prison at all, but an abandoned warehouse where he'd stored a bunch of dead bodies. He'd placed her in a room away from them, but she still had to endure that horrible stench. And we don't know if he planned to kill her or if he was trying to scare her."

I shudder at the thought. "What about ASP?"

"Nothing but a bunch of young punks." A deep scowl covers his face. "They're a problem, for sure. Bent on destruction, reckless, and fearless."

"Yeah." Guess he doesn't know I was a part of them for a while. I pull one of the chairs away from the table and sit. "Do you have any news of Martin?"

He takes the chair next to mine and props his chin with his fist. "Adrian stabbed him. He was critical for a while. Some of my friends helped him escape, but he wasn't able to travel due to medical restrictions."

"I wish I could go after Callie. I wanted to be the one to save her. It's not like I don't have training."

"I know your gumption and your heart, and when I saw your Twitter post, I realized you might be considering something stupid. Convinced my superiors I needed to speak with you in person." He rubs his hand over his buzz cut and massages the base of his neck. "Ethan, you have to trust me. I know I haven't given you a lot of reason to. But in a few weeks, maybe a month tops, there will be no more Alliance. All of the citizens will be rescued and relocated, and we will bring Callie home."

His partner steps into the room, carrying two mugs of coffee. "At least now, you can rest assured that she's safe and well fed. Those refugees are housed in great facilities, and she's in no danger from the fighting that we've seen. It very may well be that they get her out of the country tonight or even tomorrow."

Michael follows with two mugs of his own, and takes a seat opposite me. "We sure do thank you for making the trip down here to let us know."

"No problem." James accepts a steaming cup and stares into it for several seconds before attempting a sip.

Our conversation turns to Michael's craftsmanship, and by the time we've finished the coffee, James has talked him into building a custom toolbox for the back of his truck. They walk into the shop to draw out the design, but I stay.

If what James says is true, I could be sitting in this very room with Callie as soon as next week. I can't wait to tell her how much I love her. But, after all that's happened, I can't help but worry. I left her. And I won't get to be the hero who rushes in to save her. Will she even want to see me?

# Chapter Twenty-Two

## CALLIE

**AFTER TWO WEEKS** of peeling potatoes, Erma moves me to the chopping table. "Show her what to do."

A raven-haired girl with piercing blue eyes looks over her nose at me. With her Adrian-styled curls, she's almost a twisted, demonic version of him. "Do you even know how to use a knife?"

"Yes." Dad showed me. My chest tightens. Where is he now? Does he have any idea that I'm alive?

"Are you going to chop or daydream?" The girl hands me a plastic box filled with carrots. "I want circles, an eighth-inch thick. Can you do that?"

"I can." My knife flies over the carrots like the TV chefs. All that anger over Amber kissing Ethan has paid off.

Erma scoops the pieces into a stainless steel bowl. "Mallory will work out fine." She leaves us, and I lose myself to the sound of whacking knives.

Whispers draw my attention to the right. I catch Raven Hair's gaze and frown. "What?"

"I don't know what you think you're trying to hide." Her whisper is more of a hiss. She points to my neck, where my twisted locks cover the edge of my butterfly.

"I'm not trying to hide anything." I lift it so she can see. "I have a tattoo. On my neck. And I'm sure you know what that means."

"So it is, true." Her eyes widen. "Officer training, or the academy?"

I shrug. "Officer training." Not that I ever intend to use it.

"Ladies!" A woman I've never seen before marches toward us, hands on her hips.

Raven Hair points to me. "I wanted to make sure she didn't cut her fingers off. Erma told me to show her."

The woman hovers, and we go back to chopping.

Cutting circles is much easier than peeling. My fingers still ache after an hour of it, but at least the potato juice isn't soaking into my cracked skin and burning anymore. As I settle into a routine, my gaze is drawn to a new luxury—an open window.

Across the street, men move into and out of a storefront, carrying boxes inside from a ten-foot moving truck. Like my coworkers, they wear their hair curled and cropped short in Adrian fashion. I'd love to corner our fearless leader and figure out how he managed to make that happen.

After a while, the truck pulls away and another takes its place. I chop and watch them well into the afternoon.

When we stop for lunch, Raven Hair stands beside me. Though she says nothing, her posture stiffens. She moves with me, keeping her body at least a foot from mine at any given time. Why is she so paranoid? Does she think I'm some kind of spy? Does she know who I am?

We move through the lunch line and return to our posts. I start a new bowl of carrots and resume my window vigil.

A new truck pulls to the front of the store and stops. The driver gets out and meets one of the men, pausing for a second to sign something on a clipboard. He points down the street, and when the man nods, he walks away.

Fifteen seconds later, an earthshattering explosion shakes the room, sending carrots, potatoes, and turnips rolling off tables and landing at our feet. Some of the girls scream. The rest of us gawk.

Out the window, black smoke billows and fireballs balloon, reducing the entire storefront façade to crumbling bricks.

The color drains from Raven Gair's face. "My brother works in that building."

More explosions follow, and Erma rushes in. She hurries us down the hall to the stairwell.

"Where are we going? Outside?" Maggie blocks the rest of us, standing in front of Erma with her arms crossed. "There's nowhere safe."

Erma touches Maggie's arm. "We're going to the basement, an old shelter."

Maggie points to me. "I'm walking with Callie."

At the sound of my name, Raven hair gasps. "Don't you mean Mallory?" She eyes my neck and covers her mouth. "No. It can't be."

So, she didn't know. But now… I lift my chin and meet her gaze. "It is. But you don't need to worry about me."

"Let's go!" Erma drags Maggie forward and the rest of us trudge after them, along with girls from all over the factory, down four flights of steps and through a thick steel door and down a concrete staircase. The smell of smoke drifts through cracks in the windows, and my body convulses. It's too much like the warehouse.

At the foot of the concrete stairs, I stumble, and hands reach out to steady me. We file into the shelter, which is full of old crates and boxes. Dim emergency bulbs give the place an eerie blue glow. Erma lights wall sconces with a long match, and we huddle together in the center of the room.

The ground rocks beneath us. Some of the girls scream again. Lily, Ashley, Sheena, and Maggie stand with locked arms and hands held tight enough to see the whites of their knuckles. But not Raven Hair. She marches across the room and faces me. "Is it true? Are you Lord Lamb's daughter?"

"I am Callie Noland. I'm the girl he kidnapped and called his daughter, but my last name isn't Lamb."

"The girl we all watched die. I don't believe you. Why would you try to pass yourself off as his daughter?"

Maggie moves between me and Raven Hair. "I know Callie. It's her. She was brought to Monongahela against her will."

"I'm the girl you watched get shot." I lifted my shirt, revealing my scars. "I spent a while in an Alliance hospital, and longer in several of Adri… um… Lord Lamb's prisons. So it hasn't been a picnic."

"Did you escape or did he let you go?" Raven Hair steps closer. "Did he send you to spy on us?"

"Someone helped me escape, yes. But to spy? No."

"Then why are you here?"

Other than occasional sniffles, the cries quiet. About fifty girls total, all hanging on my next words.

Erma moves to my side. "Callie is here for the same reason the rest of you are. She's waiting for a chance to return home to America. She's biding her time until there's a safe transport."

"Did they blow up the building because they know she's here?" A short girl whose Adrian curls spring from reddish roots narrows her gaze at me.

Shaking my head, I press my lips together. "I think that whoever blew up the building was not an Alliance loyalist. He had his hair cropped short and wore a mustache."

Erma frowns. "How do you know that?"

Raven Hair nods. To have maybe lost a brother, she seems calm, though a vein in her neck pulses. "Callie is right. I saw him, too. He drove up in a truck and walked away from the scene. But if he's a rebel, why would he destroy a building where innocents are working?"

"I don't know."

The woman who'd hovered while we were chopping bursts into the room. Erma glares at us all through slit eyes. Conversation over. She faces the woman. "Robin, what's going on out there?"

Robin takes several deep breaths. "Three of the surrounding buildings were hit. When the first responders arrived at the initial blast, the second one went off at a neighboring building and destroyed one of their trucks."

Murmurs pass through the girls. My pounding pulse thunders in my ears.

"Why?" Erma picked at the hem of her shirt. "Who would target factories?"

"People who need God." Though my voice comes out a whisper, it feels like a shout. I swallow and try louder. "People who need God."

"You're right." Lily smiles. "And we all need God right now. At the very least, we need to thank him for sparing us. Should we pray?"

Robin and Erma stare at each other for a full minute before
Robin nods. "It wouldn't hurt."

"I'm not praying." Raven Hair crosses her arms.

"Well, you don't have to. Shut your mouth and daydream or
something." Lily drapes an arm over my shoulder. "Callie, would
you do the honors?"

I glance at Raven Hair. "Um, okay I guess. Please bow your
heads."

The girls make a circle, except Raven Hair, who backs herself
up against the wall. Robin and Erma join in, standing on my left, and
Maggie falls in line to my right.

"Dear Lord, we come to you this day with humble hearts,
thanking you for our many blessings." I chew my lip. What was it
Dad always said when he prayed? "We believe in your divine power,
that you are able to deliver us from sin and the evil in this world."

Maggie squeezes my hand. I guess that was okay.

"Be with us now, in this time of trouble, and please be with all
those who are fearful and experiencing loss." Someone sniffles, and
I swallow nonexistent saliva. "We pray for um..." I can't call her
Raven Hair. "For our sister's brother, who worked in the building
across the street. "We pray that he's safe, and not suffering."

At my amen, half the room is in tears. Ashley tears a piece of
cloth into several pieces and passes them around for tissues. "What a
beautiful prayer," she tells me. "You knew what to say."

The ground below us shakes again, and I quiver with it. "We
could sing."

"Okay." Erma smiles. "That might help take our mind off
things."

The perfect words come to mind, and I fill my lungs. "Sweet
hour of prayer, sweet hour of prayer, that calls me from a world of
care."

Lily joins in. "And bids me at my Father's throne, make all my
wants and wishes known."

Tears stream my cheeks, and my voice cracks. "In seasons of
distress and grief, my soul has often found relief."

Erma squeezes my hand.

"And oft escaped the tempter's snare, by thy return, sweet hour of prayer."

Raven Hair wrinkles her nose. "What does that even mean, the tempter's snare?"

Robin sits on a crate and the rest of the girls follow, some finding places on the floor. I gnaw on a fingernail. *Lord, please, help me find the words.*

"The tempter is Satan. The Devil. Have you all heard of him?"

Some girls shake their heads yes, others no.

"Well, you've all heard of angels, right?"

They nod.

"The devil was once an angel, who fell from God's grace. He rebelled against God and wanders the earth tempting man to sin and be separated from God."

"Oh." Raven Hair scratches her head. "So there are good angels and bad ones. Interesting."

We talk for a while longer about angels, but I turn the discussion to Christ and salvation, and why, in spite of everything, I have no fear of dying. And how much I want to go home.

"I was there when you spoke at the arena. Didn't recognize you because you're so skinny now." Raven Hair fiddles with a loose plastic piece of the crate she's sitting on. "Way back in the crowd, but I heard what you said. And I didn't understand any of it."

I search the ceiling for something to say. "Well, I am a Christian. I serve Jesus Christ, my Savior, Son of God, who created the earth and everyone in it."

"My teacher said life was formed in an explosion." Raven Hair runs her tongue over her teeth, puffing out her upper lip. "The rearrangement of star particles into primordial matter that can produce life. It's in the Bible."

Some of the other girls nod.

Lily pulls her Alliance Bible from her dress. "You've missed out on most of the story. This book is fragmented, a small portion of God's original words. And some parts added by the Alliance aren't true. The real Bible does not say anything about primordial matter."

I take the book from her and flip pages. "She's right. There are entire chapters and books missing. The true biblical account of creation is given in the book of Genesis, which your Bible is missing. "In the beginning, God created the heavens and the earth. The earth was…"

The girls fall into silence as I quote the first three chapters.

"Wow. How do you remember all that?" Sheena tucks a tuft of hair behind her ear.

Raven Hair wrinkles her nose. "Sounds like a fiction book to me."

"Believe what you choose." I hand Lily's Bible back. "I could have had a life of luxury, being ushered between political galas and charity balls. And I chose to take this stand, because I believe. Nothing I say can make you believe, but God has provided plenty of evidence to his existence."

Static emerges from Erma's belt. She twists the knob on an old, boxy radio handset. "Yes."

"We've arranged another location for ten girls. The truck will be there in fifteen minutes. We're working on two more places, but it may be a day or two."

A hushed whisper passes through our ranks. Erma's eyes fill with tears. "Robin, get the list."

Robin disappears and returns five minutes later with a piece of paper. She hands it to Erma, whose hands tremble as she glances over it.

"Hayleigh, Lily, Desiree, Bridgett, Kim, and Riley." The paper slips from her hands, and she swoops to pick it up. "Jennifer, Ashley, Brianna, and…" She swallows. "Callie."

Raven Hair shoves past me and snatches the paper. "I'm supposed to be on that list."

Erma shakes her head. "We can't, Ginny. We have to get her out. It's a matter of security. We have no guarantee they didn't set off those bombs because they suspect she's here."

"You can't take her. It's not fair." Raven Hair/Ginny lunges toward me.

I clutch the collar of my uniform, ducking to her left. Three pairs of hands reach for her. Robin twists her arms behind her back and drags her to the other side of the room, where she breaks into convulsing sobs.

Lily steps forward. "Of course Callie needs to go. She's our First Daughter. It's our duty to protect her." Turning to Erma, she bobs her head toward Ginny. "She can take my place. It's fine. If we're leaving in a couple days, I don't mind waiting."

Erma's eyes widen. "You'd let her go in your place? Lily, you were one of the first girls here."

She shrugs. "True, but I don't have a family to go home to. And Ginny's family most likely lost a son. We should help them reconnect with their daughter."

"Well, Ginny, did you hear that?" She peers over her bifocals at Raven Hair. "Lily is going to let you take her place."

From across the room, Ginny faces Lily. "You'd do that for me?"

Lily nods. "That's what Christians do. Trust Callie, Ginny. Let her teach you about God. Don't be afraid to let go of what you think you've always known."

After hugs, it's settled. The ten of us, including Ginny, make our way to a warehouse floor at the back of the factory. Amidst crates of canned vegetables, we cross to a loading dock and climb into the back of a semi. Déjà vu.

As we cram-pack into the back of the truck and sit with our legs crisscrossed like kindergarteners, Ginny presses her mouth against my ear. "I don't want to hear any of that crazy Bible talk. If you open your mouth when we get out, I'm going to tell the world who you are."

# Chapter Twenty-Three

## ETHAN

**MY KEYS SLIP** from my grasp as I fumble with the doorknob, one of the things Dad kept promising Mom he'd fix. I'll head to the hardware store and take care of it tomorrow.

The lock gives, and I push the door open as a minivan taxi pulls into the drive.

Callie? Dare I hope?

The passenger door opens, and I bound down the porch steps, my pulse racing.

Not Callie. The stringy, tawny hair. Her hollow face. Amber.

She steps out of the car and collapses into a mound on the gravel, gripping my feet with both her hands.

Kneeling, I lock her bone-thin fingers in mine and help her stand.

She glances toward the taxi, straining to face the driver. "How much?"

"Twelve-eighty two." The driver raises his brow. I'm sure he has serious doubts about whether or not he'll get any money from her. In fact, I do, too.

"Ethan?" Panic covers her face, along with a tiny hint of a pout.

I pull out my wallet and toss the guy a ten and a five. As he drives away, her eyes moisten.

"Guess Mexico didn't work out."

"No." A cascade of tears rains on my shirt as she slumps into me.

I take her in my arms and let her cry for a couple minutes, because what else can I do? Then, I lead her to the porch swing. "At least he got you to America, right?"

"Well, yeah." Her lip quivers. "But it was an awful, awful trip."

She wipes her nose with her forearm. "What about Dad and Callie?"

"I don't know." No way I'm sharing what James told me. "But I'm still hoping."

She bats her sunken, black-circled eyes at me. "I was hoping we could talk."

Please, no. If she asks to get back together, I may lose my lunch. Drawing in a deep breath, I scoot to the far left end of the swing. "What's up?"

"I need money." She says it so matter-of-fact, like I can come up with cash out of nowhere. Same as she did when we were dating.

"Amber, I don't have any more cash on me. Maybe three dollars, if that." I leap up and pace the porch. "Are you using again?"

Don't know why I asked. I know she's using again.

She knows I know, too, because she hangs her head and sticks out her pouty lip. "What happened to us? We were such a great couple."

"We were together for all the wrong reasons. Sex, parties... I want a relationship with some depth." I grip the porch railing so tight splinters jab into my skin. "I want to be with a woman who loves God and serves Him by my side. I want..."

"Callie. You want Callie." Amber sniffles.

"Why are you acting surprised? It's not like you didn't know."

She tosses her matted hair. "I was hoping that with her out of the picture, you'd maybe consider me again."

I fling my hands against my thighs. Seriously? "Please tell me that was some kind of sick joke."

"This was a mistake. Coming here, I mean." She unzips her bag and pulls out a pack of gum. Four twenties spill to the porch.

"Are you kidding me?" Raging heat assaults my body, and my pulse throbs in my neck. "You had money and made me pay for the cab?"

"This is for—"

"I know what it's for." I stomp over, kneel, and snatch up the money. "You are not going to buy drugs. I'm not letting you."

"But I'm not buying drugs."

I pocket one of the twenties. "Let's call it even, since I'm getting ready to drive you across town."

She gasps as I scoop her over my shoulder. More money tumbles out of her bag, and I crouch to pick it up. I tilt it so it can't spill anymore and carry her to the Mustang while she wiggles and squirms.

I dump her in the passenger seat and grab her bag. "If you get out of this car, I'm burning your cash."

As I walk around to the driver's side, she glares at me through the windshield. When I get in and buckle, her glare intensifies. "Where are you taking me?"

"You'll see." As the engine roars to life, she grips the door handle.

"Don't even think about it." I tuck her bag beside my left foot. "I'm warning you, Amber."

She sulks the fifteen minute drive to the detox facility, a yellow brick building with gray trim.

I pull into the parking space and face her. "I can't let this go on any longer. You've broken your dad's heart, when he's already lost so much. You're killing yourself. I mean look at you. Your teeth are all gross, your hair is like straw, and you have scabs all over your body. You need help, Amber. Please. Let these people help you."

"No way." She reaches for her backpack, and I catch her wrist.

"What are you going to do for money? Sell your body? You haven't even left yourself anything worth selling. And how will you eat? Don't you care at all?"

Her eyelids flutter, and she drops back against the seat.

"Amber, you have nothing. No family, no friends, no money, and no job. No health, no boyfriend, no parents—at least this place will give you a fresh start where you might be able to have a fighting chance."

The sobs start slow, with several quick gasps for air. Her lips contort and her eyes squint, and for the first time since I've known her, I think she cries real tears. The car shakes as her sorrow engulfs her, and I reach across the seat to wrap my arms around her.

"You know I'm to blame for this." Stroking her shoulder with my thumb, I press my forehead against hers. "I took you to those parties, introduced you to those people who got you hooked on pills. You might have gone that route anyway, but I should have been a better example."

She whistles as she inhales, and grips me tighter.

"Let's get you clean, and we can work on rebuilding our relationship—as a friend. It has to be that way. I'm in love with Callie."

"I know you are." Her whisper gives me chills. "I always knew you loved her, even when we were together. You made sure she was taken care of, and watched her when she was in the room. No one has ever taken care of me like that. Not even Mom or Dad."

Cupping her face, I force her to lift her chin. "Your dad loves you. We could have left you in the Alliance to die. We were in America. Free. And we went back for you. Martin was sick over it. Like he was sick when he caught you with the drugs."

She stares at the floorboard. "I have a confession."

My heart stops. What on earth could she confess that's worse than what I already know?

"You didn't get me addicted to drugs. I knew about Adrian. All along. From the time I was a kid."

I jolt back from her so hard I hit my head on the driver's side window. "You knew?"

"We were at Grandma's house one night. Mom and Dad let us spend the night, and of course Callie the Charmer had her full attention." Amber dabs at her blotchy eyes with her fraying collar. "I caught them distracted and took off down the street by myself. I was so mad. And Adrian called to me from a window of an old, abandoned house."

The gravity of her words hangs between us. All this time she knew.

"I went, of course, because I was such a curious kid. He gave me candy and told me I was beautiful like my mommy. Said he loved her and me, but don't tell anyone. It was a surprise."

My jaw tightens. "Did he ever—?"

"No. Goodness, no." She grimaces, drawing her chin into her thin neck. "He's creepy, but not creepy like that. Anyway, as more time passed, he convinced me he was my real dad. You didn't start me off on drugs. He did. He gave me drugs to keep me quiet. We even used together some. And I knew Mom met him on a regular basis, and he gave her gifts."

"Wow." What a tough thing for a little girl to carry. No wonder Amber's so messed up.

"I needed to protect Callie. I thought he'd take me and Mom away, and she wouldn't have a mother anymore."

I embrace her again. "Oh, Amber. I'm so sorry."

"It gets worse." Her tears spill again. "That night Grandma died, I was there. I'd hidden in the bushes, hoping I could sneak to his house and get my fix."

Oh, no. I squeeze both my lips between my teeth. What can I say to that?

"He came up behind her and I think maybe he injected her in the neck with something. But then, he used her pressure points to make her pass out and left her in the chair." Sheer anguish rivets Amber's frail body. "I... I could have helped her. But I was so scared."

Heat pulses my entire body. That snake in the grass. I almost pity him. Killing the mother who didn't want him... I bet she'd never thought her sin would have such widespread consequences.

We sit huddled a while longer. Every so often, she gasps for more air and the sniffles start again. At last, she raises her head. "Do you think I can ever be forgiven?"

Emboldened by the Bible study I had with Michael at lunch, I replay the points in my head. "Come on, Bam-Bam." She snorts at my use of her old nickname. "You remember the story of the apostle Paul when he was Saul on the road to Damascus. Don't you?"

She nods.

"And you remember how he persecuted Christians. Stoned people to their death. But God forgave him."

"Yeah."

"And you remember Peter, who denied Christ three times when he died."

She gives me a wry grin. "You're right."

"Good." I wink. "Now that we've established that, let's go inside and get you registered. Get clean, and then we'll work on rebuilding your life."

"Why do you love her?" Amber combs through her hair with her fingernails. "Callie is a whiny, goody-two-shoes brat."

Why do I love her? How could I not love her? But I'm not sure it's the best thing to say to Amber right now.

"Tell me." She clutches my collar in her fist, her voice thick with desperation. "Tell me."

"Fine. I love Callie's relentless spirit. The way she refuses to back down and makes you think something was your idea to begin with. I love how she's compassionate to older people and little kids, and how she always sacrifices her wants and needs for the greater good."

Tears build in my eyes, and I swallow hard. "I love her undying devotion to memorizing scripture, and her competitive nature. And the way she drinks sideways from a straw, and how she has that one strand of hair that always hangs in her eyes. Oh, and her laugh. How it starts as a stifled snicker, bursts across her face, and then explodes from her chest."

"Oh." Amber opens her door and sets her feet out of the car. "Let's go in before I change my mind."

When we walk up to the tinted glass doors, Amber holds her right palm to her reflected one. "I look like a zombie."

Yep. She called it. "You'll get better. When you get off the drugs, your sores will heal, and you'll put on some weight. Your hair will be healthier, too. Maybe you could get a short cut so it won't take so long to get rid of all the damage."

She pivots. "Let's go do that first."

"Okay." We head back to the car, and I drive her to Allie's Dolls, a salon in a new strip mall. She reaches for my hand as we walk in, and I lead her to the counter.

"Welcome to Allie's." A bubbling brunette with spiky red streaks flashes us a huge smile. "What can I do for you today?"

I point to Amber's brittle hair. "Something short and cute?"

"No way." Amber shakes her head.

I glare at her over the bridge of my nose. "You have to do something, Amber. It's falling out. Are you going to commit to changing or not?"

The girl holds her fingers and thumbs in a box shape and peers at Amber through them. "I think a short cut would look great on you. What's your name, sugar?"

"Amber Noland."

The girl types into her computer. "Address?"

Amber stares at her feet. "I um… I guess I don't have one. I got out of the Alliance and don't have anywhere to go."

Sympathy washes over the girl's face, and she meets my stare. "Okay, well, for now can we use your address?"

"I guess."

Thirty minutes later, she emerges with a stylish pixie cut and a smile to match it. The look's already a huge improvement. While I pay, another thought comes to me, and when we leave the salon, I walk her down the strip mall to a makeup store.

The girl in the shop is fantastic, taking Amber by the hand and leading her to a chair. She does a color analysis and skin type in about eight seconds, and sets to making Amber over, chatting the whole time about every product. Within fifteen minutes, Amber looks like a person again. And the makeup bill comes to $128.60, but I pay every dime. I want her to feel like she's worth it.

As we're walking out, she glances through the window of a clothing store, and I steer her toward the door.

"Ethan, you've done too much already." She tugs me away.

"Do you have underwear and socks? More than one outfit?"

"No." She pulls me away again. "If we're going to do this, let's go to one of the discount department stores. This place is too swanky."

"Fine." I drive her across town and she lets me buy her five outfits. I ask a clerk to help her pick out what she needs as far as underwear and socks, and even talk her into a new pair of tennis shoes and a suitcase. And, a Bible. Three-hundred and fifty dollars later, we get back in the car and return to the facility.

"I don't deserve any of this." Amber steps out of the car and sets the suitcase down on the blacktop. She opens it and places all the clothes and makeup inside.

"You can be a good person." I walk around and help her zip it then lift it to carry it in. "I'll work on a place for you to live, and see what you can do about finding a job when you get out. Think about the future, okay?"

"Okay."

After brushing a kiss across her forehead, I take her hand and walk her in to the receptionist. She cries as she fills out the paperwork, and I explain her payment situation. The woman makes a couple of calls, and we wait in uncomfortable plastic chairs for an answer.

"You're lucky. We have a space for you, and you have sponsorship." She sets the phone handset in its cradle and walks round the counter. "We have a few community members who offer to pay for treatment in a work exchange program. You owe them six months of a paid work experience after you finish treatment. This one was a local lawyer and he advocated for your admission."

Let me guess. Michael Harding.

# Chapter Twenty-Four

## CALLIE

**A FEW HOURS LATER,** Ginny sits in a corner, curled into a ball and pretending to sleep, though I feel her occasional glares. I close my eyes, resting against the wall of the semi. Every so often, the truck jostles, and I bang my head, wincing as I turn my sore neck away from the cool steel. The other girls chatter in the dark about life and who they were pre-Alliance. I miss Ethan.

"So we were on this bus," one of the girls says, "and they pulled us over and arrested the driver."

"You're kidding." Ashley drops her clasped hands to her lap. "That happened to us, too. We were on a school trip to collect geological samples, and they told us the driver had been trespassing on government property. Then, our parents came to get us, and they started talking to us about the scholarships and private schools."

"I wonder where they're taking us." A different girl speaks, erupting gripes about the canning factory and the long hours. I tune them out, reciting Scriptures in my head.

My scars itch, and my knee throbs. I'd been too busy in the factory to think about how much it hurt.

The truck makes a sudden stop, and I'm thrown forward, bumping the shoulder of the girl next to me. She squeezes my hand. "We're backing up."

"Yeah." I brace myself against the truck wall.

Light floods the cabin as the cargo door lifts. Two men with close-cropped hair lower a ramp and help us out. We follow them across a grassy field into a red barn.

The sweet-smelling hay tickles my nostrils, making me sneeze. Cows line the room, trapped in restraints and attached to hoses. They lead us to an office at the far end of the barn. A man dressed in overalls and flannel stands and smiles. "Welcome, ladies. I'm Kurt, owner of Brinnager Farms. We're thrilled to have you join our family."

He extends his hand to all of us, squeezing our fingers with his hearty shake. "Some of you will work in the barns, feeding the cattle and cleaning the stalls. Others will work in the farmhouse, cleaning and cooking meals for the farmers. The work is tough, but it will be better hours than what you're used to, and you'll have quite a bit more freedom. And, we will pay you. We have accounts set up in an American bank to transfer your salary."

"Thank you." Ashley steps forward. "Do we get to choose our jobs, or have they already been assigned?"

Kurt grins. "We'll give you some physical tests and see what you can handle. It takes quite a bit of strength to work with the cattle."

He takes us into a side barn and shows us a binder full of plastic sheet protectors holding what looks like recipes. "In the mornings, some of you will mix the livestock feed." He points to several large metal bins with gears on the outside. "You'll have to be careful, because different animals get different mixes."

"Why don't you buy ready-mixed food?" Ginny glances at a pile of overstuffed bags in the corner. "Wouldn't that be easier?"

Kurt flips through the recipes, stopping on an unprotected page with crumpled corners. "It's to make sure they get the full nutritional value, and also because it can affect the taste of the milk. And you must have been working in that factory for a while if you're under the impression we can still buy what we need in the Alliance. We're lucky to get what we have."

"Oh." Ginny stares at her feet.

I tug at a loose fingernail fragment. "It was my impression the entire population was moved into the cities. How is it that you got to keep the farm at such a remote location?"

"Lord Lamb likes milk." Kurt shrugs. "You'd be surprised. There are several good-sized farming operations in the Alliance on the outskirts of every city. The Alliance founders pressed for organic, non-processed food. When a lot of other industries failed, ours blossomed."

He crosses the room, opening a sliding door that leads outside to a wide, open field full of various crops.

We follow him out, walking past huge corn stalks to rows of planters filled with bushy green plants. The word potato is stenciled on a sign along the edges.

"We've developed irrigation and temperature-controlled processes that allow us to grow crops that wouldn't survive in this climate. Some of you will work in our engineering room, monitoring the controls, water acidity and such. Lord Lamb was adamant that the Alliance would not need to import a lot of food from America, so we could be self-sustaining."

My mind drifts as he walks us through the rest of the tour, pointing out odd jobs that we can do. The workers nod to us and go about their business.

After several minutes of walking, he lets us climb on the back of a hay-covered wagon, and drives us to another part of the farm. We pass apple and pear trees, their bases surrounded by strange electronic devices. "To monitor for poisons," Kurt says.

At our next stop, we walk through a field of grazing horses. Ashley stops beside one, grinning. "I used to groom horses back home."

"Where was home?" I stand next to her, brushing my fingers through the horse's mane.

"Tennessee." A frown flickers across her face. "My mother was a Redemption Party supporter. We moved the week the president was shot, before the Alliance even became a real country."

"Me, too." I pat the horse's neck. "I was kidnapped."

"I wondered about that." Ashley stepped toward the gate, where the other girls were hopping from dry patch to dry patch, avoiding thick, gloppy mud. "If you were really his daughter, or someone else he manipulated."

"He's my… uncle, I guess. My real dad's twin. So he says." I kneel, picking up a bit of the straw the horse has been eating from. As we approach the mud, I sprinkle the straw and we step over it.

Kurt chuckles. "We have a resourceful one here, do we?"

Ginny scowls. "She's resourceful alright. Did you know she's the—"

"Ginny!" Ashley steps between us, clamping her hand over Ginny's mouth. "I apologize, Kurt. Sometimes Ginny can be rude."

Wriggling free from Ashley's grip, Ginny harrumphs and stomps a few feet away, missing a cow pile by inches.

Chuckling, Kurt leads us further down the path to a long driveway with a row of white houses. The other girls fall behind, distracted by a huge flower garden. He walks on, and I follow alone.

"Our entire community of workers is housed on site." He points to a four-story square building in the center. "We also have a school and a couple of churches."

"And Adrian lets you do that?" I slap my lips. "I mean Lord Lamb."

Kurt meets my gaze. "Callie."

I deflate, then glance back at the girls who are still far away. "You knew."

He smiles. "I offered. Tristan was supposed to get you here sooner. I knew your dad back when I started my first job, and met Tristan a few weeks ago." Fishing through his wallet, he pulls out an old newspaper clipping from Eastern, the university where Dad worked pre-Alliance. "We're going to get you back to America as soon as we can. Tristan's capture put a damper on our operation, but we've got a few other tricks up our sleeve."

I peer at the clipping. The picture shows a group of professors standing around a shovel, celebrating the groundbreaking of the new English and Language Arts building. Dad is in the center, wearing a hardhat and grinning like he'd won the lottery. My heart sinks. I miss him.

I look back at Kurt. "You're from Kentucky?"

He folds the paper and tucks it back into his wallet. "I grew up in West Virginia, but accepted the job in Kentucky right after graduating with my doctorate. Hated working indoors, though, and quit to farm full time."

"Wow. Have you heard any news from Dad?" I press my lips together and glance at the clouds. "Or Ethan? The boy he was traveling with?"

Kurt's brow creases, and he presses his lips into a thin frown. "I know they escaped, because Lord Lamb spent days dominating the media asking for someone to come forward with information as to their whereabouts. I believe they crossed back into the US through Ohio, which is no longer an Alliance state."

So they're safe. Or maybe safe. I let out the air I've been holding and rub my temples. "Good to know. I've been so worried."

"I bet you were. Luke told me about the warehouse fire. Incredible bravery."

"I didn't know what to do, other than pray. And when he showed up in that car looking like Adrian..." I laugh. "I thought I was captured again, for sure."

"We are going to try to move you next week if we can. I have a big shipment with several trucks going out, and several stops. We'll move you to the Ohio River, and try to get you on a tugboat that will take you the rest of the way. I've got a friend who might let you work in the galley and cook for the crew. Think you can do that?"

I nod. "I think so."

"If that doesn't work out, we can connect with the American military and get you out on one of their river routes."

"Sounds great. I appreciate all your help."

We pause on the front porch of a huge farmhouse. I steady myself against a fluted white pillar and the wind rustles my hair. An older woman climbs the steps beside me. As the other girls catch up to us, she brushes her fingers through my tangles.

"They call me Mama Carol around here. I take care of everyone if you're sick or feeling kinda down. If you girls would like, we'll give you more original haircuts. We do not participate in mimicry here."

"Please." Ashley lifts her hair, exposing red roots. "I want something short so I can get it back to my natural color."

"Me, too." Kim's roots are tawny brown like Amber's.

Mama Carol leads us inside the house, through a vaulted entry, and into an enormous sitting room that could double as a ballroom. She takes Ashley down the hall and the rest of us pile on couches and wait.

While the other girls chatter, I sink into a deep armchair. A tapestry hanging at ceiling height on the opposite wall shows a wedding scene with a groom wearing the uniform of a US Marine. A bride in a billowing white gown reminds me of *Gone with the Wind*. A light touch on my shoulder sends me jumping to my feet. Mama Carol straightens my collar. "Let's get you ladies into the kitchen and find you a bite to eat."

We sit around a big oak table seating about twenty. Ginny and I take opposite chairs, and her glare slices through my core. It's replaced by a wide grin when two women bring huge platters of barbecued pork to the table.

We feast on roasted potatoes and plump green beans. And bread—softer and fluffier than any I've ever had. "This is delicious."

"I'll have to teach you how to make it, Callie. You can make some for that fella of yours, when you two get reunited."

The girls' breaths catch as Mama Carol smiles at me.

"I'd like that."

Ginny clears her throat, and we all go back to forking food into our mouths like we haven't eaten in months. Maggie places a light hand on my arm, and tears spill onto my cheeks. In another world, she and I would have a great friendship. Maybe we'll both make it back to America and have that chance.

At the end of the meal, Kurt comes in from the field, tracking dirt across Mama Carol's pristine floor. She chases him with a broom, and he swats at her with a wet towel. Their laughter hangs in the air, and we all join in.

"I like this place." Jennifer places her napkin on her empty plate. "It's peaceful here."

"That, it is." Mama Carol gives Ginny a stern look. "We work hard to keep it that way."

Six days pass. The alarm blares at five a.m., and I jolt from the bed.

Ow. My tender feet protest. My time on the farm has earned me nothing but blisters, aching muscles, and animosity from the other girls who have tired of the extra attention I keep getting. I lace up the boots Mama Carol gave me and head out to the barn.

Tomorrow's the day, at least that's what Kurt tells me. A quick glance at the skyline shows that the weather might not cooperate.

Bright lines of electricity arch between clouds that appear menacing even in the darkness of the dawn.

Something shuffles behind me. I turn, finding no one. My heartbeat quickens, and I hurry toward the barn. Kurt waits inside, and I meet his warm smile with my cautious eyes. "Someone is out there. They were following me, I think."

Kurt laughs. "It's that Ginny. She's been following you all week. Mama Carol is pretty frustrated with her, because she hasn't been able to get her to do a thing in the house." He steps out of the barn and grabs a lantern from a shepherd's hook. "Ginny, come on in the barn. You'll freeze to death out there in those weeds."

More shuffling, and her face pops out of the four-foot high thistles. When she steps into the barn, her arms are covered in burrs and her face is scratched.

"You're bleeding." I brush imaginary burrs from my own clothes.

"So?" She wipes her sleeve across her face. "Not everyone can be perfect like you."

I sigh. "Listen. We didn't get off on the right foot, but there's no reason we can't start over and try again. I'm sorry if I've made you upset."

Silence.

Kurt grabs a set of keys from a small hook and tosses it to me. "Let's feed the cats first. Their food is in that plastic tub over there. Then, you can mix the cattle feed if you'd like."

A truck engine revs in the distance. Kurt glances over his shoulder and eyes the equipment. "Let's wait on that. I don't want you to operate it alone."

He rushes out of the barn, leaving me staring after him. Why? I race to the still-open door and peek out.

Ginny trails a step behind me. "That was weird."

"I'm sure it's nothing to worry about. He would have told us to hide if it was." I squint at a dim orange-tinted light on a faraway pole. "But I'm curious."

Two headlights jostle across the field, heading toward the house, and Kurt rushes toward them. Ginny and I tiptoe across the field after him.

"Maybe someone else is coming." Her whisper echoes my fears. "Maybe." We creep to the line of bushes surrounding the farmhouse and duck behind one.

The truck pulls up to the house and turns around, backing close to the porch. Sitting in the bed, a masked man leans over something, his shoulders slumped.

The man lifts his mask. Tristan. My heart skips a beat. Guess he must have escaped.

"How is he?" Kurt takes off his cap and sets it on the truck bed.

"Knocked out on painkillers. His injuries weren't too bad. He wasn't in the main part of the factory when it exploded. We found him pinned under a couple big beams."

Luke? Is he okay?

"I had to bring him to her." Tristan glances toward the house. "I know it was risky, but I couldn't leave him. And after all this, they deserve to be together."

"No. You did right." Kurt covers his lips with his hand. Is he trembling? No, scratching his mustache.

Tristan grins. "Where is Callie?"

My breath catches, and Ginny squeezes my arm. His answer is lost to my thundering pulse, roaring in my ears.

They step toward the barn, and I lunge forward, catching my sleeve in the branches of the bush. "I'm here. Who is it? I'm here."

Kurt reaches me in ten slow paces. He takes both my hands in his, and leads me to the truck. There, Dad lies in a crumpled heap, covered in a wool blanket.

# Chapter Twenty-Five

## ETHAN

**SUNDAY MORNING,** I wake to roaring thunder and rain pounding on my bedroom window. I pull the covers over my eyes and lay there for about ten minutes then drag my feet to the icy floor. My mouth stretches into one of my famous gorilla yawns, as Callie used to call them, and I extend my fingers to the ceiling. Maybe there will be good news today.

As I stumble to the window, goosebumps cover my arms. Boy, do I miss having Dad around to turn up the heat every morning before I got out of bed.

Bright sunlight streams in through a crack in the curtains. I open them wider to a brilliant spread of red, purple, and orange clouds, which reflect from the wet road in front of the house. When I turn back to the bedroom, the brightness fades to dismal shades of dull grays and navy blue. All those times she complained, Mom was right. This place looks like a tombstone.

I move to my desk, pushing aside my two-year-old stash of Axe, Polo Red, and hair gel, and sit in my peeling leather office chair. Snagging my jacket from the crate next to the desk, I lick my dry lips and dig for my Carmex, though my finger brushes across the bag holding the engagement ring.

Callie's engagement ring.

Rocking back in my seat, I apply a liberal coat of the Carmex then take the ring from its box and loop it over my pinky. The rose-colored gold is a perfect match for the gorgeous sunrise. Wish Callie were here. Today would have been the perfect day to slip it over her finger.

I can't wait to ask her, but will she say yes? After all we've been through, will Callie even want to be my wife? She's been robbed of a normal senior year, and she may even want to go to college for a while. And yes, I know we're young and all, but we've lived a lifetime in the last year. I want to be with her the rest of my life.

In fact, we could start our new life together in this very room. Shaking my head, I chuckle. I'd have to redecorate first.

Conor McGregor stares down at me from a poster hanging over the desk, as if to ask, "Are you an idiot?" With his muscles flexed and an open-mouthed grin on his face, his tattooed chest and torso look even fiercer. I stand and snatch the poster from the wall, wadding up the slick paper and tossing it into the corner by my building stack of clothes.

I'm sure Callie wouldn't appreciate my former obsession with mixed martial arts.

Turning to my bookshelf, I grab the stack of Maxim and Sports Illustrated magazines and toss them into the same pile. My college textbooks fit well in the crate by my desk, and I set them by the door to load into the car. Who knows? I might get money out of them.

Then, I stand before my Lionel Messi poster and laugh. What am I thinking? If Callie did agree to get married, we wouldn't end up sharing my tiny bedroom. I'm sure we'd move into Mom and Dad's old room or something. Which would be… creepy.

Maybe I should sell the place. Start over somewhere new.

I rub my thumb and forefinger over my chin stubble. Guess I'd better shave if I'm going to church. I can worry about all this later.

Once I've showered, I sift through my closet for something not too wrinkled to wear. Until Mom died, she always laid out all my clothes for me and ironed them the night before. Even what I wore to college. How rotten and spoiled was I? Self-centered, demanding, and rude. Maybe it's a good thing the Alliance happened. I've learned, as Paul said, to be abased and to abound. And to not pursue everything I want for the purpose of having it.

The sun creeps farther into the room, catching one of the diamonds from the ring and refracting small rainbows on the wall. Am I being self-centered again, to assume that Callie would want to jump in and get married? Maybe I should return the ring and wait. Maybe it was a stupid idea.

In the back of my closet, crisp khakis hang with the tags still on. Paired with a plaid flannel shirt, they'll save me from ironing. I can do some exploring in the laundry room this afternoon and figure all that out, too. Angela Harding can teach me. Thank goodness for my church family. I don't have to be alone.

By nine thirty, I'm staring at my reflection in the bathroom mirror with my shoulders straight and smooth chin held high. Pretty good for what I've been through.

I grab my Bible from the living room, lock up, and head down the porch steps toward the Mustang as James pulls into the drive.

He hops out of his rental truck and blocks me from reaching my car. "Ethan, we need to talk."

"Thought you left town." I don't bother to hide my frown. How dare he ask me to trust him when he's still hanging out in Union City? He should be out looking for Callie.

He kicks a loose gravel across the drive. "I've been doing some digging into Adrian's past. New things have come to light."

"Such as?"

He shrugs.

I dart around him, moving closer to the car. "I get it. I'm not privy, right? So, why are you here?"

"Told you. We need to talk." Holding up his arm, he glances at his watch. "Where are you headed?"

My jaw drops. "Um, church. It's almost ten o'clock on a Sunday."

"Oh. Right."

I clutch my Bible tighter, resisting the urge to whack him over the head with it. "Aren't you supposed to be a Christian? Or, was that all fake lies, too?"

"Not fake. Although my faith has become weak." He rubs his right eye with his fist. "I forgot it was Sunday. When you spend all your time in a place like the Alliance, you sometimes lose track of important things like church and family. I spent all that time trying to earn enough money to take care of my wife, when I should have been by her side."

Not that I can talk. I've lost track of Sundays, too. I loop my keys over my pinky and spin them. "How is your wife?"

"Gone."

My keys slip off my finger and clink on the ground. He carries so much hurt and frustration in that single word. I draw in a deep breath. "I'm sorry."

"She was gone long before she died. They kept her on life support in that facility because I wouldn't face the truth." His jaw forms a hard line and he takes two steps back toward his truck. A couple seconds later, he pivots. "Okay, so I shouldn't tell you all this, but there were three raids conducted in the Alliance in the past week. Don't ask by whom. The teams came within a hair of nailing Adrian. They made a big capture—Agent Kevin Wiseman. I'm sure you remember that loser."

"Yeah."

"They caught him with a huge drug shipment as he tried to smuggle it across the border from America. The man cried like a baby, and spilled everything about his role in intimidating parents to send their children to the Alliance schools." He strokes his chin. "And... Callie. I have news."

I lean forward. "What about her?"

"She's been transferred to one of the extraction farms on the outskirts of the Alliance. They're planning to get her across the border next week."

I steady myself against the hood of the Mustang. "So, it's happening, then. Callie is coming home."

He gives me a curt nod. "If my sources speak truth. And I'm sure they do."

A slight breeze trickles past my neck, tickling my ear and mussing up my hair. It's almost like a tap on my shoulder, awakening my guilt. James and I had been friends, and now we have this huge rift, all because he knows I can't trust him and I've been rude. I inhale deep and twitch my lips, forcing them to turn upward. "Maybe you could come with me to church."

He quirks his brow. "Guess I could. I need to." Then, he grins and winks, pointing to my car. "You should let me drive. Been years since I've driven a sports car, and if you'll recall, a few months ago, you told me you'd let me if I helped you get back home."

"You didn't help me." I clamp my fingers over my lips. "Sorry." At his crestfallen face, the bulk of our friendship flashes through my mind. Like the day he recruited me to become an officer, promising he could get me close to Callie, and we spent four hours talking about baseball stats and laughing like hyenas. All those heartfelt prayers he'd offered, which must have been real. No one can fake that kind of emotion without slipping up somehow. All our debates about soccer plays, basketball coaches, and mixed martial arts—I think that part of our friendship was real. Even if he kept things from me and dropped the ball at times.

And to look at him now—dark circles under his eyes and worry lines around his mouth—I think maybe he needs a friend. It has to be hard to be four different people and reconcile yourself back to one when you have no life to return to.

My angry pride deflating, I toss him the keys. "Okay. Have a go."

His face lights up like Christmas as he slides behind the wheel and turns the ignition. "Where we headed? Is the church the same way I came?"

"No, it's opposite. You go left out of the drive and left where this road ends. The next road has this big serpentine curve and then you'll go under a set of railroad tracks and make a right at the top of a hill. After that, we'll be back in town, the other exit from the one you took. You could go the way you came, but it's a lot longer."

"Gotcha." He shifts gears then sets off, smiling so wide he exposes his dimples. Mad as I've been, it feels kind of good to see him happy.

I wipe away a grimy layer from the dashboard, roll down the window, and rub my fingers together, letting the dust fall to the ground. Misty droplets stream into the car, and the cool morning air makes me shiver. Pressing the button to close the window, I reach with my other hand to adjust the heat. "So, where are you staying?"

James switches the wiper blades on, and sets them to delay. "Shirley's Bed and Breakfast. But I've been thinking about finding a more permanent place. I like it here. And I've already filled out all my retirement paperwork. Need to go finalize it. When I finish with my leave, then I might settle in the area." He gives me a wry grin. "If you'll let me."

"I don't hate you. I hated the secrecy. And the fact that you let a lot of details go which compromised Callie's safety. But I understand now why you had to." We whiz past several sycamore trees, and a long road cutting to the right between two fields. "Speaking of Callie, if you turned that way, you'd get to her old house. Martin rented it, so I'm sure they've let it go to someone else."

"Yeah. I'd say you're right." James adjusts the visor. "It's bright out today. Martin told me he put all his stuff in a storage building and paid it up for a year. He was so despondent about that. And I feel his pain. It stinks to live out of storage all the time."

"It does." My heart pangs with… compassion? This must be what it's like to be Michael Harding. I meet James's gaze through the rearview mirror. "I could use a roommate. It also stinks to live in that big empty house by myself, and I've been really missing my parents. Besides," I laugh, "you're a much better cook than me. Everything I've eaten since my return has been either bought out or frozen stuff I've heated."

He blinks and turns back to the road. "I'll consider it."

"Think you should."

By the time we reach the church, we're kidding each other like old, familiar friends, but his depression hangs in the air. He's been pushed out when he prefers to be in the heart of the action. I'm guessing he doesn't feel useful anymore. And maybe even like a failure, because he couldn't save Callie. I need to stop holding him responsible for that.

As he pulls into a parking space, he leans close to me. "Since I'm being honest, I'm not here on any sort of official business. Like I said, I'm retired now." He swallows. "Adrian confided in me once that he has this secret office hidden somewhere in Kentucky with crates of ledger books and receipts detailing transactions he'd used to climb to power."

"Do you have any idea where it might be?"

"A hunch that it's somewhere in town. But finding it could be huge. There are a lot of people who participated in the social media

Cocooned

affair that are sure to pay for their actions because there's a digital trail. But others only worked through snail mail. If I don't find those documents, some will walk away free like they'd never betrayed the country. I don't want that."

"Me, neither." I clench my fist around the door handle. "Maybe I could help you look for it."

Mary Whitman snags James's arm as he climbs out of the car. The scent of her Aramis hangs in the air, and she hasn't picked out one side of her hair. Crazy old lady still using her husband's cologne. She drags him toward the building. "We're so glad you could join us this morning. Following services, you can come out to dinner with us."

James gives me this you-should-have-warned-me look. I shrug. No one ever sees Mrs. Whitman coming.

She follows his gaze then releases his arm and rushes to my side. "Oh, Ethan, you poor dear. We've been praying over you. We miss your parents so much."

"I do, too." I cringe as she leans closer and squeezes me, squishing her stiff gray hair against my temple. "You need fattening up, boy."

A couple I don't recognize crosses in front of us, and she lets me go to dash over to them.

James snickers. "That was creepy. Like Hansel and Gretel."

"Yeah. Mrs. Whitman means well. She's a force of nature." I stare after her as she corners the couple outside the church entrance. "You know, she lives down the road from where Callie's grandparents used to live, two houses down from an abandoned house Adrian used sometimes, according to Amber."

He jerks to face me.

"There's a cave on their property, and they let people go into the woods there to hunt sometimes. I wonder…"

"Maybe Adrian spent some time there. You could put in a word for me, and see if they'd let me do some exploring."

I point out Mr. Whitman, who's making his slow way across the parking lot with a cane. "It's going to take some time to earn his trust. He won't let anybody on his property. And you don't want me to put a word in, because I got caught sneaking into the cave once with a bunch of my buddies. Although, he might appreciate your military accolades."

"Guess we'll be going out to lunch with them, then." He winks. "You can sit beside the beautiful lady."

"Speak for yourself. I'll make myself a frozen pizza." I hold the door open for him as we make our way into the church. "Whatever you do, don't let her feed you anything she's cooked."

Mr. Whitman comes in behind us.

I walk James over to him. "Morning, sir. I'd like to introduce my friend, Colonel James Caudill. You may have seen him on CNN a while back."

Mr. Whitman's green eyes widen.

James flashes his dimples and shakes the old man's hand with vigor. "Pleasure to meet you, sir."

"No, no. Son, the pleasure's all mine." Mr. Whitman clamps his loose hand over James's and grips tight.

We'll be in that cave by this afternoon.

# Chapter Twenty-Six

## CALLIE

**MAMA CAROL** hums to herself as she spoons lumpy mashed potatoes from a deep steel pan to a ceramic dish. She leans close to me. "They're going to move you tomorrow."

Her whisper tickles my ear. "What about Dad?" My voice comes out sharper than I intend, and Ginny huffs from across the room.

"Bruised and we think some ribs that need to heal, but your dad is going to be fine. We'll get him fixed up and send him on. We've got a good doctor nearby who will monitor him a week or two and make sure he's up for travel." Mama Carol empties the pan and takes it to the sink. "Here, Ginny. Wash these up for me, and I'll slice some bread."

Maggie holds up a dish of julienned carrots. "What else do you want me to put in the salad? I have cucumbers, radishes, onions, and these."

"We have a few green peppers. Maybe dice those up real fine." Mama Carol tilts her head toward the pantry and glares at me.

I grab the sack of potatoes and carry it back toward the oversized closet. "Wish you could go with us."

Maggie sighs. "Yeah."

"Maybe when you get to America, we can find each other again." She smiles. "I hope so."

Mama Carol follows me into the closet and shuts the door behind us. "We've heard rumors the American Army has raided the facility where they're holding your mom. Your dad wants to wait until he knows for sure that she's safe."

Grunting, I hoist the potatoes into the bin. "Mom is a lost cause. She's a total vegetable. She can't even lift her feet anymore without someone to help her."

"All the more reason for him to save her." Mama Carol reaches into a deep freezer and pulls out a pan of the rolls we made a couple nights ago. "You have to understand about love, Callie. Your dad would rather die with your mom than leave her to suffer like this."

I shrug. "I don't think I understand anything about love. How could a man like Dad forgive Mom for what she did to him? How can he still love her?"

She dumps the rolls into my outstretched arms and reaches for another. "Once you've been bonded with someone, you never get over your love for them."

Like Ethan and Amber. I picture the two of them racing across tree-covered fields, stopping for laughs and kisses under the cover of the leaves. I'm sure they reconnected. One, I'm supposed to be dead. Two, Amber can't be around a guy for two seconds without making a move.

"Maybe I could stay and help him." I accept two more packs of rolls, then follow Mama Carol to the door. "Without Dad, what do I even have to go back to?"

Mama Carol gives me a sad smile, then pulls the chain to extinguish the pantry light. "Callie, don't you remember what it's like to live free?"

Freedom. The word sends chills down my spine. Of course I want to live free. Why wouldn't I? I don't want to live in Adrian's household again, although I'm pretty sure that would never happen. His hatred for me extends to the moon and back. But Mama Carol is right. I have forgotten the peace of sitting on my front porch, not having to worry about whether or not someone is trying to find me.

Saturday, Kurt walks me to a flatbed truck where several men hoist bales of bound trash along its edges. "They stagger the bales to give you light and some relief from the smell, should there be any. This is all paper trash, but if it gets wet, it can mildew."

"Okay." I press my hands against my thighs, trying to keep them from shaking.

The men lift three braided-back wooden chairs to the truck bed and build an enclosure around them with more bales of paper, leaving a narrow passage in.

Two of the men head into the cavity, and Kurt nods to me as another climbs on the tractor and backs it up to the hitch.

My heart pounds. Being smuggled out in a tight box months ago was terrible, but this… trapped in trash with two men I've never met? Ugh.

Kurt hands me a backpack. "Just in case. This trip will not be long. About an hour, and slow going on side roads. Then, you'll follow it to the river along to where the American soldiers will be waiting to get you out."

We set off, jostling and lurching along the bumpy wagon ride.

"You excited to go home?" One of the men, a fifty-something balding guy reaches into his pocket. He pulls out a plastic sleeve of pictures. "Name's Steve. My daughter's been missing for six months. I've been helping so many girls find their way. Keep praying that we'll come across her. Have you ever seen anyone who looks like this one?"

I look at the picture and shake my head. "Sorry. I haven't."

The other guy lifts his cap and runs his fingers through thick brown hair. "I'm Darren, and the driver back there is Gary. We rescued my girls a few weeks ago, but I can't make myself go home. So many kids left to save. And I worry about the little ones."

"What are your daughters like?" I sit on my hands, leaning forward so my back doesn't rub against the piles of trash.

The men take turns telling stories, and our ride goes by pretty smooth for a while. After about forty-five minutes, we hit a huge bump, and the wagon tilts on its side. Trash bales spill everywhere, landing on top of me as I slide from the truck bed to the cold, damp ground.

The men scramble to free me then pull me and the chairs into the woods.

"We are close." Steve scans the horizon. "I think we can walk the rest of the way from here. By the time we got everything cleaned up, we might miss our connection. They've cleared the area two miles from here. It's so remote, I doubt we'd run into trouble."

Darren points to a bulge at his waistline. "And I'm prepared if we do. Steve, you help Gary dig out and load up, and go on to the recycling place."

I take a deep breath. "Okay. Let's go."

Darren and I inch forward through thick foliage and thorny brush. He examines the area with infrared goggles every twenty steps or so, and we make the bulk of the two miles with no trouble. "About ten more yards or so there's a cairn marker where we'll wait by the riverbank." He slices a thick weed with his pocket knife and lunges forward. "Careful. Looks like we're coming on a marijuana patch."

A springy noise sounds from the bushes. His eyes widen. "Duck, Callie!"

I do, as a nail-covered board pops up from the ground beside him. He dodges it, leaping to the side as another springs up to his left, striking his shoulder, and sending him back into the first.

This time, something boings. The trees beside me vibrate, and a metal wire stretches taut as he falls toward it at neck level.

I cover my eyes and scream.

And then, thunder booms loud enough to break the sound barrier.

For a few painful seconds, I stand in the blood-spattered, knee-high grass paralyzed as the clouds darken around me and the wind picks up its pace. The wire falls slack and Darren drops to the ground beside me. He clutches his neck with fear-glazed eyes and motions me forward.

"Keep going?" Covering my mouth with trembling hands, I kneel next to him. "I'll stay with you."

He struggles to lift his arm and points again. "Get help."

"Okay." My voice quivers and his raspy whisper sends chills down my spine. "I will make that connection and send someone back for you."

To my right, the wind dislodges a long, fallen branch away from its tree, and I snatch it from the ground. As I make my careful way around Darren's body and the nail-covered boards, I hold it out in front of me like a sword, waving it from side to side before each tentative step.

After about four yards, I pass a tree with a heart carved into it. As Darren had described, it has numbers over a cross instead of letters. This is the way we would have taken if we hadn't wrecked. I step over a low wire fence into shorter grass and follow a stony path to the line of trees separating the field from the riverbank.

And then it rains. All I can see, all I can feel, and all I can smell are the crisp, clear droplets. But at least it's not that poor man's blood. Or my own. The mud sloshing around my feet gets thicker and thicker with every terrifying step. At the point where we should have made connection, there's no one. No boat, no choppers.

I fall to the ground.

Water streams from clumps of my hair like a faucet. Droplets roll down my so-called waterproof jacket and soak into my sneakers. A new level of miserable. And I'm cold... so cold.

As the water pools around me, I search the landscape for the thousandth time, seeking anything resembling shelter. The leafless trees offer no protection, and there's not even the slightest hint of a rock cubby or cave. And who knows when I might run into another booby trap if I try to explore.

I trudge onward, pulling myself tree by tree, stepping on the roots the way Dad showed me months ago. My heart aches. Will I die here? Will I ever see Dad again? If I'd known, I'd have fought even harder to stay with him.

I blink away tears. *My grace is sufficient.* I've been repeating that verse for days, but my roaring stomach protests.

A thorny twig scratches my face. Red swirls of blood accompany the rainwater on my shoe. The wound shoots across my cheek, almost reaching my right eye. That's the last thing I need—to lose my sight to a bush. Adrian would love that.

Can't worry about it now. I turn sixty degrees, spotting a leafless catalpa tree like the one we had in our backyard. Dad spent two hours one day telling me all about it, how frustrated he was by the gypsy moths that ate all the leaves. After that, wind and ice left their marks in the branches. Then, he had to wait a long time for the tree to grow leaves in the spring. Guess I'm kind of like that tree, pushing toward my own spring. Adrian's like that aggravating moth. But, as Dad pointed out, the tree endured. God sustained it. And God will sustain me, too. I have to believe that.

A raging river flows parallel to my path. Is it the chemical contamination that's attacked this particular tree?

Rainwater collects on my eyelashes. A quick wipe on my wet sleeve does nothing to help my blurred, bloody vision. I unzip my waterlogged backpack and retrieve a damp bandana. As I'm tying it around my forehead, the sky clears and the sun peeks out from behind fluffy white clouds. A hint of a rainbow spans the horizon, accompanied by a lower, more intense one. God is reminding me of His promises today.

I yawn, patting my wet sleeping bag. I can do all things. All things.

The bandana slips from my grip and lands in a puddle. As I bend to reach it, an engine roars over the rushing water. Multiple engines. Helicopters. At least three of them, and not Alliance. My connection...

Easing closer, I gasp. Cables of men dangle below each chopper. All wear green helmets and camouflage. Twenty? Maybe fifty or more? At the end of each cable, an American flag waves. They're here.

I drop to my knees, sinking into the ground. My tears are lost in the murky puddle. Seconds tick by, then minutes, and then the growl of the engine fades.

I crane to see where they land. It's too far away. Way too far. Was I mistaken? Did they not come for me? Though it's futile, I take cautious, squishy steps in their direction. My heart sinks as the choppers swing in wide arcs and head away.

Slipping and sliding, I continue onward, following the winding river path closer to the border. Twenty, maybe thirty minutes pass and I hear nothing but the rushing water.

Out of nowhere, a double-decker boat comes into view, with a four men pointing military assault rifles in all directions. I clamber up a nearby tree for a better look, easing onto a fragile branch.

It takes a moment to process the snapping limb, and another to brace myself for the impact of the muddy rocks beneath me. A whoosh of air escapes my lungs, maybe a scream, and then an intense thunderbolt of pain encompasses my left shoulder. I tumble, sliding helpless down the slippery bank, as the sharp, jutting rocks shred my skin.

Blood seeps from a cut on the side of my wrist. What can I latch onto? I clutch a flimsy trunk, which is enough to turn myself so that I'm plummeting by my feet and not head first.

My palms sink into the muck beneath me, securing my grip on a moss-covered rock, and I pull myself upright. Raising both hands in surrender, I wave at the soldiers until I come into their view.

"I'm an American!" My intent of fervor is wasted as my words blend with the frothy water. I stand taller. Can I shout louder? "I'm an American."

The boat slows, coming to rest along the bank a few feet behind me. One of the men lowers his rifle and approaches, though the others keep theirs trained on me. My knees knock, and I tumble to the water.

The soldier's strong hands close around my arms, and he lifts me into his. "I'm an American." I crumple, dissolving in tears.

The others speak in hushed tones, and he sets me on a secure rock, a few feet back from the edge of the bank. "What's your name?"

My name. Will he know who I am? I squeeze my eyes shut and blast air through my nostrils. "Callie Noland."

He glances at the other soldiers and looks back at me. "We expected to find you here. Are you alone? Do you have any proof?"

Twisting my hair, I expose my butterfly tattoo. "I have paperwork, but it's soaked."

"Where's your escort?"

"I was with three men who smuggled me off a farm on some paper recycling truck. We wrecked, and one helped me walk toward the meeting point through the woods. He triggered some kind of booby trap. Nails on boards, a long thin wire…sliced his neck. I'm afraid he's dying. Someone needs to check on him." Swallowing, I shiver. "It was… bad."

"I'm sorry." The man glances over his shoulder at the other soldiers. Three head off in the direction I point. The man rummages around and hands me a thick folded blanket. I gratefully unroll it and clutch it around me. He also gives me a bottled water and motions me to sit on a cushioned seat. We wait in silence for the men as I finish off the water. Finally, one returns.

"Think we can save him. He managed to hold his head at an angle to stop the bleeding from his neck. We've radioed for the medic to come on the next boat. Go ahead and get her out of here."

As I breathe a sigh of relief, my stomach rumbles.

"When did you last eat?"

"This morning." I chew my cracked lower lip.

"Well, we'll get you fed and take you home." He touches my forehead. "Wow. You're feverish. Hang in there, Callie. We'll take care of you."

# Chapter Twenty-Seven

## ETHAN

**IN TYPICAL KENTUCKY FASHION**, intensive flooding thwarts James's cave exploration plans. After a couple days of rechecking and pouting, he drags his luggage to the kitchen. But he does have a direct connection to information about Callie. The extraction team is moving today. She could be home within a day or two.

"Giving up?" I fill two mugs with coffee and carry them to the table, sloshing it all over the floor. Mom would have been all over me for that. Gritting my teeth, I wipe up the scattered drops with a paper towel.

He reaches into the freezer and grabs two pieces of ice then drops them into his coffee the way Dad used to do. "Maybe next week. I'm going to go take care of the last of my retirement paperwork and go through all my wife's stuff."

"Want me to go with you? Michael wouldn't mind." Trash spills out of the can as I toss in my dirty towel. And then, maybe I could talk James into taking me to wherever they bring Callie.

"No. I need to do this by myself. Take some time to grieve her." His voice catches. "Maybe I should have stayed by her side. Sometimes I wonder about my choices." He lifts the mug to his lips and takes a whiff. "Good coffee. You know, if there is anything in that cave, I'm sure it's destroyed by now. It'd be my luck."

"No. There's a chance. There are some higher places we never explored." I lather bread with butter and sprinkle cinnamon over it. "Want some toast?"

"Nah." He laughs. "Although I'm impressed. You've come a long way since yesterday."

Monica Mynk

"I try." As I flip on the broiler, my cell rings. I put the bread in
and check the screen. "Michael's calling. Oops. Missed him."

A couple minutes later, I cradle the phone against my shoulder
as I dump six browned pieces of cinnamon toast into a plate. "Hey,
Michael. What's up?"

"Forgot to tell you I'll be in court all day today. I left you a list of
some things to do. Charlie will help you with everything."

"Okay. Sounds good." As I take a big bite of the toast, the
cinnamon sprinkles over my chin.

"Catch you later." Michael ends the call before I can answer.

James winks, reaches over, and snags a piece of the toast. He
bites off about half of it.

"Hey." I air-punch him. "You said you didn't want any."

"Changed my mind." It comes out all muffled. He shoves the
rest of the toast in his mouth and snickers. "Although you could have
broiled it longer."

"You're gross, man. Whatever my limitations are on cooking,
I've got you beat in the etiquette department."

"You know, I always wanted a kid brother to torment growing
up." His face darkens. "I appreciate you giving me another chance. I
always did think the world of you and Martin."

I pass him two more pieces, cram the rest of my toast down, and
head out to the drive. A rainbow stretches across the skyline, coming
to rest behind a thick walnut tree at the end of our yard. When I was
a kid, I used to wish on all the rainbows that ended behind that tree,
hoping for my pot of gold. Now, I want it to bring Callie home.

When I get to the office, twenty Post-its wait at my desk, laid
out in a checkerboard pattern. Michael needs an intervention. His
obsession with straight lines is almost scary. But thank goodness for
the distraction, because otherwise I'll go nuts waiting to hear news
from Callie. When I finish the list, Charlie, his assistant, takes me
around to visit several sites, and by the last one, my watery eyes are
bulging and burning from my yawns.

"Tough day. I've done a lot of talking." Charlie nudges me to the
corner of the living room. "Hang in there. We're almost done. But
first, look up. See that mess?"

217

A glob of drywall mud hangs down about two inches from the textured ceiling. "That one's obvious."

He jots something on his little pocket notebook. "Yeah. You have to watch these guys like hawks. It's hard to get workers who pursue the level of quality Michael wants. And we can't be everywhere at once, so we have to keep going back and inspecting their work."

"What about the counter there? It's a good half-inch from the wall, and that caulk has settled into it." I inspect it closer. "Did they glue it that far out from the wall?"

He runs his fingers over the caulk. "Looks like it. I'll note that one, too."

"One of the bulbs in the chandelier doesn't match the others." I point to a brighter, whiter bulb. "Is that a big deal?"

Charlie chuckles. "It would be to Michael."

"Looks like they missed a few paint spots, too." I step over a pile of copper wire fragments. "When's the carpet being installed? Is this one almost done?"

He quirks his lips to the right. "Long way to go. We still have a lot of exterior stuff. Rain's held us back a lot."

"I can see that." I nod to the door. "Plus there's mud everywhere. There are huge handprints all over that one. They'll have to repaint it, won't they?"

"Maybe they can wash it. Marking it down." He flips his notebook to the next page. "Think we're about done here. Let me have a quick look at the cabinets and we'll call it a day. Michael will be impressed we got to all of them."

"It's a lot of work. I don't know how he manages all of this plus a law career, too."

Charlie laughs. "I'm convinced the guy never sleeps." He carries his level around the room and checks the cabinet installations and corners. "You've done a pretty good job today. Maybe we can get you enrolled in the courses and I can train you to do appraisals. That would go a long way helping you pay for college."

I flash him a half-grin. "Michael mentioned that, too." I point to a nick in the wall, and he adds it to his notebook. "But wouldn't it be a lot of work?"

Charlie feels along the baseboards, pressing the trim and frowning as it gives. "No reason you couldn't do both. Trust me. You might enjoy the backup income. I think you're a natural."

"I'll give it some thought. After the Alliance, it's hard to think about committing to something so... permanent."

"Yeah." Charlie stuffs his pen back in his pocket and takes a couple steps toward the door. "You never know if you've got tomorrow. That's for sure."

"Are we done?"

He mock-shoves my shoulder. "What, you hungry? I heard Angela was bringing snacks by this afternoon."

"No, I wanted to make sure that was all you were going to check." My stomach roars.

"The boss has spoken." He mock-shoves my shoulder. "Let's hit the road."

Back at the office, I help myself to one of Angela's famous turnovers. The creamy cheese and cherry filling rolls over my tongue, and as I swallow, it pulses through my veins. Real food. It's been so long since I've eaten so many good meals in a row. Guilt washes over me. Has Callie eaten?

After updating the inventory, I toss the last of Michael's Post-its and head out a few minutes before closing to stop by Kroger's on the way home. Grocery shopping feels so normal, and wrong, but it's something to do.

I roll the cart through the fruit section, picking up bananas, grapes, apples, clementines, a cantaloupe, and strawberries. Then, I grab carrots, celery, cucumbers, bell peppers, and lettuce from the veggies. After hauling a ten-pound bag of potatoes into the cart, I hit up a rustic wooden shelf with an assortment of nuts—cashews, almonds, pistachios.

And the meat—by the time I leave the butcher area, I have a cart full of fresh fish, pork, steak, and beef.

An elderly lady helps me out in the spice aisle, sending me along with bay leaves, black peppercorns, cayenne pepper, chili powder, cloves, cream of tartar, and a whole slew of others in this tower with several jars. I've never heard of most of this stuff, but hey, I can ask Angela Harding.

By the time I reach the last aisle, the cart's almost too heavy to push. I get a loaf of bread and roll past the shelves of beer and wine. Right as I'm rounding the corner, two of my former partying buddies, Bobby Jenkins and Jacob Friend, come barreling toward me.

"Dude." Bobby picks up a pack of chicken from my cart. "Heard you were back. You having a party? Looks like you're going to need another cart for the booze."

I shake my head. "No party. I'm stocking up on food."

Jacob bumps the cart, knocking a pack of shredded cheese to the floor. He bends over to pick it up and Bobby shoves him forward. They scuffle next to me.

"See you guys." I kneel for the cheese then move along.

"Where you going?" Bobby stops wrestling and chases after me. "Listen, we're all going to be out at Harper's tonight. Big bonfire and weenie roast. Heard there's going to be plenty of weed and percs to go around."

"I don't do that stuff anymore." I try to roll past him, and he plants his hands on the cart.

"What? You're too good for us now?" He snorts. "Heard Babe's back in town, too. Guess she's a free agent since you're swooning over her sister on the Internet. Think I could have a go?"

"You stay away from Amber. She's in rehab, getting clean." My pointer finger lands a centimeter from his face, and I freeze, the tension building between us like a volcano. "And mind your business about Callie."

Jacob steps between us. "Leave him alone, Bobby. He's been through a lot."

I walk away, feeling Bobby's glare piercing my shoulders. Got a feeling the conversation isn't over, but I don't have time to worry about him right now.

Once home, and after all the groceries are put away, I start the laborious inventory of all of Mom and Dad's stuff. I place a few calls to my estranged siblings and I'm surprised when they offer to come help. We agree to a meeting time, and I tell them they can have whatever they want of the furniture. They say they don't want any of the clothes, so I'll donate them to the church's benevolence closet.

After that, I'm going to see if James is interested in buying the place. And if not, I'll put it on the market. When Callie gets here, we can look for a house together. If she even wants to.

I carry a stack of flattened boxes I'd brought from Michael's stockroom up to Mom and Dad's bedroom and dump them in the middle of the floor in front of the bed. After rebuilding and taping them all on the bottom, I label the first one with a sharpie. Dad's socks.

The tears come from out of nowhere. It takes about ten minutes to gather my senses, and even after that, my cheeks remain wet. I dump Dad's sock drawer into the box, and it fills about half of it, so I add "and underwear" with the Sharpie. I stare at the words for a minute then scratch them out. Who'd want old, used underwear? Better grab some trash bags from the kitchen, too. Good thing Mom always bought the monster pack.

After stumbling across embarrassing negligée, I dump the rest of the contents of their chest into a box without looking. Someone else can do the job of sorting through all their intimates. Too weird for me.

Next, I move on to the coat closet. I'll keep all of Dad's suits and ties, now that I'm working for Michael. He sent me to run an errand for the law firm the other day, and I felt awkward in my ripped jeans and wrinkled Henley shirt. I might need to get some of them altered by a tailor, but no sense of getting rid of anything that might fit.

Suit by suit, I carry them to my closet. Once I've emptied his side, I face Mom's dresses. And… I break down on the closet floor.

Somehow, I make it through the task of folding each one and tucking them into one of the boxes. I tote the box to the living room and return for her jewelry. My sister Carrie asked if she could take it all and divide pieces out for the rest of us. Sounded like a good idea to me, but I swing its hinged drawers open anyway.

The butterfly necklace, bracelet, and earrings set I got Mom two Christmases ago hangs from a brass hook, and my heart stops. Her tattoo. The mark Adrian forced her to get that only amplified her determination to succeed in defeating him. I don't think anyone would mind if I kept it for Callie. They don't even know it exists since they haven't been home in years.

Within an hour, I've emptied the room, so I head on to Dad's study. Twenty-five years of Bibles line a shelf, each containing massive notes from past sermons. My brother Patrick will want those, since he's a preacher. All the house and tax info sits in a file cabinet beside the desk. I'll need to get Michael to help me go through it.

By eight o'clock I'm exhausted. No scratch cooking tonight.

I wash a few of the grapes and pop a frozen pizza in the oven. While it cooks, I plant myself in front of the TV, switching to CNN. The anchor's image fades into a scene of street fighting against a smoldering Charleston skyline. My heart sinks. Hope Callie is safe.

As I sit on the edge of my seat, the camera zooms out to a bird's eye view, revealing pockets of smoke and rubble. Fear engulfs me— for all the Alliance citizens and for the soldiers and rebels helping them. I can't imagine extracting anyone from a place like that.

But… what does it all mean? I should have watched the news this morning. Has President Cooper gone ahead with his threat of air strikes? Or is ASP causing all this trouble?

When the oven timer buzzes, I slice the pizza, taking a bite before it cools. A blister forms on the roof of my mouth. Reaching into the freezer, I grab a handful of ice and dump it into a plastic cup, keeping back a small piece to suck on and soothe my burn.

Once the pizza's cooled, I throw a few pieces on a plate and return to the TV. Seconds later, a furious-looking Davey glares out from the screen, his hands cuffed behind his back.

He sneers at the reporter, a pretty brunette who shoves her microphone in his face.

"Mr. Brinkle! Mr. Brinkle!"

Where are they? Ohio? Wherever it is, they're standing in front of a row of American flags.

"Mr. Brinkle, can you comment on the bombings? Why are you targeting factories with innocent citizens? What is the endgame of your organization? Do you consider yourselves terrorists?"

"ASP will continue the bombing until their demands are met. We are not terrorists. We are a group of concerned Americans doing what our government and military refused to do. We're taking down Adrian Lamb and all his blind followers." He lifts his left shoulder like he's trying to wriggle free of his cuffs. "Capturing me does nothing to stop the cause. Nothing. We will not stop until Adrian Lamb is dead."

He spits, and the reporter jerks back, stumbling into the camera. The screen bounces around and then settles as federal agents lead him away. Thank goodness Callie's already out of that mess. Can't wait until she gets here.

# Chapter Twenty-Eight

## CALLIE

**"CALLIE?"**

Mom. I must be hallucinating again. Or dreaming. Rolling toward the wall, I pull the coarse, musty blanket over my eyes.

"Callie, wake up."

There she is again, but on the other side of the room and standing straight. Sitting up, I reach for the murky water pitcher the guards left me. Maybe if I dump it over my head, reality will return. But when my hands reach it, I grasp air.

I freeze, staring at the frail woman on the other side of my prison bars. Wait. Maybe not prison bars. After blinking a few times, I reach out and grip them, again meeting air. "Mom?"

She nods, tears streaming her cheeks.

I fall to my knees, engulfed in breathless gasps. When I catch my breath, I pull myself up, bracing myself on the splintery legs of my cot. "But how?"

She dissolves into nothing, and I reach after her. "Mom?"

"Callie?" A large, rough hand covers my forehead. "Fever's up again."

Several people shuffle feet away, and a few moments later, something pricks my arm. My eyelids flutter. A soldier with a nameplate reading Dylan leans over me with a warm, wet cloth, his mouth covered by a sterile mask. He places the cloth on my forehead, and brushes my hair away from my neck. "Are you awake?"

"I…" Sweat drips from my forehead. "Where are we?"

"We rescued you, and you passed out. Do you remember falling on the rock by the river?"

I push against the thin mattress and the cool metal wall, sitting up and yawning as the wet cloth falls to my lap. When I grab it, the warmth covers my hand and my senses come rushing back to me. The woods. The booby traps. I shiver. Darren's severed neck. "I do." My voice quivers. "Is this the chopper? Will we cross the border? Can you take me to Kentucky?"

"Not a chopper, but yes, we are crossing the border." Dylan's eyes sparkle. He takes the cloth, and wraps it around my neck. "With whatever force necessary."

A glance around the room reveals faux wood-paneled cabinetry, and small oval windows that let in light from the bright blue sky. I'm sitting in a bunk bed, across from two others. Between us, four soldiers play cards at a booth-style table, also wearing the sterile masks. One stands at the counter of a kitchenette, making coffee.

"You injected me with something." I rub my arm. "What was it?"

"Antibiotic." Dylan points to a bright red rash covering my hand. "Cole over there is pretty sure you have scarlet fever. As soon as we cross the border, we'll get you to a hospital. But if that's what you have, twenty-four hours of antibiotic should have you feeling much better."

"Thanks." I follow Dylan's gaze to the man who must be Cole. He's sitting in a small leather armchair, going through the contents of my drowned backpack. At least all my paperwork is in protective plastic.

"You should know... we may encounter gunfire until we get into the protected zones. Vigilantes and officers are butting heads all over the place." Cole sets my backpack on the floor and approaches me. "Navigating the river can be tricky these days. The Alliance has disputed ownership of the waterways, and the US has negotiated safe passage through the locks in exchange for resources. We've sent men ahead to make sure that happens."

Another soldier offers me a cup of water, and I accept it with a clammy hand. "Can bullets reach me in here? Can they sink us?"

"No." Dylan pats the steel wall. It doesn't sound hollow. "This is a vessel we modified for extraction. The Alliance guard doesn't have the kind of weapons that could sink a ship like this. They're nothing to contend with. They express their displeasure that we're passing through their territory by firing a couple halfhearted sniper shots to make themselves seem scary."

"Fellas? Time to change out." The voice booms from above, where a hinged door is held open by a husky, hair-covered hand.

One of the soldiers at the table drops his hand of cards and stands. The others follow suit.

"I'm going up for my watch shift now." Dylan grins. "You get some rest and try to eat if you can. Our boy Harvey can make you this awesome macaroni chili that can cure anything."

"Or kill anything." Chuckling, Cole returns my belongings to my backpack, and sets it beside my bed. "Straight from the shiny foil packages. Awesome."

I reach for the backpack. "I've read about soldier meals before. Dehydrated and reconstituted. Not my kind of awesome. Think I'll hold out a few hours."

"They're not so bad if you get hungry." Cole pats my shoulder. "Better than starving."

"Did you find my identification card? All my paperwork should be in there. It was in a sealed plastic box."

"It's intact." Cole moves the bag closer. "Don't you worry. This will be smooth as silk. Once we get past the lock, we're verified, and we'll sail right into America."

A while later, a man calls down to us. "Snipers!"

Cole jumps to his feet. I clamp my hand over my mouth and pray.

While metal clinks and clangs above me, I curl up in my bunk and sob.

A few minutes later, someone taps my shoulder. As I turn, my eyes widen. Cole, covered in blood, but not even flinching.

"You're okay."

He smirks. "Amateurs."

Looks to be some kind of shoulder wound. A graze. He grunts and groans while they bandage him, and demands to go back up when they finish. A few minutes later, a second soldier climbs down to be doctored. I sit up, gaping as they wrap clean his wounds and wrap them in gauze.

So many times I've taken for granted how soldiers fight for our freedom. Never again. I squeeze my collar, scratching my neck and shoulder. I'm not at all worthy of this.

"You should rest." Dylan presses his palm against my forehead. "I think your fever's spiking again." Sure enough, shivers and cold sweat course my spine, and the wretched itching starts up all over again. I lift my arms, inspecting the sunburn-like bumps in the bends of my elbows.

All I can do is sit and wait while the bullets pelt the sides of the boat like pebbles.

None of this is right. It's not acceptable. How did our country get so broken that we could let this split happen? How could a man like Adrian gain power? And why am I so special that they'd risk everything to get me out of the country?

Six thousand breaths later, I sit up straight in the bunk, knocking my temple on the beam supporting the upper bed. I know why. It's not that I'm special. It's that God is special, and He has work for me to do. And it must be time, because the footsteps are quickening above me. The hatch opens a crack.

Dylan pokes his head in. "Callie, think you're up to walking? Thought you might like to be the first to plant your feet on American soil."

Arty, a soldier who wears a gold cross around his neck, scoops me up and carries me to the ladder. He lifts me to Dylan, who grips tight under my arms and pulls me to the upper level. Bright sunbeams assault my eyes, which are already dry from hours of tears. I stumble, reaching for the cool, steel rail.

"You okay?" Dylan walks me to a crate and sits me down.

"I'm fine." I blink a few times and my blotchy vision ebbs to normal.

He kneels beside me. "Want to talk about it?"

"So many people hurt and dying on my behalf. That poor man I left back in the field. I wonder if they were able to save him."

"He's going to be fine. They took him on a different boat." Dylan presses his mouth tight and looks away from me. "It's never easy to watch stuff like that. Senseless."

"Yeah. Is someone bringing my stuff?"

"Right. Your bag." Dylan calls to a young, but balding soldier. "Arty, go grab her sack. And that sleeping bag." He reaches for my hand. "You ready?"

"Guess so." I take a few feeble steps, and he helps me out of the boat. We walk along the dock to a grassy area next to a rusty truss bridge.

Through a thicket of trees, a tall, suited man approaches. "Is this Callie?"

"It is." Dylan looks back toward the boat, where Arty emerges with my bag. He waves Arty closer. "She's got her documentation."

The suited man stares, like he's trying to memorize every inch of my face. "We've got an ambulance waiting. Didn't expect to see you walking. From the message, it sounded like you were on death's doorstep. Thought we'd have to send them into the boat for you."

"She's tough. And we gave her antibiotics." Dylan takes my bag from Arty and unzips it. He hands the suited man my paperwork, and turns back to me. "Good luck, Callie."

The suited man escorts me to the ambulance, and as I get close, my knees buckle. Strong arms wrap around me, and the intense blue sky swirls into a tiny black dot.

Blurs move to my right, fussing with equipment. On occasion, I pick up a snippet of speech.

"She's dehydrated. Let's get her some fluids."

# Chapter Twenty-Nine

## ETHAN

**WEDNESDAY MORNING**, the phone blares me awake from not-so-peaceful dreams. A full week's passed and still no word from Callie or James, so I grip my sheets tight and pull myself out of the fog of nightmares.

"Hello?" I tap the screen and shake my head. "Hello?"

"Ethan, this is Michael. Got some news for you. Think you can meet me up at church in a few minutes? We need to head over to Lexington. To Central Baptist."

"What time is it?" I squint at the screen. "Five a.m.?"

"Something like that."

I jump out of bed, knocking the phone to the floor. Maybe Callie is home. Is she hurt?

As I bend over and scramble for it, he calls out my name.

"Sorry, dropped the phone. Is it Callie?"

A long, slow breath blasts through the speaker.

"It's not her."

"No." His lips smack. "It's Martin and Ella. I got a phone call about thirty minutes ago that they were on their way to Kentucky. Neither one's in great shape to travel, but conditions were so rough the extraction team went ahead and flew them out on a chopper. Kept them in the hospital in Ashland for a few hours, but Martin's made arrangements to get them an apartment in Rhoda's Place. They're going to do rehab first so he can get his mobility back."

"Oh." I squeeze my jeans between my toes and lift them within grabbing reach. As I slide my legs in, I balance the phone on my shoulder. "Give me about twenty minutes and I'll be there. But what about Callie?"

"I don't know." Michael's voice holds a slight quiver. "I haven't heard anything other than she's safe at that farm."

It's dark when I shuffle out of the house and lock the front door. I skip down the stairs, race to my Mustang, and peel out of the drive. When I arrive at the church, about twenty cars sit in the lot, and the building lights are on.

Michael greets me in the foyer. "You ready?"

"Guess I am." My stomach rumbles. I should have eaten something before taking off.

We drive the half hour to the hospital and Michael walks up to the receptionist. He gives her one of his casual grins. "Hey Brenda."

"Mr. Harding. How's it going?"

He stuffs his hand in his pocket and comes out with a ring of keys. "I fixed that cabinet lock for you but keep forgetting to give you these. If you want to move all that stuff from the teacher library into your classroom, I can get Angela to help."

"Oh, great." She takes off her glasses and chews on the frame. "I might do that Saturday if you think she'll have time."

"Call her. She should be home." He sets the keys on the counter in front of her. "We heard Martin and Ella Noland are on their way. I know you can't tell us anything, but I want to—"

She holds up a scrawled note. "They sent word to get in touch with you. I'll let you know as soon as they arrive if you want to wait in the lobby."

"Sounds good." He pats me on the shoulder. "Guess you've never met Ethan Thomas, have you?"

"No." She extends her hand and I clamp mine over it, jolting backward at her firm squeeze. "I've been praying for you, though."

"Thanks." I hide my arm under the counter and flex my fingers. "When did you start going to church there?"

"We moved about the same time your parents died." She flinches. "Sorry. I didn't mean to…"

"You're fine." I flash her a reassuring smile as her phone rings.

She answers, and Michael and I head to the lobby.

"Brenda's been a real asset to the church." He drops into a plaid upholstered chair and stretches out his legs. "She's taken over a lot of the work your mom used to do."

My breath hitches. Time passing. Everyone else moving on with their lives. I can't even begin to fathom what normal feels like, but for so many people of these people, they didn't experience anything even close to what most of the Alliance citizens fared. Maybe this is something like what soldiers experience when they come home for war. Should I look into some counseling or something?

An engine roars outside the window, and Michael and I rush to the glass. A chopper flies past. It appears to be landing on the roof. We pace for a few minutes, but no word from Brenda. A half hour later, she comes for us and sends us to the emergency waiting area.

For what seems an eternity, Michael and I entertain ourselves with relentless Tic-Tac-Toe and Hangman. When we're tired of the games, a petite blonde approaches. "Mr. Noland is okay for visitors if you'd like to see him now. He's asking for you."

"Okay." Michael stands and pats her shoulder. "I appreciate it."

We follow her through the swinging double doors down the bright hall to the last room on the right, where two policemen sit in chairs on either side of it.

"Thank you," Michael tells them as he passes through. He digs in his wallet, turns to the blonde, and passes her a stack of bills. "Would it be too much trouble for you to grab these officers a couple coffees from that vending machine out there? Grab one for yourself, too, if you want."

"Sure." She smiles. "Do you guys want cream and sugar, or black?"

"Mr. Harding, that's not necessary." One of the officers meets Michael's gaze. "But thanks for the offer."

Michael grins. "I know it's not. That's what makes it my pleasure." He turns to the blonde. "Maybe you could come back with three coffees, and if anyone wants to drink them, that will be fine."

The other officer laughs. "Thanks, Michael." He turns to the blonde. "I'll take mine black."

"You're welcome." Michael shakes his hand then slaps him on the shoulder. "I owe you about ten, Fred. Thanks for helping protect Martin."

"You know everyone in Union City, don't you?" I chuckle.

He winks. "I make it my business to know them."

We enter Martin's dim room with slow paces finding him sitting up in his bed, smiling. To his right, Ella sleeps amidst a network of tubes and monitors.

"Ethan. Michael." He fumbles for the TV remote and turns down the volume. "Great to see you both."

"Good to see you, too." His voice a whisper, Michael walks up to the bed and shakes Martin's hand. "What happened?"

Martin's jaw twitches. "Well, I guess Ethan's told you we were looking for Callie together for a while. We ended up separated, and I got in to an Alliance prison to see her. Turned out it was a setup, though. Adrian had orchestrated the whole thing." He gives me a curt nod. "Good thing I made you stay behind, Ethan, or he would have captured you, too."

"Or he wouldn't have captured you." I clench the bedrail and force a slow inhale. No sense in fighting over it now.

"Anyway…" Martin tilts his head from side to side, popping the joints in his neck. "Adrian had moved Callie into the same prison as her mom, in that old Monongahela school where she'd started. So when I went in to talk to them, Adrian came storming down the hallway. He threw knives at me. Stabbed me in three places."

He pulls his hospital gown away from his neck, and I wince at the purple scars that brush his heart. "How did she look?"

"Way too skinny, and limping around, but otherwise healthy." He frowned and reached for his Styrofoam water cup. "Ella and I had a few moments to reconcile, and that was a great strength to me during my healing. To forgive her lifted such a weight from my shoulders."

"I'm sure." Michael handed him the cup, and he took several long sips.

"Thanks. So Adrian refused to let them give me medicine other than antibiotics. He wanted them to keep me alive so I'd feel the pain and torture."

"Whatever happened to Luke and Tristan?" I scuff my foot against the shiny tile floor.

"They were captured, but escaped. Helped get me out of prison and transported me to the farm where they moved Callie." He took a few more long sips. "Where is Callie, by the way? Shouldn't she be here soon?"

"Sorry to interrupt." A nurse carrying an iPad slips in behind us and moves a chair from Ella's side to Martin's. "How's the patient? You guys can sit for a while if you want. But first, let me get his vitals."

She pokes a thermometer in his mouth and checks his blood pressure then taps the screen. "I'm going to do an old fashion double-check on your monitor here. Says your BP's one-sixty over ninety-two. Did you get to eat breakfast?"

"Yeah." He winces and lays back against the pillow. "It could have used some salt."

She chuckles. "Better not for a while. At least not until you've healed."

Michael moves to the chair and rests his elbow on the arm rest. "What's wrong, Martin?"

"They smuggled me into a factory-turned-hospital and ASP bombed it. I'm fine except for these horrid lacerations from being pinned under those beams. They're healing, but deep cuts."

Chills pulse through my spine. "Do you think we're still in danger from Adrian? Can he get to us?"

"There are eyes all over this hospital watching out for us. But we were told they're closing in on Adrian and he's holed up in a cave somewhere. They're going to find him in a hole."

The nurse reaches over Martin's bed and flips a switch, lighting the room more. "How long has Ella been sleeping?"

"About two hours. But she didn't sleep the whole trip, so I'm sure she's exhausted."

Ella's breath whistles. The nurse adjusts her monitor and taps out some notes. "When she wakes up, press that call button and let me back in here. But otherwise I'll check on her in about an hour."

After she leaves, Michael takes a chair, but I go to Martin's bedside and kneel. "Amber is back. I talked her into going to a detox facility. She's been there about a week."

Half the wrinkles leave his face. "What a blessing. I've prayed so hard for her." He grips my right hand with both of his. "And Callie? Where is Callie? I thought she'd be here."

I glance at Michael, and he shakes his head. "Sorry, Martin. We haven't seen or heard from Callie. We did talk to James Caudill, who said they'd gotten her to the extraction farm, but we haven't heard anything past that."

Martin's heart accelerates, going wild on the monitor. "I was there with her. She left for America a week ago Tuesday. But she never made it home?"

"No." Michael reaches in his pocket for his cell. "We've not heard anything from her at all."

The nurse rushes in and checks his monitors. "Mr. Noland, are you feeling okay?"

He clutches his chest, and I lower my chin. "Sorry, we all stumbled upon some unexpected bad news. His daughter is missing."

"Sorry to hear that," she picks up one of his tubes and taps it. "Think this one isn't working right. I'll get that changed for you in a few." She laughs. "We have to get that blood pressure down, though. Sure these guys didn't help you swap out your meds for a salt pump?"

"Nope." Martin grinned. "I'm on my best behavior. Promise." His smile fades. "Although, I do wish we'd have some word from Callie. Think I'm going to rest a bit, but please wake me if you hear anything."

Several hours pass and Michael and I take turns listening to Martin's snores. Ella stirs when the nurse checks her vitals, but other than that, I pretty much stare into space and wish Callie home.

As soon as I get out of this hospital, I'm going to find her.

Michael taps my shoulder. "I told Angela you'd help her with the serviceman dinner tomorrow night. Hope that's okay."

His knowing eyes. Ever the protector. And he's right. If the military didn't manage to get Callie out of the Alliance, there's nothing I can do either. My lungs deflate. "I'll be there."

# Chapter Thirty

## CALLIE

**I LEAN** against the cool window, counting the bright green sugar maples as Arty drives me past them, headed back to what couldn't be a normal life. Dad said our belongings were in storage, but would I even be interested in what had mattered to me months before?

He'd told me I might stay with Michael and Angela Harding, provided they'd not left town, or maybe someone else from church. When I called, I left a message on their machine. Said I'd be at church and begged them not to tell anyone I was coming. Last thing I need is for word to get out and Adrian to come after us again.

As the streets became more familiar, tears well in my eyes. Cars pass with teens staring at their screens, darting in and out of traffic. Has life even changed for these people? Their manicured lawns back up to impeccable homes with two-car garages and fall decor. Some bear sports banners and others American flags, but none show signs of the desperation and travesty wrought by the Alliance.

Arty clears his throat. "I'm sure it's tough to come back home after all you've been through."

"It is." I choke on the words, falling into a coughing fit. As I hack into my elbow, he signals and pulls into the lane that turns onto our bypass.

"I like this town. Union City. Seems like a decent place."

"Yeah." The horizon is void of the thick, black smoke I left behind. "You should drive through the countryside. The horse farms are nice. At least, they were. Seems like they still are."

He adjusts the rearview mirror and leans closer to it. "You're brave, I think, for not going into witness protection. It would be easy to start over with a new identity. But the Alliance's reach has been shortened. I wouldn't be surprised at all to see us back in a united country again by Christmas."

Christmas. The very word strikes a pang so deep that I sob.

Arty clears his throat. "Sorry, Callie."

I calm myself to sniffles and snatch a tissue from the console. "No, I'm sorry. I should hold myself together more. I wish I had news on Ethan. And Mom and Dad. And Amber."

"We'll do what we can to help you find out." Arty pulls too close to a slow-moving car in front of us and huffs as he lowers his speed. "But for now, let's worry about getting you settled."

"I know. I'm so glad they didn't make me stay in the hospital."

He gives me a sympathetic grin. "Yeah. You do seem to be feeling a little better. But still, you need to get some rest."

"I'll rest when I get home." I let my breath fog the window.

Town seems normal. We pass a bus from the high school where teens lean their heads against the window like me, headphones in place. Thank goodness I'm eighteen. I don't even want to think about the nightmare of trying to figure out my credits right now. Someday...

We come to a familiar intersection where teens hang out all weekend and sometimes on weeknights and afternoons. I glance at the dashboard clock. Four thirty.

A small crowd of college students has gathered outside Drusy's, a favorite mom-and-pop place that offers a cheap weekday supper. A familiar tuft of brown hair sticks out above them. They all wear UK blue, other than this boy, who sports a bright red cardinal. My heart catches. "Wait. Turn around. Pull in that restaurant."

Arty raises his brow.

"My friends. Maybe..." Dare I hope? Ethan?

As Arty pulls into a spot, several heads glance toward the car, then they return to their chatter. The brown-haired boy is in deep conversation with a pretty redhead girl. He laughs, tossing his head back, revealing a rounder chin and pointier ears. Not Ethan.

My shoulders fall, and Arty rests his head against the seat.

"Not who you expected? Do you know anyone here?"

I do know a couple of them, but no one that I have a burning desire to reconnect with. "Nah. Sorry for making you stop."

"It's fine."

My cheeks are wet again. He must think I do nothing but cry. Although, I might as well. I can't even drive myself anywhere right now. Can't get a job, can't live on my own... Although, I do maybe have the money Erma promised me. It isn't much, but it might be a start.

Wish I'd been able to talk with Dad more. He could have explained our finances and at least given me an idea of what we owned.

"You ready?"

Rubbing the heel of my hand from my forehead to my crown, I tangle my fingers in my permed curls. "Yeah."

"Three stoplights from here and then a right. Wasn't that what you told me earlier?"

"If the church is still on that property. It was bombed that day when the president was assassinated. I'm not even sure if they rebuilt. But if they're having services then I'll be good. I tried to call earlier but no one answered."

"If not, we'll run by the police station or somewhere, and they can help you find someone you know."

Anticlimactic. Away from Adrian, I'm a lost girl. And I can't lie. There's a bit of malice digging away at my heart. I'd expected some kind of fanfare when I stepped back into the country. Big, important Callie escaping the terrible Alliance beast. And I guess witness protection would be some kind of special treatment if I'd agreed to it, but otherwise, nothing.

How could all these people continue living as they have, knowing the devastation of the Alliance?

Unless... did they know? Adrian disabled communications and confiscated technology as much as he could, but if the military came and went as they pleased, someone must have snapped a photo here and there.

As Arty backs out of the space and drives past, I face the students. With the exception of two or three, they all stare at their various electronic devices. Maybe they did know. And the Alliance was nothing more to them than a meme or blog post to share or an article to spout opinions about.

Words from one of Michael Harding's Bible class lessons come to mind. A society governed on opinions is destined to fail. He'd talked about people throwing fits and the squeaky wheels causing policy change rather than the majority ruling. A giggle builds up in my throat, and I swallow it like bad medicine. Mom always rolled her eyes when Michael complained about the people who lived by the books of First and Second Opinions, and Dad always chuckled from his belly. How I miss those days.

But, do I? Do I miss the days I spent chained in my resentment of Amber and longing for Ethan? The days before I considered myself a soldier for Christ?

Arty turns onto the bypass and approaches the first light, the veins bulging in his bulky muscles. All the stories he told me on our trip… He's a soldier. Not me. He puts his life on the line to preserve freedom and justice. I quote scripture to defy Adrian.

Why had I not reached out to Ginny and pleaded with her to hear the gospel? The prison guards, yes, but they came to me in response to my defiant singing. I've got so much growing to do.

Two stoplights later, I grip the door handle as we drive through the part of town where smoke billowed in the horizon while Amber sat in jail the night before Adrian snatched me away. Bright facades decorate busy storefronts, and American flags hang from every electric and light pole.

"Looks like your town has thrived since the Alliance took over." Arty eases up to the third light and flips on his right signal.

"I guess so."

A block from the turn, the church looms proud on its hill, the old siding replaced by a blend of tan, black, and cream-colored bricks. A brick-lined marquee stands in place of the faded wooden sign.

"Church, a gift from God. That's a good one." Arty grins. "Assembly required." As he merges into the side street traffic, he bobs his head toward the parking lot. "Looks like you worried for nothing. A full parking lot on a Wednesday night. This must be some church."

"It was. They did a lot of weekend stuff for the teens." I sit taller, hope washing over me. "And, they had dinners for... well, look at the sign there. Tonight's a dinner to honor our veterans and soldiers before services. You should go in and eat."

"I can always go for a good meal."

He pulled in next to the Whitman's Cadillac. The old man still driving the same ancient car. And good old Mary, who'd always fought for her status as chief church gossip. Next to the Cadillac, Michael Harding's truck. And rows of unfamiliar cars. I empty my lungs through my nostrils. Looks like maybe the church grew without us, too.

Arty walks with me to the side of the church where cherry double doors open to the fellowship hall, which smells like barbecued baked beans and charred meat.

An older man I don't recognize grasps his wrist with both hands. "Welcome. Welcome, son. In what branch do you serve?"

As Arty launches into deep conversation with the man, I scan the room for anyone familiar. Deep plum rugs cover the wall-to-wall marble tile in the walkways and three columns now divide the wide space that used to be filled with long, rectangular tables and those metal chairs that screech whenever anyone scoots back. Men and woman in fatigues sit around circular plastic tables sporting exquisite floral arrangements. Angela Harding's work, no doubt.

Angela. She has to be here. My gaze darts to the kitchen, where women dance like bees around the counters. No sign of her, though I do recognize several of the women.

A side door opens, and grill smoke filters in. Then, my heart stops. Angela holds the door for Ethan, who's carrying a huge platter of grilled meat.

I stumble forward, steadying myself on the table nearest me, drawing a concerned look from the three fuzzy-haired men who occupy it.

He follows Angela across the room to the serving table and places the tray in an open spot. As he pivots, meeting my line of sight, he stops short, gaping.

For eternal seconds, neither of us move. I cannot speak, or breathe, or think. After so many hardships, was it this simple? To walk into the room and find him here?

I clench my jaw. Of course, it's not this simple. I'm sure he's moved on and found another girlfriend since returning to America. Why wouldn't he?

My heart pounds in an almost cartoonish beat, as though it's beating from outside my chest. The noisy bustle of the room vanishes as he takes a single step in my direction then breaks into a run.

I'm in his arms before I can blink. His hands cup my cheeks and he lowers his forehead to tap against mine.

"Callie." He steps back, studies my face, and squeezes me tight again. "I'd almost given up hope on finding you."

I cast Arty a shy glance. "Providence, I guess. I stumbled on a group of American soldiers who brought me home."

He kisses my forehead and leads me out of the fellowship room to the stairwell that leads to the classroom. "They said you were coming, but then we didn't hear anything." His grin widens. "Have you talked to your dad?"

"I saw him a few days ago. He was weak, but healing. He's staying at a farm with a man who helped us escape. Kurt."

"Right. Kurt." Ethan brushes a curl behind my ear. "Your dad told us about him. But Callie, your parents are home. Both of them."

"Home? As in Union City home?"

"In the hospital. And both recovering well."

I grip the railing behind me and Ethan helps me to a chair. He sits in the one next to me and reaches for my hand. "How did you get back to America?"

My lips quiver. "It was so terrible. Kurt sent me in this truck with these men and it wrecked. So we went through some woods to the river bank, and ended up running into a booby trap. This poor guy got nails jabbed into his skull and sliced his neck open against a thin metal wire." I take several deep breaths. "I thought it had cut off his head at first, but it sliced his neck. The army men said they'd take care of him."

Ethan reaches across the chair arm and pulls my head to his shoulder, rocking me as even more tears spill.

"He told me to go on. I was so scared. Scared to death to move, and scared to death not to. And then I found the American soldiers and they helped me get home. I had scarlet fever. Delirious, like I was hallucinating or something. But they had antibiotics and when we got back to America, I went to the ER and checked out fine."

"Well, I hate you had to go through all that, but… you're here! I'm so glad this is all over." He pulls out his cell and glances at the screen. "It's not too late. We can go see your parents if you feel up to it. Maybe eat a little first."

My heart thunders as he makes circles against my skin with his thumb. "I want to see them."

Michael Harding approaches from a side classroom and drops the bags of plates he's carrying. "Callie!" He runs to me, engulfing me in a monstrous hug. "We were so worried."

"I'm okay." I force a reassuring smile as Angela joins us. "I need some rest is all."

"You're way too thin. We need to get you to a hospital." She brushes my hair away from my forehead. "Get in there and eat something."

"I went to the hospital but they released me. They recommended I see my regular doctor and have a full physical. Maybe I can do that tomorrow." I frown. "Well, I'm not sure about insurance and stuff."

"The church can cover it." Michael pats my shoulder. "And if they can't, we'll all go in together to help out."

Angela rushes off to make me a plate, and I take a chair next to Ethan. With my first true contented sigh in two years, I lean into his arms and close my eyes.

He squeezes me tight, then relaxes his grasp as if he thinks I'm fragile enough to break. "I missed you so much. I tried everything I could—" His voice chokes up as his cheek presses close to mine.

"Shhh," I reach up and touch his face. "I know. I tried, too. But God brought us back home safely. All of us. Everything is going to be okay."

His lips brush my right ear, and warmth from his breath spreads over my neck. "I love you, Callie. Today, tomorrow, and forever."

His whisper sends waves of peace into my soul. "I love you, too," I whisper back. How amazing it is to feel so safe. So…

comfortable. I almost drift off to sleep when Ethan shifts and Angela returns with the food.

As we eat, the church members and soldiers pause at our table, all sending well-wishes, hugs, and promises to help us settle into a future. Our future. Whatever that may be.

After an hour, Michael pushes his way through the line.

"Time to go, sweetie. Angela said I have to get you home to rest. Ethan, she's safe now. We'll take good care of her and you can see her tomorrow."

Ethan squeezes me once more, reluctant to let go. Am I dreaming? Is this real? As Ethan follows, Michael gently lifts me, carries me to his truck, and tucks me into the passenger side. Ethan stands by the window, looking at me so intensely that I dissolve into the sea of tears I've held back for so long. Then, he jerks open my door and clings to me as we both have a good five-minute cry.

Michael clears his throat. "Ethan, if you want to come by for a while, you can. We'll get Callie resting and eat up all of Angela's leftover dessert."

While Ethan follows in his Mustang, Michael drives me back to their house, where Angela has prepared the bed for me in their guest room. "We'll take you to see your parents tomorrow," he promises as he leaves me in Angela's care.

Ethan pauses by the door. "Goodnight, Callie."

I mumble something that sounds like goodnight in return. Michael, Ethan, and Angela share a laugh.

"I've got it from here, boys." Angela nudges them out of the room and closes the door. "Here, sweetheart, you can change and get some sleep. You look exhausted." She's pulled the sheets back, laid a pair of flannel pajamas and fuzzy socks on the end, and a TV tray sits on table beside the bed with a cup of steaming tea waiting. As she softly closes the door, Relief, fatigue, and gratitude washes over me. This is real. I'm finally here… Ethan is here, safe. My parents are here, and even Amber. It's almost too good to be true, but… that's God's providence.

My hands tremble as I bring the warm mug to my lips. *Dear Lord, please forgive me. I do not have sufficient words for my gratitude. This outcome… so far beyond what I dared hope for. You have wrapped me in your love and comfort—that cocoon where the peace that passes understanding billows into fearless waves—and carried me home. Thank you for so many blessings.*

I snuggle down into the warm bed and pull the blankets up to my neck. *Lord, please watch over us. Protect us from Adrian, and Lord...* Saliva catches in my throat as I try to swallow. *If it's your will, soften his heart. Let him forego his bitterness and earnestly seek your comfort. Oh, and the American people... the people still trapped in the Alliance...*

Somewhere in the night, my prayers fade into sleep and my dreams fill with images of Ethan—his eyes, his arms around me, and his soft kisses.

The next morning, Ethan's voice drifts from the kitchen with Angela and Michael's. Not a dream! My heart does a flip, and I push my aching body to hurry and shower. My first day of freedom! My adrenaline races. I can see Mom and Dad. And maybe I can visit Amber. . I keep whispering, "God, you are so good!" over and over.

When I walk down the hall and round the corner to the Hardings' kitchen, Ethan's face lights up. He runs to me, wrapping me in his arms. Through breakfast, Michael and Angela shower us with questions that Ethan and I eagerly answer, melding our time in the Alliance into connected dots that lead us to this moment. As the pieces slowly fall into place, we share joy and tears. It is incredible to be here right now. All these months God had been steadily helping us, even all those terrible times when it didn't seem like it.

After eating, Michael and Ethan drive me to the hospital and force me into a wheelchair. They roll me to the door of Mom and Dad's room.

"Got a visitor, Martin." Ethan skips inside.

A few seconds later, when Michael rolls me in, Dad's smile starts slow, then explodes across his face. His eyes blink, and he covers his face with his hands, his body overcome with sobs. Michael pushes me closer, between him and Mom's bed, and her eyes flutter.

"Callie." Her raspy voice tapers and she yawns. "You're home."

"We're safe." Dad wipes his eyes with his sheet. "We're all safe and it's over now."

After asking and answering a million questions, we've filled
in the blanks of what has happened to each of us since we were
separated. We've cried together, told each other how much we love
each other, and prayed together. Michael has us in humble tears.
He's already drawn out plans to build a house for Mom and Dad,
and someone from church is donating land. It's the most wonderful
feeling to be here with my family again, but closer than we've ever
been.

Finally, Dad passes Ethan a black remote. "Turn on that TV, son.
I haven't seen CNN in months."

I shield my view as Adrian's squirrel-like face pops up on the
screen. The image shrinks to a corner, and a tall black-haired female
reporter appears in his place. "Border authorities are still searching
for Adrian Lamb, former leader of the Alliance of American States.
A state of emergency has been declared in the flailing nation, and
US soldiers have gone in to stabilize the country." The woman
squints like she can't see her teleprompter. "Lamb is rumored to
have escaped the Alliance and believed to be armed and dangerous,
perhaps hiding in the hills of Eastern Tennessee or Kentucky."

I grip the handles of my wheelchair. Even in the dim room I can
see Dad's blanched face. Mom gasps, Ethan's jaw clenches... would
he dare come after us?

Michael whips out his cell and walks toward the door. "I'm
making some calls. Adrian Lamb is not going to touch your family
again."

Dad scoots up in his hospital bed. "No, he isn't. Ethan. Go out
there and tell those police officers you need an escort. I want you
to go to my parents' old house and get my guns out of their cabinet.
We're not facing him again empty-handed."

THE END

# CALLIE

**THREE WEEKS** have passed and no sign of Adrian. If not for the fact that he'd managed to evade any sort of law enforcement and stay off their radar, I might allow myself to relax. Might.

Some think he may be hiding in West Virginia. Either way, Michael's hired two body guards to go everywhere I go.

On Monday, Ethan strolls up to Michael and Angela's house at noon. "Your dad still wants me to go to your grandparents' house and get his guns. Michael says maybe I can bring them here and he'll be satisfied that we have them. Want to come with me?"

I giggle at his shy grin. "I will."

"You sure you feel up to it?"

"We'll have to take it slow, maybe."

With our bodyguards in the car behind us, he drives me over, holding my hand on the console. Wish I knew how all these changes will affect our relationship, but I'm willing to take it one day at a time.

Once we reach Papaw and Grandma's drive, Ethan parks and rushes around to help me out of the car. He locks his fingers in mine and plants a light kiss on my forehead. [Obviously, since on the lips would be something more. ;-)]

I try not to frown as he leads me to the end of the drive while Tweedledee and Tweedledum inspect the yard. They wave us on, and we make slow progress toward the gate. "Sorry. My knee."

"It's okay." The twisted stone path still winds to the back of the brown brick house and through a wrought iron gate to the smaller white one behind it. Crumbling concrete snakes through nettles and milkweed like I remember from childhood. Weeds have overtaken the flowerbed, but I can picture Grandma sitting in her wicker rocking chair, arranging fresh-cut roses in vases for one of our church meals.

But now, I'm overcome with chills as our bodyguards brush past the house and sweep the bushes mangled with thorny brush. How many times had Adrian stood in that very spot, watching me play and concocting his plans? And, worse of all, planning Grandma's death.

"You okay?" Ethan drapes his arm over my shoulder and tugs me near. "I thought this might be hard for you."

"I'm fine." I take cautious steps over the icy walk and kneel at the edge of the flowerbed. The hollow turtle still stands guard. I lift it, raising its shell. Thank goodness. The key is inside. "Hope no one has changed the locks."

"I doubt it. It's not even been two years since your dad was last here, right?"

"Well, yeah. Grandpa died three years ago, and Dad worked on cleaning the place out a little bit at a time." I let Ethan help me up then limp to the front door.

"You need to see if they can do something for that knee." He steadies me as I try the key in the lock.

"I have an appointment for next Tuesday with my doctor. They might do a replacement." When the knob turns, I grin. "Success. Maybe this will be easier than we thought."

"Maybe so."

Once the men have checked the house, we enter the musty living room and Ethan pats the stiff, formal sofa sitting beside the door. A cloud of dust spreads over it, and we both sneeze. To know Adrian hasn't been back here brings great comfort. At least there's a small piece of my life he's never touched.

"Papaw never cleaned." I point to the Queen Anne tables at each end of the sofa. "You would almost have to carve your name in that amount of dust. At least ten years' worth."

Ethan walks over to the marble mantle sitting over the fireplace and picks up a picture of Mom, Dad, Amber, and me when I was six. "Look at you, all toothless and skinny." He laughs. "Who'd have ever thought you'd turn out so pretty?"

The tiniest flutter stirs in my stomach, and my cheeks warm. After all this, he still thinks I'm pretty. "You flatter me."

"Yep." He moves to the frame next to it. "Your dad looks so young here."

"When he was in college, I think. He was young." I move to a crowded shelf, where photo albums of various shapes and sizes have been stuffed. "We might start here. I don't think she'd have left anything out in the open, but you never know."

"Check under the couch cushions. Maybe your grandmother hid something that might help find Adrian." He nods to the couch. "And we should check under all the rugs. It would be a quick place to hide something if you're rushing off."

"The rugs?" I giggle. "Doubtful anyone would have hid anything under the rugs. And I can't imagine Grandpa wouldn't have found anything if she'd hidden it. Besides, aren't we here for the guns?"

"Hey. Just a thought." Ruffling my hair, Ethan glances toward the window. "Not sure how much daylight we'll have. We may have to come back tomorrow morning. And you're right. There may not be anything to find."

"I think the guns are in Papaw's bedroom closet. And Grandma used to have this old trunk that she kept in the opposite corner. I've only seen it once, but it was special. She brought it out when I was baptized and showed me the Bible she carried when she was a teenager. Maybe it has something related to Adrian in it. We could check there before we go."

"We'll try."

Hand-in-hand, we make our way through the dim house, up the stairs, and into the bedroom. We stand in front of Grandma's antique dresser and face each other in the mirror. His stubbled face and gorgeous brown waves far outshine my brittle straightened hair and scarred cheek.

As if reading my mind, he plants a soft kiss on the scar then backs away like he'd been shocked. He fumbles through his pocket and produces a velvety box. As he falls to his knees, I cover both eyes with my trembling hands. Is this what I think it is?

Gaping, I take a couple paces toward the bed and steady myself on the mattress. He drops to one knee and my heart sinks to the floor.

"Callie, I've watched you grow up, and I've seen you almost die. I've fought for you, I've lied for you, and I've offered a million prayers for you." He swallows, making a failed attempt to raise the lid of the box. "I didn't rehearse this speech, but I don't want to be apart from you anymore. It's been months. Other than the Hardings and your parents, we have no one but each other now, and I think we need to cling to each other. Please, Callie, will you be my wife?"

My mouth goes dry. As much as I've loved him, I can't find the answer in my heart. We've been through so much, but outside of the adventure, do we have enough to build a marriage on?

He extends the ring with a brilliant smile that fades as he studies my face. "You weren't ready for this."

"I..." Not even close. My chest heaves and I take the box from his hand, holding the ring up to the window light. "It's so beautiful. How did you get it? And when?"

He gives me a sheepish grin. "The moment I got back to America, I found out my grandfather had left me a bunch of money." A bitter laugh escapes his throat. "It's crazy. I walked into a store and bought it on the spur of the moment. A diamond for yesterday, today, and tomorrow."

I drop down beside him and he slips his arm around my shoulder.

He nuzzles his head against mine. "Sorry. I shouldn't have jumped the gun so fast. It's okay that you aren't ready. But I am planning to marry you one day. Don't you even think I won't ask again."

"I'm not saying never. I want you to ask again. Just can't think about it right now."

"Understood." But hurt flickers across his face.

We scoot back against the bed, our feet pointing out toward the old trunk. I inch away and pry myself from his grasp. "We're running out of daylight, remember?"

I cross the room and open the trunk to a wadded mess of clothes. Someone's been through it since the last time I was in there. Careful to shake out and fold each of the old dresses and shirts Grandma had saved, I make my way to the bottom. Grandma's Bible is there, and I clutch it tight in my arms.

Cocooned

"Someone's gone through this years ago. Probably Adrian. Or maybe one of my aunts. If there was anything in here worth keeping, whoever was looking has found it. I'm sure they've taken any important financial documents and such, too." I stand, huffing as the lid falls closed on one of Grandpa's old flannel uniform shirts. It lands square on a button, splitting it in two, and sending half of it skittering under the iron-framed mattress.

Crawling on my knees, I sweep my arm across the dusty hardwood and miss the broken button by a couple inches. I slide to my back and grip the frame with my left hand as I stretch with my right. My finger catches on a piece of paper, and, giving up on the button, I try to wiggle it free.

"Find something?" Ethan lifts the mattress and I slip out the folded paper—a faded envelope with something metal inside.

"A key, I think. Wonder what it goes to." Ripping through the seal, I hook my fingers on a chain and slip it out of the envelope. A herringbone necklace, attached to a shiny silver key dangles from my hand. "Wonder if it dropped down between the bed frame?"

He holds up the velvet box. I'm not sure he can even hear me.

Pocketing the chain, I give his hand a tight squeeze. I'll worry about family mysteries tomorrow. "I will be ready one day. It's a little overwhelming to think about right now."

"I know that." He moves to the other side of the closet and fiddles with the lock on Papaw's gun cabinet. Reaching up, he brushes his fingers over the top of the cabinet and comes down with a small brass key. When he opens the door, all the guns are in perfect alignment. "We'll come back tomorrow and try to go through her stuff again. Maybe your dad will know what that key is for."

"Sounds good to me."

After locking up, we nod to the bodyguards, head back to his Mustang and set off for town. He gives me a mischievous grin and flips the radio to the oldies station. "Think you can still beat me at guessing the song names?"

I snicker. "I know I can."

As we drive along, we sing and laugh like old times. How much I've missed little things, like the radio. My shoulders start to relax for the first time since Adrian snatched me away from Dad.

250

Static interrupts the song, like someone is scrambling for the microphone. "This just in…" The DJ gasps a deep breath. "Ladies and Gentlemen, the Alliance is no more. With the capture of Adrian Lamb, along with several other homegrown terrorists on the government watch list, the American military swept in and occupied the remaining Alliance states with little to no resistance."

I clutch my chest, and meet Ethan's wide eyes in the rearview mirror.

"Over three thousand children were rescued from the Alliance's boarding schools, which had become holocaust-era factories to spread political ideology and fear. Measures are being taken to reunite the children with their families, although some will find they have no families to rejoin."

The guy coughs.

"They've set up a special number to help make those connections." His female counterpart breaks in and recites the number, repeating it twice afterward.

Her words turn to mush as I think of all the people whose lives touched mine during my time in the Alliance. Dare I hope it? Had they been set free?

Ethan and I pull into the town as the bright orange sun dips its raging head over the horizon, lighting up the sky in brilliant yellows, pinks, and purples against a backdrop of blackened homes and trees. Crepuscular rays stream about a large cloud outlined in a silvery gray.

I smile at the cloud, the weight of the world lifting from my shoulders. "Lamentations 3:24."

Ethan grins.

A tear slips down my cheek as I picture Dad saying it with me. Adrian has been captured. I have to trust God and start putting my life back together. Renewal and rebirth. I'll emerge from this trial as the strong evangelistic Christian God intended me to be.

*The Lord is my portion, says my soul.*
*Therefore, I will hope in Him.*

# The Series

## CAVERNOUS

*A Christian teen battles for her soul against an extremist leader—her father.*

In a divided America, several secessions lead to the formation of a new nation, the Alliance of American States. Fueled by extremists who solicit members via social media, the Alliance has one weak point: Callie Noland, daughter of deceptive leader Adrian Lamb. When he snatches her from the man she's always called dad, he forces her into a suppressive life, training to serve in the Alliance military. Can she maintain her faith in God and stand up to the man who calls himself Lord and Master?

# COCOONED

*A Christian teen clings to her faith in God's providence while the boy she loves fights to secure her freedom.*
Pressured by the rebellion incited by Callie Noland, Alliance leader Adrian Lamb reaches critical mass. Callie Noland sits in an Alliance prison, recovering from wounds she received during a public stand for her faith which cost her status as First Daughter.

Circumstances place Ethan Thomas in a homegrown terrorist organization bent on destroying the Alliance. In his desperation he elicits their help to find and rescue her.

Meanwhile, Callie draws inspiration from Psalms 94:16: *Who will rise up for me against the wicked? Who will protect me against the evildoers?* It's as if God is saying the words directly to her. It's time to take a stand against extremist leader Adrian Lamb. The Alliance people need to know she did not die.

## CONCEDED—Coming Fall 2017

*A Christian teen yields completely to God's will and devotes her life to spreading His truth.*

When the Alliance is taken down by the American military, a Christian, Michael Harding, decides to run for president as an independent candidate. He enlists the help of Ethan Thomas and Callie Noland, who have newfound zeal following their triumph over Adrian Lamb's persecution.

They launch a campaign built on benevolence, service, faith, and Scriptures. Though their personal stand brings scrutiny and judgment, a broken America clings to their promise of hope.

Can Callie convince her divided nation that submission to Christ brings the ultimate freedom?

# Conceded Excerpt

Please enjoy this sneak peek from my upcoming full-length novel, *Conceded*, book three of the *Cavernous Trilogy*, coming in 2017

## PEACE LIKE A RIVER, YET THE RIVER RAGES ON...

I walk alongside Ethan among bright green leaves popping out from the long, thin branches hovering over us like a canopy. To our right, rushing water laps at the loose dirt along the edge of the bank, nudging the roots with its gentle, persistent touch. Cool droplets plunk on our noses and soak our hair, but my smile never fades.

With my fingers interlocked in his, and both of us safe in America, we've come full circle.

Muddy clumps of tangled branches litter the path to Adrian's cave, a reminder that our search may prove futile. If anything has been preserved in the flood, we might not be able to reach it.

A protruding root catches my toes, and I stumble forward. Ethan's arms wrap around me, and he steadies me.

"Try to walk in James's footprints." He grins as he releases me and points to a small set of paws. "The bigger ones. Not those."

A few feet ahead of us, James stops then pivots. "Are you trying to say I have big feet?"

"If the shoe fits…" Ethan's laugh makes my stomach flutter. Hearing it is surreal. "How much further you think?"

"About a quarter mile." James backtracks and helps me through a muddy spot. "I should have called some of my army buddies, but I wasn't sure if this would pan out. I hate that the flood washed out Mr. Whitman's access. Would have been so much easier to cross back there."

"Ah, it feels good to get out and walk." My knee aches something fierce. It's a minor tradeoff to be hiking with Ethan like a normal couple.

"I still can't believe you didn't tell the federal agents. Can't you get in trouble for that?" I step around another small puddle and brace myself against a slimy tree.

"Nah. This may prove to be a bust, and it would be a shame to have them use all their resources for nothing." James trudges forward, and we slosh and slurp our way through the muck to the mouth of the cave. "We'll call them if we find anything."

The entrance is more overgrown than I remember. Two tall, plump evergreens hide it from view of the path, which winds on around the other side of the hill to the back of the Whitmans' house.

"Stay back." James chops away at weeds with a machete and tosses them aside.

Ethan leads me to a flat, limestone bolder, and we sit. He nudges me with his elbow, a smirk spreading between his dimples. "You look adorable in that helmet with your big black hood. Like some movie villain or something."

Cocooned

"Stop it." Slapping the air in front of him, I dissolve into giggles. "And you look like a little boy who's getting ready to ride his bike for the first time."

He tugs the hood, letting it fall to my shoulders, and kisses the tip of my nose. "Callie, I'm so sorry. We should have had so many more moments like this. I—"

"Nonsense." I slip under his right arm and lean my head against his chest. "We have all our lives to move forward together. We'll make tons of memories and have a million more great moments."

"Yeah…" He shifts his weight and reaches into his pocket for his phone. His grin dissolves into a frown. "No service."

"You're getting obsessed."

His screen lights up with his Twitter feed, and he scrolls through the old messages. "It's a good thing, Callie. How many people have been talking about your story, and engaging in intense discussions about the real Bible? Who knows the reach it could have? After all, aren't we supposed to be going into all the world?"

I pull away. "Well, I don't think going into all the world meant spending every single moment of every single day staring at a screen."

His jaw twitches. I've gone too far.

My chest heaves, and I make circles in the mud with the toe of my hiking boots. Sometimes things feel so perfect, and others… I didn't expect to find him again and squabble all the time. Of course, it's only been a week since I've been home, and we were both under so much pressure that we're finally releasing.

"You're right, Ethan." I concede. "God is using technology to expand my feeble attempts to tell others the truth in ways I could never do on my own."

He pockets the phone, smiles at me, and pulls me close to him again. "God's ways are not our ways, and His thoughts are not our thoughts. They are so much higher than we could imagine."

I empty my lungs with a happy sigh. God doesn't need me to preach to a huge arena of people—He is reaching thousands using words from my weakest moments. And He'll get all the credit, not me. I'm good with that.

"Come on." James slides his machete into its sleeve and digs into his backpack. He pulls out a headlamp and fastens it around his helmet.

Ethan and I do the same, which sets my stomach to fluttering. It's time. Who knows what we'll find.

We enter under a canopy of "cave popcorn," the chalky white nodes formed from years of evaporation. The musty scent makes my lungs burn. Ethan casts me a nervous glance, I'm sure wondering if I need to be out so soon after being sick. He's probably right, but I wouldn't miss this for anything.

Making our way between dampened rock walls, we step over abandoned beer cans and food wrappers. Looks like the flood didn't reach this part of the cave, and judging from all the still-clean labels, the litter isn't so old.

"Watch for needles." James shines his flashlight a few feet ahead, where striated rock layers hang above us like a balcony. He raises the beam to the cave ceiling, where a six-foot gap leaves a high ledge. "Ever been up there?"

Ethan shakes his head. "We went into this ten-foot chamber. And not much farther, because it was hard climbing."

James moves closer to the base of the ledge, inspecting the rock. "Someone has climbed this spot many times. Look how worn down the rocks are in some of these spots."

"How?" Ethan steps away from me and grips the rock in several places. "You'd never get a hold, I don't see any evidence of anchors, and it's slippery."

While James feels along the wall, Ethan leans close and inspects it. I shine my light over every inch of the hanging ledge, coming to rest on something pink hanging over the leftmost corner.

"Look at that." Pointing with my flashlight, I stand on my toes and extend my arm.

"A rope, maybe." James passes Ethan a small hook with a rope attached. "Your aim is better than mine."

Ethan laughs. "I'm not so sure about that. But I'll try. You don't intend us to climb with this, right?"

"Nope." James points to the pink object. "See if you can latch the rope and we'll pull it down. Hope it's fixed to something. Stay back, though, in case something bigger falls."

As James and I focus our beams on the rock, Ethan launches the hook. It lands on the ledge, slips, and tumbles back toward us. Three trials later, he hands it back to James.

"Maybe there's another way up." I rock on the balls of my feet. My knee throbs so hard my breath hitches.

"Try this one." James hands him a folded-up mechanical object. Some kind of grabbing and reaching device. "Should have thought of this first."

Ethan unfolds it and stretches as high as he can. Still two feet shy.

They both look at me.

"Right." I shake my head.

Within a couple minutes, I'm sitting on Ethan's shoulders. James supports my back with his left hand. I extend the reaching tool, looping the pink object over one side of the grabbing clamp then squeeze the trigger.

"Careful." James raises his right hand and steadies me as I give it a light tug.

A rope ladder snakes over the ledge and tumbles past us to the cave floor, sending a cloud of dust and tiny rock pieces into Ethan's face. He sneezes and staggers, and I fall backwards, landing in James's arms.

When he releases me, pain shoots through my knee, and I wobble.

"You okay?" Ethan wraps his arm around my waist and straightens me.

"I'm fine. It hurts more today than usual." Shrugging, I retrieve my flashlight and shine it over the rope. Knots mark every couple of feet, securing metal rungs, and it hangs taut to the ground. The perfect length.

"Fancy stuff." Ethan catches the braided cord in his fingers. "I saw this rope in that hiking store at the gorge once. Durable, low stretch, and at least three-hundred dollars for any reasonable length."

James nudges him aside. "Up I go, then." He jerks the ladder. "It's secure."

He climbs far enough to see over the edge and stops. "Unbelievable. Callie, you have to get up here and see this."

# Also by Monica Mynk

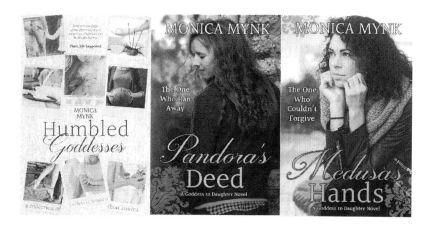

## Goddess to Daughter Series--Romantic Suspense

Years ago in rural Dreyfus, Kentucky, seven fourth grade girls studied mythology at a small Christian school. Three bore names of goddesses, and the others took on goddess nicknames.
Pretending divinity made them feel powerful until their teacher explained they could only attain true power through Christ. They promised to always be friends, following Jesus together. Then, they went their separate ways and fell deep into sin.
The Goddess to Daughter Series explores their stories of redemption and love. Available in print and on Amazon Kindle. Find more information at https://monicamynk.com

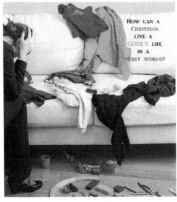

## Ungodly Clutter--Ladies Bible Studies

Have you ever been embarrassed to invite someone into your home? Cobwebs in the corners? Laundry piled to the ceiling? Mile-high dishes in the sink? If it's true that cleanliness is next to godliness, does that mean those of us too stressed and over-worked to maintain a clean home are ungodly?

Perhaps, God would be appalled to enter many of our homes... but not for the reasons we might think! Today's world is full of distractions and many litter our living space without us giving them a second thought.

How can Christian women cleanse their homes of the idols and temptations that hinder salvation?

Available for print and Amazon Kindle.

More information at https://monicamynk.com

# Coming June 2017

## Melanie Turner's taking stubborn to new heights...

When she discovers her fiance's infidelity mere minutes before their wedding, Melanie snatches Daddy's shotgun and climbs a billboard on the farm neighboring the church. As family and friends plead with her, she grows more determined. She's not coming down until that sorry Stephen climbs up and apologizes. No matter how long it takes. Problem is, Stephen's not coming, which leaves Kyle Casey in a real bind.

His grandfather left him in charge of the farm, and he's struggling with the responsibility. And as a permanently suspended ex-pro baseball player, he doesn't need the publicity her melodrama's sure to bring. His mind changes when the preacher of the church,convinces him that helping Melanie is the right thing to do. While the hours turn into days, he sits with her on the cramped billboard deck, enjoying her company far more than he should. As they both discover they've spent their lives focusedtoo much on self, can this washed-up pro athlete and spoiled-rotten tomboy find a path to peace and renewal?

# Acknowledgements

As always, there are many people to thank! I appreciate each and every one of you. This book was a labor of love, for sure!

To my readers-thanks for your support! It's an honor to present the second chapter in Callie's story.

To my Scribes girls. Forever friends and critique partners.

To my ACFW friends for advice and guidance

To Callie, Student Teacher extraordinaire, for your friendship, legal advice, and lending me the use of your name

To Deb, for the extra time and attention with the manuscript. I'm so grateful for a truly honest friend.

To Kevin Babcock and Mike Townsend, two awesome school resource officers who endure all my many questions. Thanks so much for all you do!

To Kimberly, whose honest edit helped me climb out of the deep hole. They say the middle book is the worst to write, and I couldn't have done it without you!

To Lora, who swept in and saved me when I didn't feel like I could finish.

To my beta readers who never disappoint. Your support means the world to me.

To friends and family, especially my brother Nick and sister Micki, who were great partners in pretending, and my wonderful in-laws, Terry, Sue, Lindsay and Joseph. Love you!

To my parents—my heroes. Mom, who nicknamed me Florence, and Dad, who taught me to always search the Scriptures.

To Lane, Matt, and Dana Kate, my beautiful family. Every day, my love for you grows even more.

Made in the USA
Lexington, KY
26 March 2018